WEIRD NOIR

edited by K.A.Laity

www.foxspirit.co.uk

Cover by S.L. Johnson
http://sljohnsonimages.com/

typesetting and ebook conversion by handebooks.co.uk

ISBN:978-1-909348-05-9

Contents

Introduction

K. A. Laity

What is Weird Noir?

There's been a lot of discussion about the concept of the 'Weird'—largely an enterprise of the VanderMeers, Ann and Jeff, who do an admirable job of quantifying just what the genre (or sub-genre or non-genre) is, and their award-winning anthology *The Weird: A Compendium of Strange and Dark Stories* established the benchmarks of the genre. Its parameters were deftly encapsulated by Stephen Graham Jones' flowchart[1].

I can't say when it was that I decided to pursue the idea of 'Weird Noir' but I slipped into its waiting tentacles without much thought of escape. I had been drifting into crime like a penniless ex-boxer down on his luck. I blame Paul D. Brazill who lured me into writing a story for his *Drunk on the Moon* anthology. Once you have your way with a werewolf detective, you never go back.

But there are others in this dark wood, though some closer to the edges than others: John Connolly who blazed a trail of supernatural crime and Sarah Pinborough who lit the fire behind him. And looking back, what are Algernon Blackwood's John Silence stories but a kind of supernatural detective fiction (and the direct inspiration for the comic I did with Elena Steier, *Jane Quiet*). And what about William Hope Hodgson's *Carnacki, The Ghost Finder.* Once I started to make connections, there was a lot more there to discover, including an awful lot of television: *Kolchack, The X-Files* and more modern fare like *Supernatural* and *Grimm*.

I've always had a bit of problem with crossing genres; a problem not for me, of course, but for a lot of editors, publishers and readers who don't like that sort of promiscuous

---

1   http://weirdfictionreview.com/2012/05/flow-chart-of-the-damned-stephen-graham-jones-on-weird-fiction/

wandering back and forth across the tracks. I have written and do write mimetic crime fiction, but it's as if the landscape of my mind slopes down toward the weird and I find my steps returning to its uncanny streets. I love noir because it's as much about mood as what happens in the tale, though it's likely to be something bad and characters will end up damaged, or dead. Atmosphere defines noir. But what about weird?

I'm not really the flowchart type; I'm more of a duck test woman. So if it walks like it's weird, quacks like it's weird and wraps itself in a trench coat, it's Weird Noir for me.

When I wrote up the pitch for the Weird Noir anthology, I used this description:

'On the gritty backstreets of a crumbling city, tough dames and dangerous men trade barbs, witticisms and a few gunshots. But there's a new twist where urban decay meets the eldritch borders of another world: WEIRD NOIR. Featuring thugs who sprout claws and fangs, gangsters with tentacles and the occasional succubus siren: The ambience is pure noir but the characters aren't just your average molls and mugs— the vamps might just *be* vamps. It's Patricia Highsmith meets Shirley Jackson or Dashiell Hammett filtered through H.P. Lovecraft. Mad, bad and truly dangerous to know, but irresistible all the same.'

Honestly, I had no idea what I'd get for submissions, but the results exceeded my expectations. This is a lean, mean, uncanny collection of tales that surprise, alarm and delight. The stories have oodles of atmosphere and just the right chill of the uncanny.

Of course once we had the fabulous cover image by S. L. Johnson, everything fell into place.

As soon as I read Chloë Yates' little freak show tale, 'A Kick in the Head', I knew it had to kick off the collection. She's got a way with salty language that will make you laugh out loud rather than simply type the three letters LOL. You'll find her dentally-challenged main character as bracing as a plunge into polar waters. The voice is audacious and reckless, careering into surprise and change without warning and yet remains completely believable within the weird world she's created.

The elegant Mr Glamour himself takes the next slot with his seductive 'Violet and Furs'. Richard Godwin evokes a dark and sensual London that hides a multitude of secrets. You can scent the blood in the air even as you sway to the music—and you know that everyone's not going to make it to the end.

Karina Fabian offers a cynical PI who just happens to be a dragon. He mutters like Marlowe, but the problems he faces have a lot more to do with magic than anything that gumshoe ever faced. Add the first set of brothers into the mix and the world starts to lose it cohesiveness; sometimes we have to pay for 'Sins of the Brother'.

On the dusty border between Texas and Mexico, a brujo kneels in the dirt by a tree that bears remembrances of those who have disappeared. I love the magic worker in Hector Acosta's 'Across the Border' because he's something of a confidence man—not because magic isn't real, but because it's hard work and he wants to take the easy way out. Of course that's not going to go wrong, right?

People tend to think of noir as dour, but there's often a streak of black humour running through it. Jan Kozlowski's 'Corkscrewed' captures that perfectly: even the name is utterly brilliantly funny. The realistic portrayal of the emergency med tech's life slips seamlessly into the surreal with chilling ease.

I'd like to see Andrez Bergen's 'East of Écarté' filmed by Dario Argento. In my head it was as I read it—though with far better dialogue than his giallo ever manages. There's a teasing play with the conventions of the hard case shamus and an elegant turn to ballet. Bergen's a writer after my own heart: rules? Boundaries? Who needs 'em?

The surrealist poetry of 'Three Kings' and 'A Mark in Blue' come from the pen of Carol Borden, who is one of the stars behind the Cultural Gutter—folks who show how the mundane has all the riches of the elite. Monster movies, comics, pulp fiction: these arts traditionally treated as disposable and yet the wreckage is strewed with gems. Look for the sparkle.

What can I say about Mr B? He's a pal, he makes me laugh and I never would have known him if he didn't write some damn fine noir that also usually provokes you to laugh out loud at some morbid absurdity or a blackly humorous turn of events. In 'Black Moon Rising' we get a little more background for the werewolf PI Roman Dalton, but also for his mates the barman Duffy and his former partner Ivan Walker. The secrets in their past just seem to get darker and darker.

Jennifer Martin takes us into the mundane darkness of any city life, where the young and disenfranchised gather. Her nonchalant serial killer smugly assumes that he's the only predator in town, but he's easily cowed by the feral gangs at the club. He needs to find a victim, but kids these days—are they always what they seem?

Katherine Tomlinson's 'Identity Crisis' hits close to the heart for me. Who's more invisible in modern life than a middle aged woman? But who's more prepared to make the most of that underestimation? Talk about not judging a book by its cover—oh, the ways we can be surprised.

I have only met Jason Michel in dreams. He has been kind enough to buy me drinks there, so I have nothing but good will for him. Yet I can't help but think I need to keep an eye on this one, so clearly mad, bad and dangerous to know. His characters are too; lust for power takes all kinds of forms and there are appetites that cannot be satiated. This we know.

Asher Wismer's 'Evil and Life' runs along like a fairly regular PI insurance investigation. There's a weary recognition of the disappointments of life—not all wrongs can be redressed after all. But the facts don't add up. The investigation requires a leap of faith that doesn't come easily to someone grounded in facts, figures and medical reports.

With Michael S. Chong's 'Gus Weatherbourne' we step into the mythic, a place I love. Nonetheless we don't stay there, instead returning to the almost obsessively mundane, where the powers of the gods offer no help. Love undoes us all. Power cannot save you from heartache.

I know that 'Wonder Woman Walks into a Bar' sounds like the set up of a joke. Leeyanne Moore runs with the premise and keeps it balanced delicately between realism and the fantastic, between humour and heartbreak. It's a tough row to hoe, and she manages it with aplomb.

I figured at this point in the anthology we need a big blow out of fun; Christopher L. Irvin's 'Charred Kraken with Plum Butter' rolls in to offer adventure and larger than life characters, tied up with intriguing mystery that gradually unravels into wild turns. Reading this made me run out and get some sushi, too.

Joyce Chng's elegant 'Yao Jin' brings us back down to earth with ethereal violence, passion and mystery. The heat and the humidity seep through the lines and a languor fills your body, as if some enchantment snakes through the pages; you find yourself caught in this world.

W P Johnson's 'Train Tracks' had an uphill climb. When I hear the words 'coming of age story' my face tends to look as if I am sucking limes gone bad a week before Tuesday. That's because so many of them are overly sentimental bromances that drown their narratives in saccharine memoir. Johnson's tale has no truck with that. And immediately I knew this story would bookend with Yates' punch in the kisser. This tale is the snifter of cognac by the fire, when the embers have burned down and the truth can be told. There's the sucker punch of loss, the elusive gold of that first real friendship and the cold reality of the broken heart.

Enjoy. Read them all. Feel free to create your own order, but come back to the start and read them all again.

They're weird. They're noir. It's a genre. Yeah.

A Kick In The Head

Chloë Yates

The knife was hot and sticky in her palm but no matter how much it made her want to heave, Maxxie Vickers wouldn't drop it. Thinking about what was dripping from it wasn't going to help her. Even as the car screeched to a stop in front of her and she could have sworn her heart stopped with it, she held on. The once vital organ became a static lump in her chest and it felt as though it wanted to choke her, but she held her ground. If she was fucked, these shitkickers were going down with her. All she'd wanted to do was earn a little extra money to pay for new veneers and now here she was, dead body at her feet, blood splattered all over her favourite dress and a carful of cropped haired trouble heading in her direction. Life was a fucking bitch.

Mr Mo had offered her the job that morning. He always asked and she always turned him down, but since Lover Boy had fucked her over with the rent last month and spent the lot on junk, she figured she might as well do it. Mr Mo ran his operation from the back of the club she danced in. She'd been taking extra shifts cleaning in the mornings to help pay for her new teeth but she knew she was never going to make enough to cover the rent too. It wasn't vanity that was driving her; it was the hole where several of her bottom teeth should have been. Lanky Lottie Stilts, the circus act freak show that went on after her every night, who somehow made enough in tips to rent a penthouse overlooking the river and a boob job every other year, had whacked her in the face with one of her extra legs two weeks ago and Maxxie had been spitting blood for days. They might have been limp and useless, but swung the right way those legs were a lethal fucking weapon.

10

She'd tried to get her to cough up for the dental treatment she needed, but Lottie was blowing Big Curly three times a week and, as it was his club, what he said went. So Maxxie had been reduced to cleaning up puke and mopping out the toilets in a dive that was barely palatable front of house. The departure lounge, as Big Curly called it (and didn't he laugh like an A-class ass every time he said it), was a lower circle of hell. So when Mr Mo had made her an offer yet again that morning, she'd accepted. It wouldn't do any harm to step over the line just a little, she'd thought, just this once.

Just this once.

Were there three other words that could get you into shit faster than you could spit? Right now, Maxxie didn't think so. At this point, amnesia would be a godsend. She wanted to forget all about the package. She wished she'd never had anything to do with any of it but, like they said, if wishes were horses …

'Maxxie, you good girl, you making an old man very happy.'

'Yeah, you said that already, Mr Mo. Now spill, what've you got for me.'

'So young, so impatient.' Mr Mo laughed. 'Well, is easy enough. You got to make sure the package makes the train.'

'Is that some sort of code?' Mr Mo laughed again at that. His mouth was ridiculously large considering how small his head was. It was made even more incongruous by virtue of every tooth in it being gold. Rather than putting her off, it made Maxxie want part of the action everyone else seemed to be making good on. She needed new teeth too.

'No, my little Maxxie flower, is as simple as it sounds. I have a package – now that is code, in this case it means a per-sonage – and that package needs to catch a train out of this shit hole at quarter to three this afternoon. Central Station. Platform five. Some folks will be waiting to take it off your hands. Think you are up to it?'

'Sounds easy enough. Sure, why not?'

'Excellent.' Mr Mo whistled and nearly seven foot of meat-head came barrelling through the door to his office. 'Get the boy, Gerard, and try not to break anything this time.'

11

The urchin Gerard the Lug brought in was way younger than Maxxie had expected. Kid couldn't have been more than eight or nine years old and he was cradling a plastered arm. Gerard had obviously been clumsy. She looked at him for a moment, then back at Mr Mo.

'This the package?'

'Certainly is.'

'He's just a kid.'

'He's a package. Can you handle or not, Maxxie my love? Don't waste Mr Mo's time, baby sweet.'

The kid just stood there staring straight ahead. Something about him gave Maxxie the creeps but was oddly familiar at the same time. She looked at him for a long moment. He didn't blink, not once. Finally, Maxxie shrugged and smiled at Mr Mo.

'Okay, I'll do it. He's not my kid.'

'Excellent. Boy? Boy!' The kid finally blinked and turned his head in Mr Mo's direction. 'You go with Maxxie here. She takes you to lunch then gets you to the train station. Do as she says and your bitch won't have to pull your teeth out of your arse. We good?'

The kid nodded. Maxxie wondered who the kid's bitch could possibly be. He didn't seem like the type to have 'bitches'.

Mr Mo went to his desk, pulled open a drawer and took a wedge of cash out. He handed it to Maxxie, who thought she might pass out from the sheer amount of dough he was giving her.

'Take what you need to feed the kid, get him to the station and buy his ticket. Keep the rest.'

'That's a lot of money, I can't ...'

'It might not look much but this package is important. Some real ugly people are waiting for delivery and I can't have it fucked up. I give you plenty of money, you get job done without flinching. That's the way I like it. Now go. And don't forget the package.'

'Okay, no problem.' Maxxie headed for the door, grabbing the boy's good arm as she went. He complied without hesitation. Somehow that bothered her more than if he'd put up a struggle.

'And Maxxie?'

She turned to look at Mr Mo once more. 'Yes?'

'You fuck this shit up and I'm going to enjoy beating more than just what's left of your teeth out of you. We good?' Maxxie swallowed hard, and then forced a bright smile to her lips.

'Of course, Mr Mo. Don't worry about a thing.'

Don't worry about a thing? She was currently drowning in some deeply worrisome shit. Maxxie watched the buzzcuts get out of the car. There were only two of them. Mr Mo obviously didn't think she was going to put up much of a fight. She suddenly remembered clearly when Winnie Fango, that fish-faced fan dancer with a bad attitude and three eyes, had tried to steal a couple of bottles of hooch from Mr Mo's hooky stash. He'd put six thugs on her, to 'set an example'. What had been left of Winnie was hardly worth mentioning. Just one flipper and the remnants of her bright green Afro; Mr Mo liked a souvenir.

As she watched the goons approach, Maxxie flexed her grip on the slick knife. It was slippery but she couldn't hold it too tightly, she needed to be able to slice from any direction and stiff knuckles would slow her down. She loosened her stance, ready to roll should the need arise. She hadn't grown up on the wrong side of the Harbour tracks for nothing. Her mother, the gods rest her lecherous drunken soul, had made sure she could take care of herself on the streets of the city. After all, she'd only been a little older than the boy when she'd first been sent out to work them. She had learned her lessons well. If only old Mother Vickers had taught her what to do when deals with someone like Mr Mo went tits up; she could have done with some sage advice to draw on right about then.

'Evening Maxxie. Mr Mo sends his regards.' Gerard the Lug, breaker of little boys' arms, was grinning like the Empress had just sent him a telegram. Quel homme.

'Hey Gerry. I'd say it's nice to see you, but it's not.'

'Yeah, whatever. Don't matter how smart your mouth is, you been really stupid. Time to pay the piper, the boss says, but first hand over the boy.'

Sitting in a corner booth at the Mighty Gerund Laundrette and Diner on the corner of Trotter and Campus, Maxxie watched the boy eat. He clearly wasn't normal, not even for that messed up town. She didn't know if it was nature or nurture but either way he sure could eat. Kid had barely come up for breath as he'd ploughed through a triple helping of Sea Egg omelette and toast. He was sweating by the time he finished – which was exactly three minutes after it had been set down in front of him. If she hadn't seen it for herself, she'd never have believed it.

'Where you from, kid?' The boy just sat and stared at his now empty plate. 'Not a big talker, huh? Well, me either usually, but seems you got my jaw all loose. Do you want anything else?' The nod was unexpected. The kid must have those famous hollow legs. 'Same again?' He shook his head this time, grabbed the menu and pointed at another dish. He held up three fingers again, put the menu down and settled back into the cracked plastic upholstery. Maxxie sighed, waved for the waitress, who took her own sweet time to grace them with her presence, and made the order. The waitress raised her eyes onto her forehead in surprise. Maxxie shrugged, the waitress answered with one of her own, her eyes settled back into their sockets, and she went off to holler at the short order cook. The kid just sat there, still staring at the empty plate the waitress hadn't bothered to pick up.

Maxxie tried to focus on the money and not let the weird kid bother her. When the waitress delivered the next heap of food, the kid just dived right in, barely letting the plate hit the table and it was gone in not much more than the blink of an eye. When Maxxie asked him if he wanted anymore, she was joking.

'What, really?' She stared at the boy, watched him nod again, and wondered what the fuck was sitting in front of her. Growing lad and all that he may be, but the kid was eating like a pro-wrestler and he was barely five feet tall. He was scrawny too, his clothes were threadbare in places and she doubted if his hair had seen a comb recently. Maxxie sighed. Poor kid. His life was hardly going to get any better. She wasn't stupid enough to believe she'd be handing him over to his guardian angels at the station. Still, she needed those veneers and if that was what it took to get them, then that's what she'd do. No one had ever felt sorry for her.

'If you eat anymore, kid, you'll explode.'

'Won't.' Maxxie was so surprised she jumped.

'Jeepers, kid, give me a heart attack why don't you?'

'Won't explode. Need food. Make strong.' So he could speak, but he was hardly Hozzamun Harshtongue, Wit of the Seven Cities. Maxxie looked at him for a long moment.

'Do you really want some more?' He nodded. 'Okay then.' She signalled for the waitress who came over with their bill. When Maxxie ordered yet more food the other woman looked at her like she was crazy.

'If the kid pukes on the floor, it's gonna cost ya.'

'Yeah, yeah, whatever, just fetch the kid his eats.'

Three platefuls later and the boy was flushed but smiling.

'You done?' Maxxie almost giggled when he grinned at her and nodded. Giggled. Maxxie Vickers did not giggle. Was she letting him get to her? She focussed on her teeth. She needed those teeth and this kid was going to pay for them. 'Right then, get your stuff. We need to get gone.'

The walk to the station was easy. It was what happened once they got inside that turned the day to cock. The kid was fine, following Maxxie without a word. She didn't even feel like she needed to hold onto him and it irritated her that he was so fucking compliant. This wasn't a city that bred trust in its young and she found herself worrying about his future. She was fairly bristling with it as they headed towards the ticket booth and, just before they had reached the back of the queue, it happened.

The Kick.

Her cycle had always been regular; she wasn't prone like her mother was to it, coming on with strong emotion. She'd had episodes no more than three times a year for as long as she could remember and then only when the Moon was on the wane. Yet as they walked across the marble floor, her high heels clicking, his battered sneakers scuffing, Maxxie felt the familiar thrill lick up her spine like a sizzling hot fudge sundae. Thick, sensual, forbidden.

She tried to shake it off, but the feeling intensified, tendrils of want and fury unfurling from her core, pulsing through her muscles, aching in her throat. Her mouth watered.

She needed to feed.

It was fully on her now. It always happened like that, a swift surge that propelled her into a world of sensation common sense had nothing to do with. It was all about instinct, want, hunger. Her innate desire to feed was the driving force now and she knew which side of her would win.

The side she wanted to win.

The side that took and never apologised.

The side that made her powerful, that made her feel as though, finally, she was the one in control. If she'd been able to see through the blood lust, she might have mused on the irony of that.

The kid was handing the money over for his ticket by the time the sweats started. Maxxie could feel the soft run of her bones as they shifted, yielded, unctuous as they metastasized. It was heaven and it was always the glorious same. She exulted in the change, revelling in the way it elevated her, swept her away from the crassness of mediocrity and into the realms of deity. She was mighty, the mistress of the puny ordinaries all around her, and she would feed.

The kid swung away from the booth and stared up at Maxxie, a frown marring his almost anonymous features. He swallowed and took a step back, but Maxxie grabbed him, pulling him along behind her as she headed for platform five. Common sense was long gone, but the feeling of anger at his helplessness was stirring something inside her, something protective? No. She couldn't (wouldn't) name it, but as she swept along the platform, clocked the delectable gentlemen waiting for their shiny package, she felt a rage so deep, so effervescent, that she had no choice but to unleash it.

All things considered, the first of the three men was lucky. His severed head was bouncing along the train tracks before he even knew there was any danger. Maxxie licked her arm clean of the blood with her swollen tongue and stared at the other two, daring them to step up, to take her on. The one on the left had barely got his hand to his inside pocket, looking for whatever weapon he had concealed there, before Maxxie was on him. She ripped off his head in one go too and gulped at the jet of blood that shot from the severed neck. It was hot and warm on her face, in her mouth, and she swallowed greedily, filling her stomach with visceral goodness. By the time she had finished gorging herself, her predicament forgotten in the ecstasy of feeding, the remaining goon was gone. People were looking. Not even in this City did mid-afternoon murders in a public place go unnoticed. The boy was sitting on a wooden bench not far away watching her impassively. He seemed to have grown in the past few minutes; his cheeks had a healthy glow and was his hair going green? Maxxie shook her head. Post feeding, her senses were on overdrive. She was imagining it.

'Come on, kid, we've got to split.' Thankfully her wings were fully powered now, and as she grabbed the boy's hand, she felt them peel away from her back, tearing her clothes, stretching, testing until finally, hummingbird strong, they propelled them straight up into the air. This was her natural state, Maxxie thought, as they climbed into the sky, leaving the filth of the City far below them. She was strong, powerful, glorious, just as nature had intended her to be. If only it were permanent, then she'd bust this shitty joint and make her fortune some place good, some place clean. Somewhere she wasn't just another cog in the wheel. Somewhere she could be adored.

Nearly overcome with the euphoria of her fantasies, Maxxie suddenly remembered the boy she was clutching in her arms. She had urgent matters to attend to. Using her heightened sight to scout the land below them, she forced herself back to reality. They needed a safe spot to land

The harbour.

The day was beginning to fade and there were plenty of places to hide down there. They could lay low until she figured out what to do. She knew things were royally fucked up but she was confident she would come up with a plan. This was why she loved the Kick. Even while her common sense told her she should just fly like a bastard out of there, the Kick told her she could handle whatever shit came her way. The puny creatures below were no match for her, no match for …

'That was my husband, you bitch.' Maxxie nearly dropped the boy when he spoke; she'd been wrapped up in getting them to safety and it wasn't like he'd been a chatterbox up until then.

'What?'

'You ate my fucking husband.'

'Your what?' She'd heard him all right, but what he said didn't make any sense. Only then did she realise how heavy he'd become. He must have tripled in size since they'd left the train station. Something was as sure as shit not right.

'What doesn't make sense, Vickers? You. Ate. My. Husband. Get it now?'

'Shit.' Maxxie swooped down towards the water, skimming the boy's legs across its surface before pulling up slightly once she'd managed to gauge his weight correctly. She pushed on a little further before setting them down behind a large container. Once her wings had settled back into place, she cautiously checked the boy over, noting with some astonishment just how swollen his belly had become.

'Now, what the fuck are you talking about and what's happening to your guts, kid? You look like you swallowed a blimp!'

'My husband was one of those guys waiting at the station.'

'What are you, nine years old? Mr Mo said …'

'Mr Mo is a fucking ballbag.' Maxxie flinched in surprise. Seemed like the kid was finally letting loose. 'He likes to talk big and make out like he's a player, but he's a two-bit hoodlum who needs taking down a peg.' Maxxie was too concerned with the colour the kid's face was turning to pay attention to what he was saying. Deep red blotches had bloomed across his cheeks and were spreading down his neck at an alarming rate. His temples were pulsing, his forehead beading with sweat and for the first time Maxxie was genuinely scared. Something was way more than wrong with the boy and she didn't like it, not one little bit.

'Holy fuck, kid, what's going on with you? You look like you're about to burst all …'

Tempting fate. Her mother had always warned her against it and she should have known better but, as the kid's head exploded, all Maxxie Vickers could think was 'shit.'

Splattered by head meat, she tried to back away, but the rending noise that punched through the air rooted her to the spot. Her mind tried to refuse to take it in. The kid's meat-suit split down the middle and fell to the ground, the slap of flesh and organ on the concrete floor like the sound of a thousand beef tomatoes falling out of the hole in some giant's shopping bag. Maxxie gagged. If the sight hadn't got to her, the stench would have done. Doubling over, she heaved, bringing up most of the blood she'd drunk at the station. Straightening up as quickly as she could, not wanting to be more vulnerable than she had to be in a situation where she clearly had no clue what the fuck was going on, she looked to where the boy had been standing moments before. Standing in the middle of what now looked like a mad butcher's bad acid trip, was a woman. A woman with flippers instead of arms. It took Maxxie a couple of heartbeats, but only a couple.

'Winnie?' Winnie Fango. As she lived and breathed she couldn't have been more surprised if she'd tried. She hadn't been imagining the green tinge in the kid's hair after all.

'Darn fucking tootin' it's Winnie. In all that's holy, Maxxie, what the fuck is wrong with you? All you had to do was get me to the station and on that train. Mr Mo would never have been any the wiser. But no, Maxxie Vickers, tart without trace of a heart, let alone an ever-loving brain, has to come along and fuck it up.'

'Why didn't you say anything?'

'I was incubating, bitch. Honest to gods, you're thicker than molasses. The kid was a cover, not to mention a place to lick my wounds. Regeneration, y'know? It ain't just for starfish.' Winnie ran a flipper through her bright green Afro, her eyes glistening with unshed tears, her face tight with anger. Maxxie could understand that. She could understand fuck all else, but she could understand that. 'Did you really think I'd let that greasespit Mr Mo get away with what he did to me? No fucking way. My husband and me came up with a plan to shake him down. He thought he had the kid of some dentist the Wanger Banger gang have been putting pressure on to help them out. Y'know, fight-related fixings, dentures, the lot. Those creeps have got a thing about dental hygiene. Fucked up is what it is. Anyway, she's been resisting and they want her bad. So when he thought he'd stumbled across the woman's kid, Mr Mo thought he'd found the winning ticket. The dumb twonk. She lives in the Big City, not down here in this shit-infested hole and the kid can't be more than nine years old. What'd he be doing down here on his ownsome? Idiot. Still, his greed was our main asset and I knew we could count on it. A couple of sessions with the Meat Mages on Gardner Street and we were set. Body suit, regeneration module, call it what the fuck you like, it worked. Until you stepped in and shot it to hell.'

Maxxie stared at her old friend. The last she'd seen of her had been a disembodied flipper in the dumpster out back of Big Curly's place. She wasn't even sure if she was really seeing her, if this wasn't some fucked up shit left over from the Kick. Even as she thought it, Maxxie realised how much of her strength had already gone. She was barely even tingling anymore.

'So now what, huh? That's what I'd like to know.' Winnie hopped gingerly out of the remains of the kid and took a step towards Maxxie, the anger on her face darkening. Her top lip curled back under the two air holes that sat just over her mouth, exposing far too many razor sharp teeth. She intended to do Maxxie harm, that much was obvious. 'I'm thinking there's some recompense coming my way. How about an eye for an eye?'

Hot fudge.

It sizzled along Maxxie's cerebral cortex like an old friend.

The Kick wasn't done yet.

Without thinking, she let herself react. The knife she kept in her boot was ready, as always. Lightning fast, she pulled it out and swung it up and into Fango's throat. As she pulled it out again, Winnie's eyes bulged, her mouth opening and closing spasmodically. She gargled for a few moments, blood spurting from the wound. Maxxie was destined to end this day covered in blood one way or another, she reasoned, so she stood her ground, not wanting to slip or be caught out. She licked her blood soaked chin and grinned. This might still be fun. Suddenly Winnie reached for her, sharp edged flippers snatching at the air in front of Maxxie's face, and then just as suddenly she gave up, her lifeblood easing down to a trickle as one minute she was standing, the next she was slapping down into the torn meat suit on the ground. Dead.

That's when Maxxie heard the car.

She should have known there wasn't any getting out of it. Mr Mo would have heard what had happened at the station and sent his goons out after her. He might know nothing about Winnie Fango's plan, but he knew he'd sent Maxxie on a job and that she'd fucked up royally. He was going to get his pound of flesh.

The knife felt hot and sticky in her palm but Maxxie refused to drop it. It was all she had left now. The Kick was gone again, leaving her like a washed up addict hankering for the next fix even as she swore she'd never shoot up again. Don't worry about a thing, Mr Mo, she'd said. She almost laughed as the two buzzcuts got out of the car. She flexed her grip on the slick knife. She was ready.

'Evening Maxxie. Mr Mo sends his regards.' Gerard the Lug had a shit-eating grin plastered across his ugly face. He was clearly going to enjoy ending her days. Well, he wasn't going to get away scot-free, that was for sure.

'Hey Gerry. I'd say it's nice to see you, but it's not.'

'Yeah, whatever. Don't matter how smart your mouth is, you been really stupid. Time to pay the piper, the boss says, but first hand over the boy.'

Maxxie did laugh then. She couldn't help herself. She laughed so hard she thought something deep down inside might burst. Her chest ached and her jaw cracked. One of her teeth fell out. Wouldn't you just know it? Maxxie laughed harder.

And then it happened.

The tingle that had all but gone flared up suddenly, cracking through her veins like wildfire. She was burning up from the inside out; the change was coming on more quickly than it ever had done before. Mind you, she'd never stood waiting to die before. She'd been in some sticky situations, but old Mother Vickers hadn't let her girl out into the world without some know-how. She was going to get out of this. The power flowed through her, from her – the bright light spilling from her eyes, her mouth, punching through her skin in a million places. The buzzcuts took a couple of steps back, clearly frightened and they had good reason. The air around her pulsed with it as Maxxie tilted her head back and roared – exploding in a ball of fire and bright white light, scourging the ground, searing anything she touched. The buzzcuts were obliterated instantly. The flare could be seen all over the city; the power of it shook buildings and stirred the water into a boiling frenzy. It knocked down power cables and stopped trains right in their tracks. No one failed to hear it.

No one but Maxxie.

Violets and Furs

Richard Godwin

She stands on stage and holds the microphone a few inches from her lips. There is pallor in her face, as if some silent parasite is consuming her vitality. The spotlight highlights her full mouth, the ruby red lips, as she eyes a man in a bright white shirt, who sits in the front row. He seems to her to stand out from the crowd, which is a blur. They are always a blur when she performs. Their faces are amorphous, a sea of nothing. People have lost definition for her as she searches for the song. She singles this one man out and notices his eyes. They seem unnaturally alive.

'My man's gone now,' she sings.

The notes are plaintive, haunting, as if she is singing of a time before her life was altered in some way. To the man in the front row she seems lost in sexual struggle, as if she's trying to recover from some malaise.

It's a perfect rendition. She holds the audience. She moves her body slowly, sensually, as if she is alone with a lover in her room. Her cocktail dress hugs her figure as she caresses the mike. The performance is so revealing and sexually charged the audience's temperature rises. She seems unaware of where she is, lost in some private ecstasy.

The man in the front row watches her intently. He is in his late twenties, maybe older. The absence of lines on his face confuses the eye. He is hard to assess. Something evasive and knowing lives inside him. His body is still, his hand clenched on the arm of his chair as he gazes at her there, singing, alone on the stage just for him. When she stops, the concierge comes on. He raises his hand.

'Barbara Dauphin, ladies and gentlemen.'

The applause and wolf whistles rouse the man in the front row, and he looks around, registering that he is in a packed bar, the side room of a pub he can't recall entering. He recognises his thirst and what it entails as he stands and wanders over to the bar where she is laughing with the barman.

'That was pretty good,' he says.

She turns and he looks at her eyes. They seem to him to belong in a bracelet, hung on an empress's wrist. He sees sapphires and diamonds. She seems better than humanity to him.

'Only pretty good?' she says.

There is laughter in her eyes and she sees hunger in his face. It is a hunger she recognises.

'It was the best rendition of Gershwin outside Nina Simone.'

'Thank you.'

'Can I get you a drink?'

She turns to the barman who is wiping down a glass.

'Should I let this young man buy me a drink Mike?' she says.

He shrugs.

'You know what happened last time. Better get his name first,' he says.

'I'm Barbara,' she says, extending her hand.

He touches her and sees the images.

'Joe,' he says.

'So, Joe, mine's a double Glenfiddich.'

He holds a twenty up to the barman.

'I'll have a Bloody Mary, two shots of vodka.'

They sit at the bar. He can see his reflection in the gleaming glasses set on the counter, he can tell what has happened, and tries to recall the preceding days as they talk.

'So, Joe, what do you do?'

'I'm a reporter.'

'A journalist?'

'If you can dignify it with that name.'

She wags a finger at him.

'Do I detect a touch of cynicism?'

'You detect a touch of scorn actually, a deeply rooted hatred of the men whose deeds I report.'

She turns towards him now, swivelling on the stool.

'What do you report?'

'Local London politics. The kind of shit you read about, corruption, sleaze.'

'You're not a fan of politicians?'

'No.'

He sips his Bloody Mary.

'Neither am I,' she says.

'They hardly inspire trust, do they?'

'And trust is a valuable commodity.'

'The trustworthy are rare as gold dust.'

Outside they talk in the wind. Debris is flying across the street and Joe looks at the sign on the pub, searching for points of reference as the haze lifts and everything comes into sharp focus. The Dog and Duck has seen better days, the summer flowers are rotting in the untended baskets that swing against the peeling paintwork and someone has thrown up next to the side wall.

'Can I buy you something to eat?' he says.

He looks at her and sees she is shivering. Overhead the gibbous moon is unyielding in the crimson sky, and its light alters her face. Her eyes are asking a question. Joe can smell blood.

'OK, Joe,' she says, taking his arm.

It is a delicate gesture that surprises him in its tenderness and they walk out into the street.

'Plenty of places to eat in Soho,' she says.

They wander arm in arm to Greek Street and enter Zebrano.

The waiter sits them at a table in the back.

'You hungry, Barbara?' Joe says.

'I am. I always am after I do a session; you have no idea the nerves I go through, I can't eat all day, I lose pounds on stage, and then I pig out.'

She laughs, and Joe looks at her white teeth.

'Like pearls,' he says.

'What?'

'Your teeth.'

'Oh, yeah.'

Barbara orders the butterfliedbutterfly chicken breast, and
Joe the 8oz burger.

'How would you like that done, Sir?' the waiter says.

'Raw.'

The waiter looks up from his pad.

'I'm sorry.'

Barbara laughs.

'He means rare.'

They order more drinks. Joe finishes his by the time the
food arrives. He asks for another, vodka, neat. The images are
fading with the alcohol and he sinks his teeth into the meat,
smelling Barbara beneath her cocktail dress and her laughter.
He can feel her body throb beneath the table and the nature
of her sexual needs.

'You look like you could do with a shot of red meat,' he
says.

'Do I?'

'You're pale.'

'You have no idea how much I used to eat.'

'So what did happen last time?'

'You mean what Mike said?' She leans towards Joe. 'The
last time a man took me out for a drink it ended badly.'

'He left you to pick up the bill.'

'I ate him.'

'Maybe he was a shark, your name is Dauphin, after all.'

'It's just a stage name, my real name is boring.'

'I can't believe anything about you is boring, Barbara.'

'It's Canis.'

'Sounds Latin.'

'Everything sounds Latin after midnight.'

She watches him chew ravenously on his burger, picking at
her own food.

'I'm interested in what you said, Joe.'

'About?'

'Politicians.'

'Oh?'

'Something happened to me, well not me personally, a few
weeks ago.'

'You dated a politician.'

'I'm serious. My sister, Annie, was dating one, Alastair Holmes.'

'I know him.'

She leans forward. She smells on heat to Joe.

'Do you?' she says.

'His reputation.'

'I met him once. Hated him on sight.'

'You have good judgement.'

'I don't know why I'm telling you this. Well, I do—because you're a journalist. He beat my sister up. He wanted her to do some sex things she wasn't comfortable with, and she turned up at my flat covered in bruises.'

'Did you call the police?'

'She didn't want me to, she begged me not to. He had something over her. Then she disappeared a few days ago, I've been out of my mind with worry. I've called all her friends, no one's seen her. I called the police then. I didn't say anything about the attack. They took a statement but have done nothing.'

'I get the feeling you want my help.'

She looks at him, lays her knife and fork down and takes his arm.

'I need to find her.'

'What do you think I can do?'

'I can't afford a detective. You're the best I've got.'

'Because I'm a reporter.'

'You must know how to get information, besides you said you knew about Holmes.'

'I do. And he's not someone you want to fuck with.'

'I don't want to fuck him, Joe.'

He sets his fork down on the pink rim of his plate. He wipes his mouth.

He looks at Barbara, at the desperation in her eyes. It is a feeling he knows all too well.

'OK, I'll help,' he says.

'I knew tonight was going to be lucky,' she says, looking at the moon through the restaurant windows.

Richard Godwin

Barbara's flat is a studio overlooking Covent Garden.

When they go back there for coffee Joe watches her slip out of her stilettos. He touches her arm.

'You're cold,' he says.

They sit and sip Irish coffee as dawn breaks across the polluted London skyline, Billie Holiday singing Violets for Your Furs out of Barbara's iPod. It sounds to Joe as though she is in the room, the sound crystal sharp as he sees the images of the song and feels Barbara so close to him she opens like a book of smells.

Then she touches him. It is a simple unassuming gesture, full of promise and reward, an unmistakeable sign. She lays her hand on his chest and says, 'My heart hurts, Joe.' He turns his face to hers, lost in the image of the softness of her skin.

Her mouth tastes of whisky and seeds. He picks her up and holds her, his mouth on hers. She bites his lip and it bleeds on his white shirt and Joe puts her on the bed and peels off her dress, hungry and alone, the odour of sexual need filling the air.

He touches her and feels alive again and she pulls him towards her, making small rhythmic gasping noises that increase in volume as he runs his hands over her body and she removes the last of his clothes. There is craving in her hands.

He looks down at her, naked in the intoxicated dawn.

'You're fucking beautiful,' he says. 'I need someone like you, I'm hungry.'

'Joe, your skin is so smooth, I like that.'

She is running her soft palms over his chest when he enters her later that morning.

She drags eight long nails across his back by the time they are finished.

At noon they bathe in her small bathroom and she tends to his wound.

She has his skin beneath her nails.

'It doesn't bother me,' he says, looking up at her as she bends over the tub.

She looks into his eyes and sees the pleading look of a deranged animal there.

Barbara makes them steaks for breakfast and they sit at the table away from the unmade bed in the cramped flat that smells of sexual arousal.

'I don't make a habit of this,' she says.

'What, steak?'

'Sleeping with guys I meet at bars.'

'Some habits are good.'

'Will you help me?'

'Yes.'

'What do you know about him?'

'Holmes is working his way into some important positions. He's got his finger in the porn industry and sends his mates hookers in his pay. It's all covered up by a paper trail and I haven't cracked it, but if I get the scoop on it the only place he's going is prison. He's got a lot of ministers where he wants them, vulnerable positions. He says a word to their families and they're finished. That's how he likes to operate. He uses drug dealers. If your sister has a habit that could be what he's holding over her. He'll use his power to get someone out of trouble with the police. For a price that involves their flesh. He trades in flesh of all varieties. I think he's kidnapping some of the women.'

'Do you think he's abducted my sister?'

'I plan to find out.'

Holmes has an office in Shoreditch. Joe enters the building with a MagLite. He finds files and paperwork on various activities, none of them incriminating. Joe is looking for Holmes's connection to a prostitution syndicate.

He goes through Holmes's drawers and finds invoices, bills, and the usual documents associated with a business selling furniture. Wherever Holmes is conducting his secret business is well hidden. His girls aren't on the streets. There is nothing there at the office, no indication of any illegal activities. Holmes also owns a club. Joe suspects it is a front.

He spends hours chasing his tail. Hours, then he finishes and meets Barbara at some club where she's performing and takes her out to eat. Or they return to her flat and make love in the dark. She lies there afterwards asking Joe how he's progressing with the search for her sister.

He looks into her eyes and sees something fleeting there behind their surface.

One morning he finds pills in her bathroom cabinet, 'Scroivenex'. He writes the name down and GooglesGoogle's it. Nothing. He digs around Holmes. He finds out he owns an entertainment business, which he's concealed effectively among his many interests. It is the perfect vehicle, since it involves purchases of the kind expected for entertainment. It is almost a month later when Joe finds cheque stubs made out by Holmes to Cachet Services. He even finds the address on one of the invoices, on which someone has scrawled, 'Personnel'.

The Talent club is in Mayfair. And he makes his way there that night with Barbara as London pours with rain. He wants to go alone, but when he tells her he's found the club she says, 'If my sister's hurt, I want to be there, she doesn't know you.'

'OK,' Joe says, 'but you need to do exactly as I say.'

It is heaving with bodies, twenty somethings with too much dough. The men all look over their partners' shoulders at the other women, who wear few clothes, checking themselves in the mirrors that line one entire wall as bouncers stand with arms crossed over burly chests.

Joe figures that the brothel lies beyond the mirror. Security is too watchful of it, as if it holds a closely guarded secret.

He buys a drink and sits in a corner watching them dance, as Barbara says, 'This looks like any other club.'

Holmes has done a good job.

Joe checks out the toilets. He wants to see if there are any corridors that might lead to another part of the building. A bouncer loiters at the end as he goes into the men's.

It is happening again. Through the open window he sees the full moon ride the savage sky and feels it crawling up his skin as his mouth becomes dry.

He clenches his fist, drawing blood as he knows it is too

late. His face in the mirror shows no signs yet, but it won't be long. He has an hour, maybe two.

He finds Barbara and says, 'She's not here, it's not here,' and takes her by the arm and out of there as she protests beneath the red sky.

'I'm not going anywhere,' she says. 'I know what you are.'

He looks at her. That knowledge was there in her eyes the first time he saw her, but something is wrong, she seems deadened in some way he doesn't understand.

She pulls his mouth towards hers and he feels her teeth with his tongue.

'You know me in bed, Joe,' she says.

'But you're not changing.'

'If you could find a way to stop it, wouldn't you?'

The pain is immense now, as he feels it coming on.

'No,' he says, 'I wouldn't.'

The bouncer is still there at the end of the corridor when Joe walks up to him.

'No access,' he says.

'What's on the other side of the door?'

Joe's skin feels as though jagged bones are breaking through its surface. He breaks the bouncer's jaw before he opens his mouth to answer. He smashes his fist straight through the bone and hits him again, knocking him to the ground, laying him out cold.

There is a storeroom nearby and Joe puts him in there and kicks in the door at the end of the corridor. He kicks it off its hinges.

Barbara watches as two guys on the other side lunge at him and he throws one of them straight through a partition wall. He lifts the other one up by the throat, as talons lash out from his bleeding skin and he removes the bouncer's Adam Apple, as a spray of blood showers outwards from his throat. The world is red and men are prey now.

She follows him through the broken wall, where Joe can see the women, half-naked, running.

He walks into a corridor off which rooms lie and goes into every one looking for Annie. Some of the women look like pros, probably placed there to keep the others in line, the ones Holmes has kidnapped. He can smell the women, their sexuality. An acrid odour fills the air.

More bouncers are making their way towards Joe and he takes them out, one by one. He can see the fear on their faces as they come towards him, faltering, hesitant. He smashes one's head against a door, opening it up, and tears another's face open. They look at him with terror, and a couple of them run. A heavy comes towards Joe with a knife. Joe slashes his throat, watching the blood spray the walls. The final bouncer flees along the corridor. Joe catches him at its end and he takes his neck in his hands and hears it crack. Joe eats half of his face.

There is another corridor and it is full of frightened women. They have obviously been kidnapped. Annie is standing at the doorway of one of the rooms and as she sees him she begins to scream.

Barbara calls out her name.

She takes her in her arms, then Annie faints as Joe lifts her out of there and to his car, leaving the door open for the other women to escape.

As he drives away he watches them flee half-naked into the street.

Annie sleeps as he drives her to Barbara's flat.

She and Barbara talk as Joe showers.

He shaves and looks at his body under the steaming water. When he gets out of the shower Annie is sleeping. He gets into bed with Barbara.

'I knew you'd find her,' she says.

'When did you know?'

'When I first saw you.'

'When did you know about me?'

'In the beginning.'

'So what are you?' Joe says.

'A wolf like you.'

'But you're not affected by the moon.'

'I'm taking pills for it.'

'Where did you get them?'

'Annie.'

'Holmes you mean.'

'She told me that's where she got them, they're in their experimental stage.'

'So she knows about you?'

'Oh yes.'

'Is she?'

'No.'

She kisses him and he tastes the seeds in her mouth again as the moon rides the sky.

'She's scared but she doesn't seem hurt,' she says.

'What did she tell you?'

'That he abducted her. Forced her to have sex. He's been giving them drugs, she doesn't know what. I'm hoping they'll wear off soon. He's got hundreds of women he's forced into prostitution.'

'I let a lot of them escape.'

'Holmes is not going to like that.'

He knows a man like him isn't going to let this go.

The next morning as Annie sleeps and they have breakfast Barbara says, 'Annie told me some of the women were having organs removed.'

'Holmes has got a number of businesses.'

'What is he doing with body parts?'

'Selling them on the black market.'

He knows he has to go after him. He knows he has to shut Holmes down for good before he comes for Annie.

That night Joe drives to London with Barbara in search of Holmes. The sky is bloodshot.

He has a number of addresses for Holmes and starts at an office where he trades in personnel. He finds among his papers an address for a clinic where Holmes is sending a lot of money.

They go there at midnight. The beam of his MagLite shows them that the building contains an operating room. There's blood on the walls.

'It looks like some of the operations have been botched,'

Joe says. 'I figure Homes has hired some doctor who's under qualified to hack the hookers open.'

'So what happens to them? Their street value must plummet if they have scars.'

'That's what I want to find out.'

He stares out at the night.

He has one more address and plans to visit it by day.

It is a lockup in a rundown business district on the edge of the East End. Broken glass lies outside the door and graffiti adorns the stained walls at the end of the lot.

The warehouse has a padlock on it, which Joe cuts.

He and Barbara enter the darkness. It is cold in there and a rank smell hits his nostrils.

The MagLite shows piles of boxes against the walls. Joe opens one.

'Pills,' he says.

'What are they?' Barbara says.

'Convovulus, I've never heard of it. It looks like this is a storage space for his experiments in pharmacy. But what is he doing with it?'

Joe continues to look through the boxes.

He sees the name, 'Scroivenex'.

'Familiar?' he says, handing a bottle to Barbara.

'It was to control the changes.'

Joe continues looking through the warehouse.

Then he hears it. He thinks someone is choking in the dark and he spins round, pointing his torch. There is no one there. At the end of the warehouse he can make out a door with a smoked glass screen. A hand is tapping at it. As he moves forward he can hear a groaning noise. The smell becomes overwhelming and almost makes him retch.

Through the glass he makes out a shape. Then it shatters and they come through. Joe can't tell whether they are human at first. They cut their ravaged flesh on the shard that stands jagged against the pale light that leaks from within the office at the back of the warehouse. He makes out stacks of syringes in a locked cabinet.

They are all women. They have holes in their sides. They

stare at him with the vacuous expression of the comatose. Their clothes flap about their rotten flesh like rags. They lumber towards him. They raise their hands and sniff the air, smelling night-time..

They come towards him waving leprous arms, and Joe picks one up and hurls her against the wall.

Barbara runs out into the yard and Joe follows, as a limo screeches to a halt. He can see the security cameras lining the wall.

Two large guys get out and Joe makes out Holmes in the back seat.

The moonlight turns the yard red and Joe howls as he rips one of the bodyguard's chests open. He pulls out his heart and sprays the other heavy with blood as he tries to get back in the car. Joe pulls him out and opens his neck. The body-guard staggers about the yard, as the zombies tear him apart.

Barbara locks herself in Joe's car.

Holmes climbs into the driver's seat of the limo and is trying to get away as Joe gets in.

'I was making drugs,' Holmes says.

'You were making zombies.'

'You don't understand, they were experiments, those women were nothing, of no use to society.'

'Do you think you're of use to society?'

'I can control things society has never conquered, I can change humanity.'

'You're in the black market of zombification.'

'I could stop what happens to you.'

'I don't want you to.'

Joe severs his neck with a talon, turning his head to face him as he ends his life there in the yard that is now peopled with zombies.

Joe herds them back into the warehouse, lifting them and throwing them inside as he locks the doors.

He opens the petrol tank on the limo, sticks Holmes's shirt inside and parks the limo right next to the warehouse door. Then he sets it alight.

He drives away with Barbara as it goes up in flames. He parks his car in a quiet street to sleep the change off.

He gets out of the car to take some air. There is a park nearby and he lies down on the grass. He shuts his eyes. Barbara watches him sleeping. There are some violets growing and she looks at them against Joe's fur, as it fades from his skin and she hears Billie Holiday sing into the moonlit night.

The next morning they go to Barbara's flat.

They make love as Annie sleeps.

'No more pills,' Barbara says.

'Such knowledge exists between us, you can't stop what we are.'

'Don't you think the world looks desperate sometimes, Joe?'

'It does when I'm a man.'

'It's the alienation that drove me to stop it, I felt like I was losing every time.'

'And now?'

'I feel alive again.'

'The beast rages against the dark, there's nothing hopeless about him.'

'I crave the change, it's like a drug.'

'It's deeper than addiction, an undoing of man, but the body knows its ecstasies.'

The story about Holmes is in all the papers. The police are still trying to figure out what they found in the warehouse.

The fire brigade can't read anything from the cinders. Barbara tells Joe she feels more alive than she has in months. She carries on singing. She and Joe carry on changing.

Sins of the Brother

(from the Case Files of DragonEye, PI)

Karina Fabian

Dante assigned Judas his own special place in Hell for betraying his Savior. What horrible sin had I committed to deserve my own unique inferno?

I slunk my way along the streets of the Faerie side of Los Lagos, trying to ignore how the glare of neon signs and pixie flash did nothing to dispel the gloom. A temperature inversion had trapped the noxious fumes of Mundane technology, shrouding the autumn afternoon in a dismal, dirty gray fog. People had been warned to stay indoors. The Mundanes, insular by nature anyway, gladly holed up with their televisions and Xboxes, but the Faerie were still too new to this dimension to give up their social ways. The many races that made their homes in this 'brave new world' wouldn't let a little smog get in the way of their gossip and shopping.

With my treasure left behind in the mountains of Caraparavalenciana, I didn't have the means for shopping— even if dragons did shop—and I had hoped to avoid any gossip about why the resident undersized drake was prowling the streets. Unfortunately, the higher you got, the thicker the air; my nose balked at the idea of flying. I kept to the back alleys until I got to my destination, then flapped my way to the second story of a ramshackle hotel that dared to call itself The Ritz. It was putting someone on, that's for sure.

I didn't care about the digs. I'd come to visit another Judas in his hell.

The rusted fire escape made a precarious perch, but my

friend saved me the effort of scratching at the window by flinging it open and stepping back to let me in.

'Vern! Thank God you got my message.'

I blinked. Brother Abel, breaking his vow of silence? I gave him the dragoneye as I looked him and his flop over. The tiny room hardly rated the rats I'm sure he shared it with. Maybe I'd do him a favor and snack on them before I left. With a stylish Mundane haircut and civilian threads, he didn't look like a religious, even with the second-hand clothes, and with his clean-shaven face, he could attract many a fair damsel despite his religious vows. Right now, those good looks were as clouded as the sky outside the filmy window. I knew what that meant.

'What's Cain gone and done this time?'

Abel started to pace, wringing his hands like an old woman. Couldn't blame him. This wasn't the first time Little Brother had stuck his head in a noose that Abel—with my help—had to get him out of. In fact, the last time, it had almost been a literal noose. Guess the blood didn't run so true in Abel's family.

Still, even then, he hadn't broken his vow of silence. Believe me, it put a crimp in our rescue mission. The fact that he'd break it now did not bode well.

'I don't know. He was so excited at first—still is—but now, he feels afraid. Trapped.' Abel hugged himself.

I bit back a sigh. Corsican twins are the stuff of myth and comic books in your world, but in the Faerie, psychically linked twins are rare but real. Years of training had helped him block Cain's emotions, but sometimes, love trumps training. He'd always know when his 'little' brother, younger by mere minutes, had gotten himself in deep, and fishing him out was as much for himself as for Cain.

Of course, how's a monk on the wrong side of the Interdimensional Gap going to save his wayward kin? That's where I come in—DragonEye, PI, the professional problem solver for people on the right side of Good but the wrong side of the law, or who want to keep things off the Mundane lawman's radar.

'Anything more specific? There a dame involved?'

'No nobility this time—and no women, either, aside from the usual...you know...' He shrugged, clearly uncomfortable with what his psychic eavesdropping had encountered.

Human mating didn't concern me. 'The Mundane world is a big place. You sure he's in Los Lagos?' The last time, we'd had to cobble together a cover story about the need for a new plow, then travel a hundred miles out of our way to save Cain's hide. Or rather, I had to lie; Abel acted dumb—in both senses of the word. I didn't think that kind of trip would work now, even without the lies. The Gap between our dimensions had only been open a few years. Faerie-born humans could travel at will; humanoid species would raise eyebrows; a three-quarter ton, twelve-foot North African Wyvern, on the other hand, would probably start a panic. Hey, even in Los Lagos, people still pull their teenage daughters protectively behind them when they see me. Kind of funny, actually, considering some of the girls. Guess what Daddy doesn't know...

'I saw a map.' He went to the dresser and pulled out a map he'd torn from the phone book. His long fingers traced a route. 'Fifth and Thatcher, then Peak. It was important to him. And he was reciting things—spells, names. They didn't seem to mean anything as a whole. It was like he was memorizing random facts.'

Prepping for a role, most likely. 'What were the names?'

'Carson, Hillfield, Sern...and Mage Willard Whitehaven.'

The names didn't mean anything to me, and I had a pretty good memory for the Who's Who of the Los Lagos underground. 'Carson Hillfield, or Carson and Hillfield?'

'I don't know. I'm not even sure they're people, but those names are on his mind a lot. Maybe he works with them. Perhaps we can do this like last time—find out where he is and ambush whomever he's working with and make off?'

'Perhaps you don't tell me how to do my job.' Ambush, yeah, great idea. Dragons can't be killed, part of the reason I'm in my current pickle, but we still feel pain—and the Mundane pain giver of choice among the local lawbreakers is the bullet. I've been shot; even when it bounces off my scales, it leaves a welt that lasts for days.

If Cain was involved in illegal activities, chances are the local heat already had a bead on him, and that's why he's frightened. That would be the best case scenario. Worst case, he'd gotten neck deep into something even I couldn't extract him from.

'What are you thinking, Vern?'

The trouble with Corsican twins is that anxiety goes both ways. Cain would pick up on his brother's worry. I'd rather it stay unfocused. 'I'm thinking you owe me. Stay here and stay low. We don't need anyone mistaking you for your brother. I'll figure out what I can and get back to you tomorrow.'

I headed out into the streets, letting instinct direct my feet while I mulled over the names. Not much to go by, even with Mundane technology to help me search. I'd become good friends with several search engines. Too bad I couldn't intimidate them like I could humans.

I'd gone a whole block before I realized I hadn't discussed my pay. Inversion must have made my thoughts as thick as the air. Or maybe it was just that I was thick with Abel.

It's not easy being me. One upon a time, I was top of my game, top of the food chain, top of my personal piece of the world. Once upon a time, I'd have laughed at bullets and certainly would not have concerned myself with the petty cares of two human brothers.

Then came George.

Yeah, St. George, similar to your saint, but when I knew him, he was just a high-powered mage with a Holy Calling. Since dragons can't be killed, he decided to co-opt one into service for his Church. Dragons have their own 'personal relationship' with God, no human Savior needed, so let's just say I didn't volunteer. However, I am now in service to God through the direction of His petty little humans—with all of my size, power and magic as their hostages. Ironic, right? I started out not much bigger than a lizard; in 800 years, I've worked my way back to pony size, with my flight and some of my magic and knowledge, but no fire. Damsels and Knights,

I missed my fire! I've been through seven kinds of hell and then some, but I've also had some glimpses of Heaven...like my time with the Silent Brothers.

It was shortly after the Faerie version of a World War, only ours was against the Devil himself. Personally. The Church assigned me to track down and destroy an artifact that should have been a power for Good, but which you humans had perverted like so many other things you touch. Much as the Church wanted it destroyed, Satan wanted it used...as did a lot of others who had the best intentions.

You know the saying about good intentions.

Anyway, the mission left me scarred, inside and out, and after the war, I was assigned to the Order of St. Osgood the Silent in Northern England to cool off. One day, 'cooling off' meant trying to drown myself in a vat of wine, and when that didn't work, slamming myself against the cellar walls in hopes of beating myself into a coma.

Abel had thrown himself between me and the stone walls. I suppose I owed him.

Then again, I thought as I turned a corner, I lied so he could go help his brother. We were square. Weren't we?

What'd it matter? Not like I'd get much from a monk with a vow of poverty, anyway.

A sudden movement caught my attention, and I stopped before bowling over a kid who got pushed into my path by some bigger urchins. He looked about eight, though he smelled closer to twelve—pre-adolescent hormones just biding their time. He had a camera around his neck, a cheap digital job that he clung to like a lifeline. He looked like he might faint. I gave him points for not wetting his pants.

But not many. I was on a case, and he was in my way. 'You need something, Snack?'

'P-Please, can I take your p-p-picture?' He raised his camera slowly. His eyes widened to saucers—red-lined, leaky saucers. Still, the glassiness probably had as much to do with the air as his fear. He gave a glance to the pack of snickering fools hiding in the alley. Wondered if he was more afraid of them than me.

I was feeling magnanimous. Must have been the air. 'Why not? Step back and get ready.'

I reared back and flared my wings, baring my teeth in a fierce display.

Thwock! I heard the release of a bowstring just as the iron-shrouded arrow pierced my wing's membrane and pinned it to the building.

The child took off. The others followed, their laughter fueling my rage as I tossed my head and roared. I brought it down to come muzzle to muzzle with a .44 Magnum.

'You'd better be glad I can't breathe fire,' I snarled at the dark meat holding the gun.

He cocked a brow, daring me to out-move his trigger finger. I glared, but stilled, again cursing my life.

Seeing he had the upper hand metaphorically, he lowered his literal hand and stuffed the gun into his jacket pocket. His big, deep jacket pocket. Which held other things that smelled like trouble for the dragon.

Great. The one time I could use a little help, and I'm stuck in an empty alley with no one around to call the police except a scared kid cowering behind a building with his camera. I'd wish for him to run for help, but I didn't want to bet he could outrun this guy's quick draw, and I had no idea how I'd explain that mess to the Sheriff.

'Got a message for you from Bordello.'

'No kidding?' Iron poisoning spread fire along my wing. The arrow was a custom job, too, with the entire shaft bearing sharp edges that fanned outward toward the nock. No ripping my wing free unless I wanted to lose my flight on top of everything else. I had no idea who Bordello was. 'Look, I got no beef with your boss—'

'Keep it that way. Stay away from his business. Stay away from Cain.'

Then, just to make sure the message got through my thick skull, he whacked me upside the head with an iron pipe.

By the time my head cleared, Message Boy was gone. I set myself to worrying about my wing—or more to the point, worrying at the arrow still pinning my wing to the wall. That must have been some bow to have sunk the arrow so deeply into the brick. Back and forth, pull and wiggle, my neck twisted at an unnatural angle so I could use my teeth rather than slice my tail pulling the blasted thing out. I'd curse the Fates, but they never messed with me. Apparently, I provided them enough amusement all on my own.

'Mr. Dragon?'

The kid's voice caught me by surprise—just enough that my grip slipped and I nicked my lip on the sharp edge. Roaring with pain and annoyance, I swung my head around until I was eye to eye with the alley rat. 'What?'

He was breathing so fast I thought he'd hyperventilate; he smelled of fear and adrenalin; yet he stood his ground. 'I-I'm sorry. I didn't know. I—'

'What'd he pay you?'

'N-Nothing, I swear! The other kids, they dared me, and I thought it'd be so cool and— I didn't know it was a trap. I didn't know they were going to shoot you. I'm sorry.'

'Yeah, well, talk is cheap. Get out of here before you get into more trouble.' I returned to freeing myself.

I heard a click of something hitting the concrete, and then footsteps. When I'd finished, I found the camera at my feet.

I had a huge headache by the time I schluffed my way to the run-down warehouse that comprised my lair and the 'offices' of DragonEye, PI. I couldn't afford a wizard, but a vet who owed me one cleaned out and bandaged my wing. Nonetheless, the iron had gotten into my system. My joints ached. Staying away from Cain sounded like a really good idea.

I settled myself onto my nest of cushions and mats to consider my next move. Once upon a time, I would not have had to consider, except perhaps to weigh the gastric advantages of finding this Bordello and eating him for having the gall to threaten a dragon. Thanks to St. George, though, I now had to deal with messy things like loyalties and human morality. Having a tasty Bordello for dinner might benefit me in the short run, but who knew what God would think? Just like for every good act I do, I get back some of my dragon abilities, every deed immoral (by human standards) sets me back. The only path to my former greatness was the straight and narrow.

God bless St. George, magically overpowered pain in the tail.

Stay away from Cain. Could be the best move—certainly the safest—but what if he were in trouble himself, and I stood by and let him fall? Sin of omission, black mark on the dragon's record. Never mind that a dragon's natural role was that of watcher. No, I had to get in the fray, put myself at risk just like so many mortal beings did for each other.

Did for me.

Abel broke three ribs that day saving me—and his brother had had to deal with the pain.

With a sigh, I pulled the Snack's camera and thumbed through the photos. A mom and a couple of sisters. Didn't look like there was a father in the picture, literally or figuratively. Had to admit, the kid had talent. Got a good shot of me before the arrow, and one of the attacker. Too bad it was after he'd lowered the gun—not that I wouldn't remember that for a good long time.

Yep, definitely one for the scrapbooks…and perhaps something more practical.

One thing I'd learned fast about the Mundane world was the usefulness of computers, especially as I started getting more serious about this PI gig. Despite sacrificing a lot of meals, I could only afford a crappy PC that couldn't play WoW without lag, but I did have a decent scanner and facial recognition software.

'Well, Snack, looks like you're forgiven.'

Soon, I was settled in front of my computer to see what the Internet pulled up on Dark Meat, drink at my side—a gas can with a PVC pipe for a straw. Yeah, it looks silly, but it killed the pain.

Didn't take long to discover what a celebrity I'd had my photo op with. Angel Lamont, 34, had made quite a name for himself—a name most often seen in the company of words like 'allegedly' and 'suspected' but seldom with 'convicted.' Somebody's health care program included a good lawyer.

I had fairly well mellowed when I heard the cars pull up to my lot—a familiar SUV followed by a sedan. I shut down my computer fast and tucked the camera aside. The last thing I needed was the sheriff seeing me in a compromising situation with America's Allegedly Most Wanted.

I settled myself behind my desk at the far end of the warehouse and waited. The desk was for the humans—a kind of familiar barrier that made them feel safe. The long walk was for me—a sign that if you wanted to see the dragon, you would make the effort. Of course, the whole thing would have been more impressive had the walk been through stone-hewn tunnels or lined with gold and precious treasures like my home in Caraparavalenciana. Instead, cardboard boxes and other dreck abandoned with the warehouse lined the walls. I'd flame them all, or would if I'd had fire-breathing abilities. Besides, I went through them when I was bored. Exceedingly bored. The previous owner had been some kind of discount resale dealer; beanie baby knock-offs and plates with presidents holding kittens does not compete with jewels and artifacts. 'An exercise in humility,' Father Rich calls it. If my humility got any more exercise, it could compete in the Olympics.

Of course, Fr. Rich always counters that if it competed against my ego, it wouldn't stand a chance.

I put on my 'contemplating things ineffable to Man' face and waited for them to approach. Sheriff Bert's buddy wore a dark blue, pinstriped suit—expensive, unless you got it on sale. The shoes were expensive, but older and evenly worn. He shrugged as he walked, trying to get his shoulder holster settled more comfortably. A Fed whose work usually involved sitting at his desk.

Interesting, but not as interesting as the bag Bert carried. I tried not to drool as he approached.

Bert, however, smelled something else. His nose wrinkled in distaste. 'You drinking again, Vern?'

'It's medicinal.' I tentatively unfolded one wing to show him the bandage. 'Some punks in an alley. Won't be flying for a while. But that's not why you're here, is it?'

'Brought you something from Natura.' Bert set the sack on the desk.

Lamb lightly sautéed in wine, with a touch of mint. My nostrils twitched, but I warned my stomach not to growl. 'What do you want in return?'

Bert started with his 'Don't be that way' routine, but the Fed jumped in. 'We need some information.'

I tilted my head in Bert's direction. 'This the kind of information I should have a lawyer present for?'

The Fed's eyes narrowed. 'Are you guilty of something?'

'Not guilty. Wary. Mundanes have several reactions when first meeting me—and 'professional suspicion' isn't on that list. Whatever you think I did, Fed, I'm innocent.'

Bert sighed. 'Vern, we just want to ask you some general questions—but if I'd known you were going to pull an attitude...' He reached for the bag.

I set my paw on it first. 'It's fine. Inversions make me cranky. What do you need to know?'

His offering and its conditions accepted, Bert relaxed and pulled up one of the cheap roll-away chairs I kept for potential clients. 'What do you know about a mage named Willard Whitehaven?'

I said a small thanks that he hadn't asked me if I'd heard of the man. 'Nothing. Tried Google?'

'He's a Faerie,' the Fed said. 'Some kind of expert on magical theory.'

'And he didn't show up for a meeting today at the college,' Bert concluded.

'Maybe he got waylaid by the glamour of your shopping mall.' The Faerie and Mundane worlds had only been connected for a little over a year, and indoor shops and food courts cast their own kind of spell on visitors from my world.

The Fed's expression soured. Guess he didn't have much of a sense of humor. 'He was supposed to have been met at the Gap by the college shuttle, only its tires got slashed. By the time they got there, he was gone, and he never showed at the meeting.'

'Security camera got a shot of him entering a car with this

guy.' Bert called up some footage on his cell phone and passed it to me. The cameras around the Gap station were the best in the market—or at least the best the government would shell out for. I got my first look at Whitehaven, a portly mage with a braided beard, wearing a suit cut to Mundane style but with the needlework popular in Faerie. Not a bad combination, as far as outfits go. Too bad I couldn't say the same about the company he kept.

I watched as a smiling Cain swept his arm toward a vehicle as the driver hastened to open the door. Not just any driver, either. Looked like Dark Meat was a man of many talents.

I handed back the phone. 'I don't know the guy or anything about him. Anything else?'

Fed leaned his hands on my desk, an aggressive move designed to provoke reaction. Yeah, right, as if a predator like me had any reason to feel threatened. He was not endearing me to his cause, however. 'Whitehaven was studying how to increase the flow of magic through the Gap into this world. Our theory is someone wants him to do that for them. Since humans can't use magic—'

'Whitehaven looks human to me.'

'*Normal* humans—*Mundanes*, you call us.' He snarled the last.

Not that I blamed him, but I didn't make up the name any more than I did 'Faerie.' I just use it along with the rest of the universes. 'So you think a Magical did this?'

Bert shrugged, clearly not comfortable with the theory himself. 'Or a mage seeking to increase his power here. Aren't they pretty limited? We already know that the farther you get from Los Lagos and the Gap, the less magical influence there is. Prof at the college said it's an exponential decline. By the time you hit Colorado Springs, you can't summon enough to light a candle, he said.'

'Depends on the inherent power of the mage and how much he stores before crossing over, but I get your point.' I turned a baleful glare at the federal agent. 'Sure you have it right? Maybe it's a *normal* human wanting to find out how to cut off the trickle of magic instead of increasing the flow. Or are we disregarding that line of investigation because you'd just as soon see that happen?'

Who needs posturing when a few well-placed words can provoke such a reaction? The agent's face turned Fiery Federal Red, his lips compressed against an angry tirade I knew he longed to unleash. His fingers curled, squeaking on the cheap finish of my desk. If he'd had claws—or didn't bite his nails to the quick—he'd have left scratches.

'We'll be looking into that, too, Vern,' Bert said, but with a pause that made me think I'd brought a point home for him. 'But you know the Magicals, especially those that might be looking for trouble. Can you put out some feelers, see if anyone knows anything?'

'You taking me on as a consultant, then?' Rent was over-due. I could use the greenbacks, and maybe, just maybe, I could play this behind the scenes and let the cops get Cain out of his mess. He might spend some time behind bars, but it'd probably do him good. Better than the noose he'd have gotten in Faerie.

'One-twenty-five a day, plus expenses? I don't plan on you getting into danger—just nose around a little.'

'I think we'll keep the hazardous pay option open,' I countered. I knew my luck, especially with a case like this.

'Deal.' Fed started to sputter a protest, but Bert slapped his hands on his knees and stood. 'Tony, give him your card, so he can call you if he finds something hot. After all, it's your case. I'm just providing local support. See you later, Vern.' He shelled out a day's wages in cash and headed to the door without another look back.

The Fed fixed me with an angry stare—I think his face must have froze that way as a kid—and slapped a business card on my desk. 'Let's get one thing straight, dragon. I don't like 'consultants,' and I like your kind even less. You gather information, then you call me. That's it. No getting involved. *Capice?*'

I glanced at the card: Agent Anthony B. Soussan. No wonder he had an attitude; probably got worse every time he had to put last name first. '*Capito*, Agent Soussan, B. Anthony.'

It was a cheap shot, but it was all I could afford.

I wolfed down my meal and headed out myself. Thanks to my unexpected visit from the Heat, I had a couple of leads, and while the Internet might not hold the answers, I knew another source that might.

The receptionist behind the desk stopped filing her nails to smile at me as I entered. She pulled out an ear bud; I could hear some guy nattering on in a well-modulated tone about personal success. 'Hi, Vern! Long time, no see! Come to visit Shiny?'

'He available?'

She nodded, then leaned forward conspiratorially. 'Between you and me, he could use some cheering up. He's lost his luster lately.'

'Brasso and Windex?' I suggested.

'You know how he hates that!' She giggled and waved me to the small office. The lighting was low, but not dim, and scented candles filled the room with lavender. A simple but comfortable chair faced a large gilt mirror. I pushed the chair aside and sat on my haunches.

'Mirror, doomed to affirmation, I'm looking for some information.'

The glass smoked, then a face appeared—noble, compassionate, understanding radiating from its eyes...

Then it saw who was talking to it and dropped the façade. 'Vern! By all that is clear! What a relief. Get me out of here.'

Oh, no. I was not carrying this conversation in rhyme. 'Bad day at work?'

His jowls drooped and circles darkened around his eyes. 'You have no idea what it's like—having to find nice, truthful things to say all day long. These people are so...needy!'

I shrugged. 'It's this or back to the vaults in the Vatican.'

'It's not fair!'

'You're the one who took a confident queen and turned her into a megalomaniac—'

'Hey! I warned her beauty was fleeting, and she *was* the

49

fairest in the land until her stepdaughter just...blossomed. I mean, seriously! Did you ever see Snow White? What a dish. But you know, at least the Queen believed me. The losers I get in here are always *doubting* me! Me! The Magic Mirror who sees all and speaks truth. But no! It's always, 'I still think my nose is too big,' or 'You haven't seen me without make-up'—'

'Babbling mirror of affirmation, I came here for information!'

Shiny huffed, but he could not resist a command in rhyme. 'Fine! At least it's a change of pace. What do you need, O Great Dragon of the Church?'

I hated when he called me that. 'Mage Willard Whitehaven—what have you got?'

'One moment, please.' The face disappeared, replaced by an hour glass that kept flipping. Cute.

After several long moments that I spent dozing off the food, alcohol, and pain, he returned. 'Willard Whitehaven, Mage of Natural Magics, Seventh Level, theorist more than practical. Wonderful beard—quite vain about it, too. Has some very nice mirrors in his office as well as at home. Quite popular at university—particularly with his fifth-level interns. Likes them smart, but not too much—'

'Annoying mirror, full of gossip; cut the crap.'

The mirror raised his brows.

'That's it.'

'Well, what are you looking for?'

'He was doing research on the transference of magical energy across the Gap—large scale, generalized transfer, is my guess, not contained in relics or artifacts. How close was he to a breakthrough?'

The mirror laughed. 'Depends on who he was talking to— Sorry, no gossip, just facts.' He released his mirth with a sigh and spoke slowly as he pulled truth out of the complexities of university politics and (apparently) romantic pursuits. 'He has some interesting ideas and much confidence, but they still know too little about the Gap. No one's even sure that magical energy does spill from Faerie into this world. I mean, it stands to reason there is, or I would not continue to function and you would not be able to do whatever magic it is you do when not harassing honest mirrors like me. However, some say we carry that much magic within ourselves and our time is running out.'

I thought back to what the receptionist said. 'Do you think you're losing your edge?'

The mirror's face tilted back so far, there was only shadow and the outline of chin. 'Oh, how would I know? I'm used to dealing with royalty; now, I'm reassuring the rabble that their pitiful existences have meaning. They do, don't get me wrong, but it's on such a different scale. No one's content being a peasant here, and they blame their status on themselves or on others. What is it about this world that makes people always want more?'

Being an impoverished creature of greed, I didn't have a good reply. 'Could he do it, though? Given time and study?'

Shiny met my eyes. 'I wouldn't count on it. More likely, his spells might damage the Gap. He's playing with arcane fire, and his university knows it. That's why he was coming here. Mundane ignorance is his bliss.'

Magic Mirrors—better than a search engine. Now for the winning question. 'Can you see where he is now? Most likely he's on this side of the Gap.'

Shiny closed his eyes, searching the mirrors around Los Lagos for as far as his magic would stretch. 'The latest was this morning...a gas station...corner of Peak and Hillfield.'

'Hillfield?'

'Enchanted mirror speaks true. Heed what I tell you.'

Even magical mirrors had limits. My time was up. 'I'll put in a good word with the Bishop.'

'Vern?'

I paused at the door.

'I have been here six months, trying to help these unfortunate souls see the true good in themselves. They all want to believe in magic—but they don't want to believe me. Haven't I paid for my sins with the Queen? How long will the Church leave me to this?'

'When I can answer that question for myself, I'll let you know.'

I hailed a cab to take me to the gas station on Hillfield and Peak. The place had seen better days; the only improvements in decades had been to get credit card readers on the pumps. The bathroom was outside, unlocked, the mirror cloudy and unwashed with a lovely view of the urinal. I gave Shiny points for sullying himself on my behalf. The place stank so bad, I didn't think I could pick out Whitehaven even if I had known his scent. No amount of bleach would help this place, just a torch.

The kid at the counter hadn't seen anything, but then again, he barely noticed my entrance, and I'm an 850-pound, scarlet-and-red, winged dragon. 'Course, he nearly jumped out of his skin when I pressed my nose against the safety glass, so my ego wasn't too hurt.

I had the cab take me to a strip mall in town, then walked the rest of the way to Abel's hotel.

I found my friend sitting on the edge of his bed, a bag of ice pressed against his face.

'What happened?'

'Mistaken identity. Big, Italian-looking man. Thought I was running out on…whatever. Hit me a few times, told me to get back 'there' or he'd kill me.'

'Did he say where?'

Abel winced when he shook his head. 'But Cain knows, obviously. He's reaching out to me, but it's mostly messages to stay away. Do you know where he is? Can we get him out of this?'

I settled myself on the floor. 'This is not like when he convinced an earl that he could weave magic cloth. That was a simple case of noble embarrassment. This time, he's helped kidnap a high-profile figure. The FBI is looking for him and his buddies.'

Abel muttered a prayer of desperation. 'What do we do?'

'We're not in Faerie, Abel. I can't fly in, roaring threats, and swoop out with Cain like some kind of prey. The cops have a cage at the zoo they'd love to toss me in, and the bad guys are going after me with cold iron—plus, I got some goon named Bordello warning me off—'

'Bordello?'

I did not like the look on Abel's face. 'You know him?'

He was pale. 'Cain does. He's afraid of him—really afraid.'

'Well, that knights the virgin. This is out of my league. I'm giving the police all the information I have and letting them take care of it. Your brother's going to have to take his lumps. Maybe he'll learn something this time.'

Despite his pain, Abel leapt to his feet. 'You can't! This is my brother—'

'And look how well he's treated you. He knows what you go through. Yet how many times have you saved him? You should count your blessings that last time he only tricked an earl and not an emperor like the bards say. They have a word for your behavior in the Mundane. Enabling. He needs to accept the consequences for his actions—and if that hurts you, too, I'm sorry, but he has to be stopped.'

Abel sank back onto the bed, defeated. The ice pack slipped from his hands to fall at his feet. 'What if I get him to turn himself in—that means something here, doesn't it?'

I nodded. 'They might go easier on him. Depends. Soussan didn't sound like the most forgiving sort. Don't worry—we're talking jail time, not noose around the neck. You're better off leaving him to hang dry on this side of the Gap.'

'I don't know…'

I reared up and stuck my snout so close to his face, he had to lean back. 'Well, *I* know. Listen to me, Abel. You've been your brother's keeper for long enough. You deal with his agonies while he goes off to find more ways to hurt himself. You run to his rescue when he gets into hot water. Then, you set him free with a simple entreaty to be good that he never follows. You make it easy for him to sin—is that what you want?'

'I…' He shook his head, more bewildered than denying.

I moved in closer, so he had to brace himself to stay sitting. 'You tip your brother off, and I'll set the police after you as an accomplice. If he won't pay for his crimes personally, he can do it through you.'

'You'd do that? After all I'd done for you?'

'Gratitude is cheap and easily forgotten. I'd have thought you'd have learned that from Cain.' I backed off, and Abel fell forward, gasping. 'I'm heading back to my office to tell the Feds what I know. You'd be smart to head back to the monastery before they find out Cain's twin knew about his antics all along.'

It was a long walk home, but I didn't want to blow any more dough on a cab. In fact, I was debating holding off another day before calling my information in, just to rake in the next $125. Nah, probably be stealing, and with all the cops around…

Why were there so many cops around—and why was that plainclothesman in the unmarked car giving me the fisheye? I gave him a nod, friendly and good-citizen-like, and took a casual left down an alley.

I should have known better. Sirens wailed and sedans blocked both exits. It was kind of amusing, actually, thinking that a couple of Chryslers could stop me, but I wasn't in the mood to be amused.

Agents piled out, using the cars as shields while they pointed their guns at me. Definitely not amusing.

A pause for me to take in my situation, then Soussan stepped out of the car and approached.

I sat on my haunches, tail tucked around me like a cat, and exuded nonchalance. He'd have to do better to impress me. 'This how you treat all your consultants?'

'You're not my consultant,' he snarled. His heart pounded so hard, I could see his pulse in the carotid artery; sweat beaded at his hairline that had nothing to do with the heat, and he smelled of stress and aggression. Something very bad had happened, and he'd decided to blame me.

'The Sheriff's, then. Sorry for assuming you were on the same team. Maybe I need to ask for hazardous pay for talking to you?'

'Can the crap, dragon. Where's the kid?'

'What kid?' It hit me: they were combing the neighborhood, the same neighborhood where I'd had my photo—and my wing—shot. 'You mean Snack?'

Wrong words! Every agent around me stiffened, and I smelled the spike in adrenalin and the subtle shifting of men ready to shoot at a for-real dragon.

'I didn't eat him!' I hollered for all to hear, then said more quietly to Soussan. 'Look, all I know is that some kid on a dare took my picture today. I called him 'Snack.' I do that; I don't mean anything by it. Scrawny thing, dirty blond hair, brown eyes, more guts than his size suggests. Same kid?'

'Can the innocent routine. He was last seen taking a photo of you, and now we got witnesses that you were carrying a camera—as if dragons take photographs. You obviously took it from him.'

'I did not!'

'Oh, he gave it to you, then? What did you do in exchange—eat him quick?'

Okay, that was harsh enough to surprise even me. I gaped, and then started talking fast. 'Listen, Soussan, while you're making wild accusations, someone else has the kid, and they may actually be after those photos, which, yes, he *gave* to me.'

'Where's the camera?'

'My office. Look, we can help each other; there was a one guy—'

Soussan dropped to the ground.

I wasn't stupid, I shot into the air like a bat out of hell, a swarm of bullets slicing through the air I'd just vacated and pocketing the wall. Apparently, he'd believed me when I'd said earlier I couldn't fly; he didn't have anyone watching the skies. I disappeared into the dirty gray haze.

I didn't go far, though. They'd expect me to fly off, and my wing wasn't that well healed. Besides, something didn't add up. If he thought I ate a kid, why the concern about the photos—and why bullets and not tranqs? Not that I enjoyed being drugged and waking up in a zoo, but it's not the first time the police had played that card.

My species might be the greatest predators in the world,

but eight centuries of growing back from lizard size had taught me the usefulness of stealth. I hid inside an air conditioning vent, stilled my breathing, and listened as Soussan sent the cops scurrying in cars and on foot to search me out. He stormed to his car, but rather than cranking the engine, I heard him flip out his cell phone.

'It's me. Yeah, he has them. Yeah. Well, your man should be more careful next time. Whatever—not my problem. They're back at his place. Figure you have twenty minutes. No, that's the last place he'll go; he'll expect that we're waiting for him. What, am I stupid? I sent my men to search the neighborhood; I'm heading to his lair myself and will call for backup if he shows. No! Don't do anything with the kid. Just get the camera and wipe his hard drive. You have nineteen minutes now.'

He snarled and hung up, then started the car and tore off with a squeal of tires that made me wince. Great. Not enough that I had to deal with a wayward brother, a kidnapped mage, and some underground hothead who wanted me out of his business, but the world added a kidnapped child and a dirty cop. No going to Sheriff Bert. What little evidence I had waited back in my lair—along with who-knew how many thugs and soon a federal agent who had no qualms about putting holes in the dragon.

Bert has a saying: When you're going through Hell, keep on going. I think Dante might have appreciated it. I launched myself high into the air where I wouldn't be seen and started back toward Abel's place.

I knocked Abel over as I flew in through the window and swatted the curtains shut with my tail before backing off him. 'Where is he?' I demanded.

'I don't know.'

'Don't, Abel!' I roared. 'Do not play games with me. There's a kid involved—a human child. You really want that on your conscience?'

'A child?' He sat hard on the edge of the hotel bed.

'Neat kid. Got guts. Might be a knight someday, if he lives

through this—and we're going to make sure he lives through this.'

Abel dropped his head in his hands. 'I told him to get out. I told him!'

'You...what?'

I got quiet—the kind of quiet that said the next thing out of my mouth would drown a person in flames. If only I had my fire back. 'When did you contact Cain?'

'He found me.' Abel moaned. 'We met at the coffee shop down the street. We traded clothes. He had money; I told him to run for the Gap while I created a diversion. That's when I got beat up. The guy, he hit me and threw me into a cab.'

'To where?'

'I don't know. As soon as my head was clear enough, I jumped out when we stopped at a light. I was scared, Vern!'

Since I couldn't breathe fire, I started to pace, back and forth, like a panther in a cage, close enough to brush against Abel's shins. I wanted him to remember that he had something to fear right in front of him. 'Think! What address did he give the cabbie?'

'No address, just... Thatcher! Thatcher and Hillfield.'

Hillfield again. I pulled out his map and spread it on the floor. He dropped to his knees beside me to look. I found Peak and Hillfield, traced on to the address with my claw, a few miles further out of town from the gas station, and before the street turned into a state highway.

'There's no Carson Road.' Abel examined the legend. 'What's at Hillfield and Thatcher?'

Looked like national forest, for the most part—federally protected wildlife...and...

'Military depot!' I pointed to a small circle, too small to hold a name, just 'FCA.'

'Bet that's an annex of Ft. Carson. Hail us a cab while I make a call.'

* * *

Forty minutes later, we hid behind some bushes on a hill overlooking a small, abandoned military complex. Concrete buildings and razor-wire fences, overturned vehicles, and a couple of manikins in the windows—must be where they practice invasion techniques. Too bad they hadn't protected against an invasion by a criminal mastermind.

With eyes and nose, I counted six humans, male, Mundane, armed; plus Whitehaven and the kid.

While we cowered and waited for the cops to arrive, I heard them interrogate Whitehaven about his work with the Gap—mostly demands accentuated by the meat slap of hard fists on soft flesh. A voice that sounded remarkably like Abel's said, 'We don't have to continue this way, Whitehaven.'

'All right,' I told Abel. 'Looks like Little Brother ain't so good at listening. Cain and another goon are roughing up Whitehaven.'

'No!' he hissed.

I ignored him. 'They're unarmed, as best I can hear. Two more are with the kid, and two are pacing the perimeter. You get Cain and Whitehaven; I'll get the kid. You may have to do things you'll need to confess later.'

Abel nodded and muttered a quick prayer as I listened to Cain working Whitehaven.

Cain paused in roughing up the mage. 'We only want your cooperation, Willard. Isn't that what you were offering the university? Help with the flow of magic problem?'

'I want to increase it, not cut it off.' The statement ended in a bubbly cough.

'I just want to help my brother. Life doesn't give us guarantees—but I can guarantee this: if you don't cooperate, neither of us is going to live very long.'

'Even if I would help you, I don't know how!'

This time, the slap ended in a clattering of wood—they must have knocked him over. I heard a chair being set upright, and Cain spoke again. 'You know, if you don't care about your life, you might at least think of mine.'

Whitehaven laughed. Had to give him credit for bravery.

'Fine. Maybe someone else's life then. Get the kid!'

Abel interrupted my concentration with a smack on my shoulder and pointed. A tall, thin man, his shirt off to expose wiry muscles, exited one of the cement hovels, Snack slung over his shoulder and kicking for all he was worth. His feet impacted helplessly on the bruiser's shoulders. I could probably chew those muscles for days.

They were heading to the shack where Whitehaven was being held.

'Let's go before he adds murder to his list of sins!' I bounded off the rock and soared toward Slim Jim and the kid.

Slim Jim gave a startled 'Urk' and hit the dirt as I swooped toward him, making it easy to snatch the kid in my claws. Momentum carried me into the plaza. I heard a gunshot and felt something ping against my scales as I strained to alter course. My injured wing burned with effort. At least Snack was smart enough to not struggle as I carried him to the safety of the woods. I found a sizable Ponderosa Pine with an opening in its foliage, and plopped him onto a sturdy branch. Holding him steady with my tail, I sliced through his bonds with my claws.

'They won't see you from below,' I told him. 'Stay still and stay quiet. I'll be back.'

He trembled like an aspen and gripped a branch for all his life was worth, but nodded. Good enough. I expended a little magic to lift my weight from the tree and push off toward the camp without disturbing the branches of his hiding spot. I paused to scan the highway. Where was my back-up?

I couldn't wait—I'd sent a monk out to do a copper's job. Maybe I'd better schedule some Confession time, myself. What hell did Dante assign to the well-intentioned?

Please, let Abel be all right.

I found Slim Jim still unconscious on the cracked cement of the plaza, bleeding at the forehead from a wound I didn't cause. Someone had hit him with a rock, a big one, and his gun was gone. Had I missed the backup, or had my gentle monk picked up a few things from his wayward brother?

A shot whizzed past me. Goon must have been pretty scared to miss something of my bulk at such close range— that, or God had taken a special interest in my well-being.

Either way worked for me. I turned my back on them and high-tailed it to the building where Cain held Whitehaven. If I could, I just wanted to collect Whitehaven and Abel, and leave the sheriff to sort the rest out.

I slammed claws first into the wood door, the dragon version of kicking it down that sent splinters flying through the room. As everyone ducked, I lashed out with my tail and took out Dark Meat who allegedly worked as Cain's personal bruiser. Once 'round the ankles and jerk. He cracked the Formica floor with his head. I'd have to confess the satisfaction that gave me..

'Abel! Grab Whitehaven and let's go! Cain, if you've any sense left—'

My instructions died in my throat. Whitehaven lay unconscious on the floor, and Cain held a gun to his brother's temple.

'I told you, Vern! I told you to stay out of my business. Why couldn't you listen?'

'Stay out of your... *You're* Bordello? How did you get involved in the Mundane underworld?'

Cain shook his head. His grip on the gun wobbled, but not enough. I could not believe how calm Abel remained, how still. Waiting. Why wasn't he talking his brother into letting him go? Great time to return to his vow of silence.

Fine. I'd do the talking for both of us. 'Why, Cain—or should I call you, 'Bordello'? Did you plan on bottling magic to sell?'

'No! No money. No magic! Please, Vern, I need you to understand. Help me—or, if you won't help, at least walk away. This world...it harbors so many temptations—so much freedom. Too many perversions. And now—and now, we would add magic to the mix?'

'I don't think that's our call.' I settled myself down catlike in front of him, a bit toward his gun hand. No matter what my size, God graces me with a long tail. A sneaky, quick tail. I just needed a chance. 'God tells us to conquer our temptations.'

'You don't understand this world. You can't—you're not

human. There's so much here, but these Mundanes! They'll want more. They're never satisfied! They'll take our magic if we let them. They'll pervert it to their pleasure—and they'll do the same to the Magicals. To you, Vern! They don't care about you. You're a novelty! If they can't keep you in a zoo, it's only a matter of time before they find some other way to use you to feed their desires.

'Help me, Vern. We have to make Whitehaven see reason. We have to stop the flow of magic through the Gap.'

'The Magicals will die,' Abel protested, his voice just above a whisper.

'No. They'll return home. They'll have to. You'll see! You'll—uh!'

Abel hit himself in the stomach. Cain folded with a grunt and I nabbed the gun and threw it aside. Abel twisted around his brother and got him in a restraining hold. From the way both grimaced, I couldn't tell who was causing whom pain. Then Abel shrieked as Cain spit blood out of his own bitten mouth and dashed away. I bunched muscles to pounce.

A shot exploded through the air and struck Abel in the throat.

Cain screamed and folded.

I changed targets and let my full weight fall upon Dark Meat, crushing his right arm and several ribs. The gun fell from his hands, and he howled.

Abel's mouth opened in a soundless shout, and he staggered to his brother. He knelt over him, sobbing, the bullet wound in his throat healing as an identical one flowered bloody red on his brother's.

'Vern,' Cain croaked.

I leaned toward him.

'I did it for you. I'm sorry.'

Sirens wailed in the distance, moving closer, but it was too late.

I could only pray his words of apology were to God and not me.

I showed up at 'Abel's' hotel room with the most expensive bottle of Scotch I could afford. While 'Abel' was making arrangements for his brother, I'd put in a little overtime digging up evidence connecting Anthony Soussan with Bordello and his posse. Maybe the word would get out among the authorities that they should treat the dragon with more respect next time. If not, at least I'd staved off the creditors for another month. In this world, I take what I can get.

'Abel' had packed, and his bags waited by the door, but he accepted the bottle and topped off one of the motel glasses. 'Kid okay?'

'Snack? Yeah. Apparently achieving new popularity as a result of his adventures.'

He nodded, studied his glass. Silence stretched.

'Arrangements done for the body?'

Again, the distracted nod.

'How's it feel to be half a Corsican twin?'

'Exactly like that. Half. I cut myself shaving this morning. Felt it, too.'

'Welcome to the rest of the world.'

He gave a halfhearted laugh, which ended in a shaky sigh. 'Vern, I…'

I waited, and when nothing else came out, stood and stretched. 'Well, I should go. You probably want to get back to the monastery.'

'Wait, please. I have a confession to make.'

'That's what Father Kirkpatrick is for.' I sat down nonetheless.

'I'm, I'm not going to the monastery. I'm not who you think I am. I.. I'm Cain.'

'I know.' I grabbed his glass with my tail and poured its contents down my throat.

Cain blinked. 'How?'

'I figured it out at the shack. Cain wouldn't have cared one way or the other about Magicals. What I can't figure out is why you called me in the first place. Why the lies about being Abel and trying to find your brother?'

'I didn't think you'd believe me, and I desperately needed an ally. It's my fault—so many years, the emotions I subjected him to—highs as well as lows. I didn't know what I'd done to him. I came here, just like he said, seeking new temptations, new perversions. He followed me, but this time, he wanted to join me. One week, he said—one week, we'd indulge all our basest appetites, then return home to confess and sin no more. I think he hoped that if she shared my debauchery, I'd share in his remorse.

'He couldn't do it. It was so contrary to his nature to sin, but he stayed with me, nonetheless. It didn't matter what he did: he saw things, being with me. Things he might have guessed at but never knew, and he heard people talking—*Mundanes* talking. The things they'd do with magic and Magicals.'

Cain curled in on himself. 'I don't know how he found those men working for him. I can't even imagine how he recruited Soussan. He knew Whitehaven, though.' He laughed. 'He pretended to be me pretending to be him, can you believe it? I tried to talk sense into him, but he wouldn't listen. He said he was protecting me, just like he said he was protecting you, Vern.

'All my life, he protected me—and this is how I repaid him! Oh, God! What do I do now?' He raised the bottle to his lips.

I wasn't God, but that didn't stop me from answering. I jerked the bottle out of his grasp. 'First thing, you give that back.'

'What?'

'Do you mean what you say, or are you just looking for pity? Because dragons don't do pity. Your brother went through seven kinds of hell for you; now, you can pay him back. Take his body back to the monastery—and then stay awhile.'

He blinked at me, disbelieving. 'You think they'd take me, after all I've done?'

'Winter's coming—plenty to do to get the monastery ready. Come spring, they'll need someone to pull a plow. They'll need a brother.'

'I...'

I saw denial on his face, but he screwed his eyes shut and took a deep breath. 'Yes. I'll go. Thank you, Vern.'

That night, I dreamed of the time I lay in the wine cellar of the monastery, recovering from my self-inflicted wounds. Abel had brought me a copy of *The Inferno*, and I hadn't had the energy or heart to tell him I'd read Dante's first drafts. In my dream, I experienced again how glad I'd felt for my silence, as I opened the book and found a note in Abel's scratchy writing:

Sometimes, the trip through Hell is worth it if you can bring a soul to Heaven.

Across the Border

Hector Acosta

The tree sheds one of its panties just as I step under it. The underwear lands on my foot, and I pick it up without thinking. The fabric feels soft and frayed underneath my fingertips, its colors having been beaten away by the sun long ago, like most things around here.

'How do we know he's really a *brujo?*'

I look up from the panties and towards the group. There's a man kneeling on the ground, hands tied behind his back, two big, identical looking guys on each side of the captive, their meaty hands pressed down firmly on each of his shoulders. An old woman accompanied by her pretty daughter stand to the side, both of them wearing black dresses, which have to be soaking in the rays of the sun. It's the daughter who asked the question.

'Bianca shut up,' the old woman says. Then she turns and apologizes to me, 'I'm sorry señor Blanco. Her sister's death has made her say nonsense.'

'*Mama,*' Bianca says, 'You're paying him a lot of money. We need to be sure.'

'They caught *el pendejo* taking advantage of another girl under this tree, how much more sure do you need to be?'

I expect the man to speak up now, but he doesn't. So I walk over to him and say in Spanish, 'Last chance.'

He looks up at me and I see a smashed up nose; a broken faucet from which bright spots of blood trickle out from. 'I didn't kill her. She paid me to take her across the border yeah, but she didn't even show up on the agreed upon day.'

'Liar,' the old, small woman shouts and moves towards him, only to be restrained by Bianca. 'You kill my *mija*,' she says between sobs. 'She trusted you and you dragged her to his place and...' She's doesn't finish, burying her face in the crook of the younger woman's neck and crying loudly. 'I told

65

her not to hire a *coyote*, to just wait and we would find a safe way to get her to *Los Estados*.'

'I didn't do it,' the guy says, staring up at me with fury in his eyes.

Shit. I was hoping he would have confessed by now.

I glance back to the tree. I hear that up north they call them Joshua trees, a name apparently given to them by some churchy settlers that thought the branches looked like hands praying to the heavens. To me, the way the branches stretch out in all directions have always seem like they are doing their best to try to get away from the land. That's probably why the *gringo* name hasn't stuck. Though I still prefer it over what most people down here have started to call them - *arape* trees, a twisted little example of Spanglish in action.

We're standing a couple of miles away from Tijuana, near the U.S border, and under a blazing sun that presses down on my back like an unwanted lover. Around here, arape trees litter the desert, though most of them aren't garnished quite like this one. Depending on who you ask; the underwear either acts as a reminder or warning of the horrors that can transpire under the shadow of this type of trees.

That's why I'm here today. I'm supposed to invoke one of those horrors back to the surface, so that it can testify against its murderer.

Reaching for the small leather bag around my waist, I keep my eyes on the tree, watching a polka dotted bra hanging from one of the branches. I suddenly have the urge to reach out and pluck it down, and the more I try to ignore the urge, the more I want to do so. My fingers tickle.

'I just think that if we're going to rely on your word to sentence this man, we need to be sure that you can do what you say you can.' Bianca breaks the trance I was in and I look at back at her. If she wasn't making life so difficult for me right now, I would enjoy the way the heat is causing her dress to cling to body and reveal a shapely figure.

'You doubt what I can do?' My voice is smooth and calm, even as I feel a bead of sweat slide down the bridge of my nose. *Appearances are everything,* I remind myself. *She's not the first you have had to convince.*

'I just think that if we're going to rely on your word to sentence this man, we need to be sure that you can do what you say you can.'

'I didn't kill her,' *El Coyote* mutters.

'See,' Bianca says, 'He doesn't say that he didn't,' she pauses, and I imagine her trying to get the word 'rape' out of her mouth. At the end, she fails and says 'Do those things. Just that he didn't kill her. Why admit to one and not the other?'

'I didn't kill her,' the man says again, this time louder and directed at Bianca. 'I swear to *la Virgenita* that I didn't kill her.'

'You want proof,' I say, 'Fine. What would you like me to do?'

'One of the articles of clothing on the tree is my sister's. Take it down.' I can hear the dare in her voice, and it angers me, even though she's not wrong in asking. It's what I would do if I was in her position. Too many people are quick to take things at face value.

'You're asking me to break the sacred accordance,' I say, 'You know, you all know, the reason why we allow the clothing to remain as is.'

'So that the evil spirits remain trapped in the tree,' one of the cousin whispers. See what I mean about people taking things at face value? Everything I had just said was bullshit, but they're happy to not only believe it, but add to the lie. All just because it lives up to their expectations of tradition and culture.

Nevertheless, I nod and say, 'Correct.'

'I saw you pick up one from the floor,' Bianca says. I swear I see a smile of triumph flash across her face.

'I'm sure your mother taught you better. Once they fall to the ground, we are allowed to retrieve them and burn them. Never before.'

'So you can't do it.'

Before I can answer, I hear motion from the side, and look

just in time to see Coyote cut through his knots. One of the two that's supposed to be guarding the man has instead been watching Bianca and I argue, and he doesn't notice Coyote until it's too late. Next thing he knows, he's holding his belly and trying to keep his guts in while Coyote runs.

Already he's shifting.

I draw my revolver out and aim. The sound of the gun going off surrounds the otherwise quiet desert and sends a nearby perched bird flying. The Coyote keeps running.

Aiming again, I watch as the man begins to change. His arms jerk in all directions and his run becomes like something reflected out of a fun house mirror, full of high angles and leg spasms. I pull the trigger, and this time see a tiny burst of pink where Coyote's head should have been, like a stripper coquettishly showing her goods for the first time. Coyote drops to the ground, still twitching.

'Why didn't anyone tell me he was a *nagual*?' I ask. *Why didn't I know he was a nagual?*

They look at me. The guy that got gutted is laying on the ground, his brother hovering over him. The mom and daughter are standing nearby, neither saying a thing. They're all in shock, and I don't blame them. It's not every day that you get to see a skinwalker.

'Put him back in the car, and here, make sure he swallows this,' I say, opening up my small bag and sifting around until I find a small white pill.

The guy looks at me when I hand it to him. 'Is it safe?'

'As safe as oxycodone is. We need to get him back to Tijuana though.' I'm already walking towards the nagual's body.

Fuckity fuck fuck. This was supposed to have been an easy job. I was supposed to go up to the tree, put on a show for the family, and after a few minutes, turn around and finger the guy for the deed.

Hey, don't look at me that way. Asshole was a confirmed rapist. So he might or might not have killed that specific girl, I was pretty sure he'd killed some girl at some point. Pinning one more death on him wouldn't really tip the balance of things. In fact, what I was doing could be seen as a public service if you really thought about it; the family gets to walk away with some sort of closure, a bad dude is taken out of the equation, and I get paid in something other than the usual food and bar drinks. A win-win for everyone. Well, everyone except the Coyote. And the dead sister I guess.

I stare at what's left of Coyote. His body's a taxidermist's wet dream, caught in between human and coyote form. Legs are long and sinewy, thick calf muscles covered in grey fur. His long, stretched out arms remind me of the bubblegum prostitutes play with as they wait for customers. It might have taken two shots, but my aim was good in the end, spilling gray, red, and pink into the ground.

A coyote *nagual* that decided to do business as an actual Coyote - the term we use for the people that help illegals cross the border. If he hadn't made me waste two of my bullets, I would admire the guy's sense of humor.

Sifting through the Coyote's last thoughts with the toe of my foot, I don't see either bullet anywhere. With no other alternative, I pop open the cylinder of the revolver and steady my breath.

'Ayudame abuelo' I mutter, my thumb rubbing against the hammer of the gun. Every time I do this, the process gets harder on me, as referenced by the headache that rolls through my brain now. Sweat trickles down my face and the hair on the back of my neck stands up. I shut my eyes tighter and fight the headache, picturing the words I'm chanting building a fence around the parts of my head that hurts the most. Finally, the earth opens up beneath me, giving me a glimpse into *el mundo muerto* I suddenly know what an ant must go through every time they're about to be stepped on. It's the sudden and gigantic realization of how small and insignificant you really are. No, scratch that, it's worse than that. It's the knowledge that the world you live and work so hard to fit into, is really nothing but page one of a one thousand page novel, and you'll never get to read the ending.

The mundo explodes with color around me. The desert looks like a sea of red, rich salsa made only with the ripest of tomatoes. The horizon in front of me is a true blue, what children probably imagine heaven to look like when hearing the Sunday sermons. And yet behind me I know lies a darkness I'm not prepared to face. Above me birds scream, though I don't look up. Did that once, first time I was here, and it took me most of a year before I could even be near any of the baby chicks in our farm.

Bet you thought I was all show huh? Believe it or not, I do have some abilities. They're just kind of a pain in the ass to use, so when I can, I try to take shortcuts.

'*Que quieres niño*,' my grandfather says, standing by my side. People that knew him tell me I'm the spitting image of him, which I generally take as an insult. He's a bald, gap-toothed, old man, with a bent nose and busy eyebrows, all the features working together to make one hell of an ugly face. And that's before you get to his slit throat, the bottom flap of skin hanging like a flag of surrender. He stares at me, leaning on a cane he doesn't really need.

Abuelo here is less of a spirit and more a memory tied to the gun I held. Years back, my mom looked up a *hechizo* to try to bring her recently departed father back. The spell had required an item that the deceased held as important to them, something that could entice and ground them back to the world of the living - hence the gun. Sadly, by the time mom tried to pull the spell off, she'd already gone ass deep into her alcohol and drug phase, and so the best she could do was bring back a memory of abuelo Blanco.

Basically, the thing next to me was just a memory that thought he was the ghost of someone that was long dead and gone. Yeah, I try not to think too hard about it either.

'I need you to find my bullets,' I say. In here, the words coil around my tongue before spilling out and sinking into the red sand.

He scowls. 'This is why you bring me out? To find two bullets?'

'They're hexed and I don't want to go through the whole trouble of getting the required chupacabra milk to make a new batch.'

'So you just wake up a poor old man to go looking around for them, is that it?'

'You can't sleep,' I remind him, 'So I didn't really wake you.'

He hits me upside the head, and it hurts. That's when I realize something is wrong.

'No, no, no, no.'

Even though I never felt myself move, I'm no longer in the desert. Instead, I find myself in front of a massive wall, extending out from both sides as if it's about to give the world's biggest hug. Like the mundo I left behind, the color of the wall is sharper than anything in my reality, and I finally understand the phrase 'white as bone'.

Layered one atop the other, bones of all shapes sizes, from leg bones (connected to), hip bones, and even finger bones, all lacking any meat and cleaned a stark, naked white. Skulls too, grinning, frowning, and watching me with eyes that are sunk in, yet show no shadows.

Shit. I'm at the goddamn border.

I try to relax and close my eyes, focusing on breaking the connection that will send me back to the world of the living. But I find that no matter how hard I try, I can't get my breathing under control, and my hand won't release its grip on the gun.

'You need to calm down,' abuelo says, 'Just relax.'

'What's going on? Why did I go down a level without real-izing?' I use the word 'down', but the truth of the matter is that directions are pretty much meaningless in this world. I just have an easier time managing with the idea of a world of the dead if I wrap it up around a familiar concept. I use the same theory when wrapping bacon around food stuff I don't like to eat.

A thought waltzes into my head, and it's even harder to relax now, 'Did something happen to me up top?'

Delving into the mundo muerto leaves one's body com-pletely unprotected, a human ragdoll basically. And while time is different in both worlds, so that an excursion here means only minutes in the real world, that's still minutes for anyone to come up and do anything they like to your body.

'I'm dead' I say. Funny, I thought I would at least make it past my thirties.

Abuelo stays silent for a moment, and then pokes me. 'You don't seem dead to me.'

As strange as it might sound, that reassures me. And that's when I really have to fight not to completely lose it, because having the memory of my dead grampa say something reassuring while I stand on the border of the dead is a little bit more than my mind can handle.

'So then why am I here?'

He shrugs. 'I'm guessing you want to be here.'

'Bullshit. You know this place is off limits for me.' It's true, and also the reason why I had been ready to fake my way through a summoning up with Bianca and her family.

Another shrug. 'Then someone wanted you down here.'

The wall is beginning to hurt my eyes, so I turn away from it, only to find that in here, the world turns with me, and once again the wall is in front of me. Yet another reason to hate this place.

'Fine, someone wants me here, I'll buy that for now.' I start walking alongside the wall, because that at least something to do. Abuelo follows me.

Before long, I see the line of dead men and women.

It stretches back across the leveled land as far as I can see, straight as a knife cut. The people standing in line only move when it does, otherwise remaining perfectly still, their eyes up front and their hands on their side. They all wait with an unnerving patience, and it doesn't look like any of them are curious to find what's on the other side of the wall.

So I'm the one left wondering. Reward for the ones that have been good and eternal damnation for the ones that weren't? Another chance? Nothing? The possibilities are endless really, and strangely enough, I never thought to ask anyone.

The only thing I do know for sure is that I'm not dead. Otherwise, I would be in that line.

'See, told you,' abuelo says, reading my mind.

Getting nearer to the line, I expect someone to acknowledge me, but it doesn't happen. They just continue to wait for their turn to pass through the wall. Glancing towards the beginning (or is it the end?) of the line, I see that the wall looks exactly the same. There's no entrance, no gaping mouth, nothing. Just a part of the wall that becomes permeable for the dead passing through it.

I stand before the line and try to figure out what to do next, when I hear a familiar voice. 'You.'

In the time that it took me to hear that simple little word, I've moved away from the wall and am now father back along the line, standing almost next to the Coyote.

He's still in line, but instead of his eyes being fixed towards the wall, they're staring directly at me. From the pained expression on his face - yes, he has a face, and a full head, I can see how much effort it takes to do just that. I don't even want to think how much effort it took him to bring me here. That means that apart from being a nagual, he was also a brujo.

Another thing I missed.

Even here, in this place he stinks of the *magia*, of ashes and blood mixed with earth and charred meat. And there's more too, long, gleaming black tendrils seductively snake around his body, wrapping around his arms and neck like a woman wraps her hands around her man's cock. The tendrils are a physical representation of not only the dark things he'd done in his life, but the power he once wielded.

Wields, I correct myself as one of the tendrils lashes out and I barely manage to throw myself out of the way before it strikes the ground, cracking it.

'Be careful,' abuelo says. And he should know. That cut on his throat happened down here, and just like I was told the first day I started learning the craft, whatever happens in this mundo, also happens in the real world. So kinda like a reverse Las Vegas.

'You,' Coyote repeats, looking at me. The tendril he sent out returns to him and wraps around his left leg. Another one wraps around his right one. 'You know I didn't kill the girl, and you still killed me.'

'Judging by those,' I point to the things snaked around his limbs, 'You done worse than just kill a girl.'

'You didn't know that,' he screams and takes a step out of the line.

His movements are like that of a marionette that dance on the *mercado* streets, and I realize that it's the tendrils that are allowing him to do this; they're the strings controlling his body. The hole that he leaves in the line it is not even filled by the person behind him, just remains a gaping wound.

Out of the line, Coyote flexes his arms and smiles at me. 'I couldn't believe that you were so stupid enough to enter the mundo that close to my body.'

That's how he managed to pull me here. There's a reason why there's normally only one brujo per town or city. Our magia isn't a self-contained thing, it can be tapped and used by other brujos. Especially if you're sloppy like I was.

'I think I preferred you when you were begging for your life,' I mutter and jump as another of his tendrils hits the ground where I stood. 'If you're that powerful, why did you run?'

'I am..was a *moribundo,*' he says.

Fuck again. Moribundos get their power from death, whether it be chickens they cut the throats of, or worse. Basically, he being here is like a fat kid in an eating contest. An automatic advantage.

He uses that unfair advantage to send a number of his snaky friends towards me. With no hope of dodging them, I take a step back and mutter, '*Protegeme abuelo.*'

'*Pinche pendejo,*' abuelo curses at me, but does as I command, stepping in front of me and letting the tendrils crash into him. I would feel guiltier if I didn't know he couldn't feel pain.

'Is that all you can do? No wonder you're peddling your gifts to anyone,' Coyote says. Or really, growls, because he's starting to shift.

The tendrils cocoon him, and from within his self-imposed prison I hear another deep growl.

'I'm not protecting you from that,' abuelo tells me.

So I run, or try to, only to have another of his damn tendrils grab my leg and trip me. I scream at the cold touch of the tentacle and kick it with my free leg, to no avail. It drags me towards the cocoon, which has already hardened into a marble like surface and is beginning to crack.

'Do something boy,' abuelo says, standing next to me.

'I'm open to ideas if you got them.'

'You could always try shooting him.'

Oh right, I have the gun. I have never had a need to fire it in this world, so I'd completely forgotten about it. Taking aim at the tendril wrapped around my leg, I squeeze the trigger.

I half expect for nothing to happen, so I'm relieved when a bullet shoots out of the gun. And because nothing here can have any sense of normalcy, it leaves behind a thick trail of gold dust, as if I'd just shot a fairy. Figuring that at this point I would even take Tinkerbelle's help, I squeeze the trigger a couple of more times.

The tendril squeals, actually fucking squeals, which is a frightening thing all on its own, and then releases me, returning to its master while bleeding ink. I scamper as far back as I can and hold the gun with both hands, aiming it directly at the cocoon, now riddled with cracks.

From one of the cracks I can see a glowing yellow eye. From another there is a whiteness of a tooth that sets me on edge.

'You gotta get out of here,' abuelo says.

'You don't think I'm trying?

'Try harder.'

We're interrupted by another growl, and I watch as the cocoon completely shatters, revealing Coyote.

It's hard to judge heights and measurements here, so I'll go with saying he looks humongous. I doubt that he could have changed into this when he was alive, but here in the world of the dead, where everything is augmented, it makes sense that his form would be too. Which is kind of unfortunate for me.

Glowing yellow eyes act as searchlights and quickly find me, the big drops of saliva scorching the ground when they drop from his tooth filled mouth.

He lopes towards me on all fours, and no matter how many times I squeeze the trigger of the gun, it doesn't slow him down in the slightest bit. He's almost upon me when I get up and throw myself at him.

Coyote's not expecting this, and while he should have easily just swatted me away, he instead lets me crash into him, sending us spilling onto the floor. Claws swipe at my side and burn and I dodge his jaws as they close on the spot where my head was just a moment ago. I know I don't have a lot of time, so I try to be quick.

Like I said before, brujos can steal each other's magia if they're not careful. And considering Coyote here did it to me, I figure turnaround is only fair play. I had never attempted to use anyone else's mojo, but having a snapping beast on top of you is incentive to learn how to do it fast. After some light probing from my senses, I find that Coyote's form works against him as much as it does for him. It left the animal side in control, and I'm at least a more competent brujo than an animal. So it doesn't really take much for me to slip through his defenses and begin to siphon out his magia. I felt the coldness once already, but it still gives me a shock to now have it coursing through me, instead of just wrapped around my leg. Directing his and my magia into the gun, I focus all the energy, all my strength and fear into the bullet on the chamber. Then I squeeze.

It sets us both on fire, but only Coyote screams as the bullet tears through him, breaking apart his form and melting his tendrils. It leaves only a naked man, and a second later, it leaves nothing.

'I'm impressed,' abuelo says.

'Go to,' I'm about to say hell, but figure that would be a short trip for him right now. Then I wonder what happens to someone that dies in the world of the dead. I find both thoughts funny, so I lie on the ground and laugh. Abuelo Blanco watches me and shakes his head.

'You're a strange one, Juan.'

I can still feel Coyote's power moving through me and the gun, and for an instant I can understand the path he went down on. It feels so good to have that much power in you. For the first time in my life I feel in control. Getting up, I stretch and try not to think of how sore I'm going to be in a few minutes.

'You ready to go?' abuelo asks.

'In a second.'

In my powered state, it only takes a second for me to find Bianca's sister in line. She's just as pretty as Bianca, which leads me to believe that their mom would have been a looker back in her day. At first, she doesn't talk to me, just does the same as everyone in line and stares straight ahead. But then I tell her who I am and why I'm here. The short version anyway. That gets her attention.

The return trip knocks me on my ass, and I never been happier to have my pants stained with blood and brains as today. It takes a moment to get readjusted to this reality, with its subdued colors and all, and once that happens, I stand up and look at the body of Coyote. Soon enough vultures and other cravens will feast on it. But that's not quick enough for me, so I pump it full of bullets. It's stupid I know, but it makes me feel better. And fuck it, I'll go through the hassle of milking a chupacabra.

I then walk back to the group. I'm sore all right, with every muscle in my legs and arms screaming vengeance at me. With every step I take, more and more of Coyote's magia seeps out of me, so by the time I get back to the group, I feel like my usual self, magia wise.

Not sure if that's a good or bad thing.

'We been calling you for the last few minutes,' Bianca says.

Ignoring her, I limp my way to the tree and grab the polka dotted bra, which I throw at her. 'This was hers,' I say. 'And he,' I point to the uninjured twin, 'killed her.' I shoot him with my last bullet.

He goes down holding his destroyed kneecap. The mom and sister look in shock, and they're going to have questions, but they can wait. Stepping over the bleeding guy, I move to the car. 'Hey Bianca, your sister says to start having some trust. Not everyone is out to con you.'

Corkscrewed

Jan Kozlowski

The discordant opening chords of Marilyn Manson's MASH theme pulled me up out of my foggy-grey half-sleep. It was Randi's ring tone. I fumbled the phone off the nightstand and propped it against my ear.

'I'm up.'

'No you're not, Randi chirped. 'You've still got horizontal voice.'

'All right, smart ass, but I am *going* to get up and go to work today.'

'Are you sure? It's only been two weeks since the accident and...'

'Seventeen days.' I lifted the phone away enough to see the time. 'Seventeen days, three hours and four minutes.'

'Okaaay. Good to see you're not obsessing or anything. Look Joss, I know you're Ms. Tough Paramedic Girl and all, but sweetie, you were in a bad crash. I talked to Dr. Drake, he understands, *everyone* down at the clinic understands that if you need more time...'

'Time is the one thing I don't need more of, Randi. All I've had lately is time. I can't go back to work at the ambulance company because of the investigation. I can't go see my partner because he's still unconscious in the ICU. I can't even take a vacation because I'm broke and not supposed to leave the state anyway. As pathetic as it sounds, being able to grab a few part-time hours at the clinic is about the only thing keeping me sane.'

'You're right, that is pathetic.'

'Fuck you, you yeast-infected gutterslut. Fuck you very much.'

'And right back at ya, Twat Waffle. Want me to meet you at the usual spot with the usual beverage?'

'Give me 45 minutes.'

'Because you're an old, messed up bitch, I'll give you an hour.'

It killed me to admit it, but after struggling for five minutes just to attain verticality, I knew even Randi's ETA was going to be optimistic. Ever since I'd made that garbage truck our ambulance's hood ornament and turned my partner into an eggplant, everything I did took longer and hurt like a motherfucker. And every time the pain flashed through my body, the little voice in my head laughed and screamed 'eat it bitch, it's not even a fraction of what you deserve.'

Everyone from the on scene medics to the cops to the ER staff that morning made it a point to tell me how I was lucky to walk away with only cuts and bruises. Everyone but my partner Lincoln Jefferson Garroway, that is. Linc isn't saying shit to me anymore, or his wife or their kid or anyone else for that matter. He wasn't as 'lucky' as me and that was my fault too.

I showered, eased myself into my scrub shirt and pants and carefully made my way downstairs to my faithful old K-5 Blazer. The Beast was almost 20 years old, guzzled gas like a street drunk with a jug of Night Train and shook like the same alkie two days into detox when I pushed her above 60mph. Painfully I scaled the running board and hauled my aching ass up into the driver's seat. The tiny, sensible voice inside my head asked if I was having this much trouble getting into my own vehicle, how in the hell was I going to function at work today? I growled at it until it shut up, took a deep breath and headed off for the clinic.

I'd only driven once since Day Shift Commander Kenny and his partner Al sprung me from medical observation the morning after the accident and caravanned The Beast and me home. That time the physical pain had almost shut me down before I could turn over the engine, but the fear of not seeing Linc alive again drove me even harder. His wife was kind and generous when she saw me lurch into the ICU waiting room. She even thanked me for saving his life…and I think she even meant it, but I'm sure that's before the reality of his situation fully hit her. And lying sack of shit that I am, I had the balls to look into those moist, grey, trusting eyes of hers and mumble, 'I'm so sorry, Angelina. I did what I could.'

Yeah, I did what I could all right. A mental flipbook of Linc and I on our break an hour before the accident - uniforms undone, bodies feverishly banging together, telling each other this is *the* last time, that we weren't kids anymore, that this was so wrong and yet we didn't stop until dispatch interrupted us with that last call, the one we never made it to.

I could feel the self-loathing boiling up inside of me, becoming a physical manifestation. It had been like this since the accident, first the images, flashbacks of the crash mixed with ones of Linc and me and then the projectile puking would start. I pulled over into an empty parking lot, grabbed one of the fast food bags off the floor and waited it out.

I was running about fifteen minutes behind by the time I finally pulled into the sprawling medical complex that included not only the shiny new hospital where Linc was currently vegetating, but also a scattering of medical office buildings, clinics, out patient facilities and the enormous, creepy parking garage that served them all.

Randi was waiting for me as I wheeled into our usual section, Level 3 Orange, right next to the door to the skyway that took us across Garden Street and into the former hospital building where the Central Connecticut Women's Clinic was located. I could see the look of relief on her face as she recognized The Beast and caught the subtle movement of her hand as she slipped the can of pepper spray back into her pocket.

'Bout time, Bee-atch!' she called hurrying toward me.

'Sorry,' I said, pitching myself out of the seat and slamming the door shut before she could get a whiff of the barf and month old burger aroma that now permeated the Blazer's cab.

'Well at least you made it in...shit, I was going to say one piece, but look at you girl.' She scanned me from head to toe and wrinkled her nose like she could smell the vomit from where she was standing. 'You look like you died three days ago and someone forget to tell you to lay your ass down.'

'Yeah, purty, ain't I?'

'Purty ain't the problem. No one gives a shit about a few bruises, but you're dead white, even for you. You're sweating like a football player in August and you look like you're going to hit the ground any second. Here, let me help you back up into the monstrosity. Sit for a few minutes and then we'll...'

'No. I'm okay, really. I'll be fine as soon as I can get back to work.'

'Joss, there's no way in hell Drake, or any of the rest of us, are going to let you work today.'

'Randi...please. I can't take being alone in the apartment for another second. I can't do it. Please.' I was standing there begging her while she stood there appraising me and, in that minute, I hated her. I understood, but I hated her. I hated that she had that kind of power over me. And I hated myself even more for my weakness...for all my weaknesses.

'I'll tell you what, come upstairs with me and let Dr. Drake take a look at you. If he clears you to work, then I'll do everything I can to help you get through the day. If he says no go though, you'll shut the fuck up and let us take care of you. Deal?'

'But...'

'No buts. That's the deal, take it...or I leave you here in the parking garage to fight off the murderers and rapists by your sick ass self.'

'Bitch.'

'Yep, now come on, give me your arm. If you go down, I'm not going to throw my back out dragging your fat puss upright again.'

Fifteen minutes later, or about ten minutes longer than it usually took us, I was stuck in one of the waiting room chairs outside Dr. Drake's office and fighting off my co-worker's fussing over me. Medical people make the worst patients and I did my best to live up to the tradition. I could hear Randi and Drake's voices through the door, but there was too much clucking going on around me to make out what they were saying. I had just hit maximum overload on offers of tea, cold packs and make up advice and was looking for an escape route, when Randi reappeared and escorted me into the dark paneled sanctum that was Dr. Drake's domain.

I had worked at the CCWC for over two years, but this was the first time I had ever been in Drake's office. He was head of the clinic and a well-respected OB/GYN surgeon, but he had little to do with day-to-day operations. He had welcomed me aboard on my first day as we passed in the hallway but since then, our entire relationship had been a series of nods as we each went about our respective business. I couldn't say that I liked or disliked him; I simply had little knowledge of him beyond his faded movie star looks and political candidate demeanor.

'Ms. Kane,' Dr. Enigma said, standing up as Randi led me to the large floofy chair closest to his desk. 'Ms. Freburg was just filling me in on her concerns about your condition and your ability to assist our patients today.'

'Dr. Drake, I can do my job.'

Across the wide expanse of expensive mahogany, his sea green eyes pinned me to my chair like a frog to a dissection tray, evaluating me. It seemed there was a lot of that judgy-wudgy shit going around today. I did my best to calmly hold his gaze, but I could feel my stomach beginning its old pitch and roll again.

'Ms. Freburg, I'd like to have a private word with Ms. Kane, if you don't mind.'

Randi nodded, shot me her concerned mother hen look and hurried out of the office. As soon as the door closed, Drake pushed out of his sumptuous leather chair and glided around to my side of the desk. For such a large man, I had never noticed how gracefully, quietly and… bonelessly he moved, almost as if he was swimming through the air.

'Ms. Kane,' he said, leaning in so closely that I could see his nostrils flare. 'I have, of course, heard about your unfortunate accident a couple of weeks ago. I understand you wanting…and perhaps needing, to return to your normal schedule as soon as possible, but I have certain concerns.'

'Dr. Drake…'

'Please let me finish. I have the feeling there's more going on here than the after-effects of a traumatic motor vehicle accident.' He paused and seemed to take a long sniff of air before continuing. 'You are perhaps, having other symptoms, ones you haven't mentioned to the doctor overseeing your case?'

'Yes…but it's just the stress…and the pain…my partner… and…and…' And that's when I lost it. Flashbacks exploded in my head like fireworks. Linc half dressed, pushing into me, my arms and legs wrapped around him on the office couch. Linc's torn body landing on top of me as we lay in the wreckage, blood streaming from the jagged hole in his neck. My hand scrabbling toward the open wound, jamming my fingers into the hole, slowing the river to a dribble. Linc, in the ICU bed, more machine than man now, his wife holding his dead fish hand, weeping.

The tears poured down my face, the grief, guilt and anger boiled up out of my throat in a series of incoherent gibbering and wet, slushy sounds. Drake simply sat and let me spew it all out. He didn't try to hug me, there-there me, or hurry me along towards the next stage of emotional closure. He watched and he waited, silently, like he had all the time in the world.

I have no idea how much time passed, but eventually the waterworks wound down and I was able to think and speak again.

'I'm sorry, Dr. Drake.'

'Nonsense. A completely normal and healthy reaction to everything you've been through. I'd be a lot more worried about you if you didn't have an emotional release, believe me. I am a little concerned about a few things I noticed though. Would you mind if I asked you a few questions and maybe took a quick blood sample, just to triple check that you don't have anything going on that they might have missed down at the ER?'

'Will you let me work my shift today, if I agree?'

'Well, how about, depending on the test results and how you're feeling, if I either let you work, or give you the day off with pay in exchange for the blood test and answering some questions? Fair enough?'

'Deal.' I didn't even have to think twice about it. I've never been the kind of girl who worked the cushy, indoor jobs that came with Christmas bonuses, days off with pay, or even health insurance beyond workman's comp.

'Excellent! Questions first and then I'll draw the blood myself. No sense sending the clinic grapevine into overdrive.'

'Thanks, Dr. Drake, I appreciate that.'

'Okay Ms. Kane, first of all, humor an old OB/GYN man, when was your last period?'

'Um...about a month ago, I guess.'

'So your period is due any time now?'

'Yes.'

'Are you on any medications, birth control, asthma meds, vitamins, anything like that?'

'No, birth control pills make me sick and I don't take anything else.'

'How about recreational drugs?'

'No, I never got into them.'

'Smart girl. Alcohol?'

'Just when we go out after work sometimes.'

'That's fine. Any chronic illnesses or diseases?'

'No.'

'STD's?'

'No.'

'Allergies?'

'None that I know of.'

'Okay, good. Now one last question, is there any possibility that you're pregnant?'

'What?'

'You said you don't use birth control pills. Other methods are a lot less effective. Have you had unprotected or under-protected sex over the past month that might have resulted in pregnancy?'

I wanted to lie so badly. I wanted to be the good damsel and play the mildly outraged, smug I'm-not-that-kind-of-girl card, but I was that kind of girl, that kind and worse.

'Yes.'

'Yes, you might be pregnant?'

I let my fist fall onto my thigh. The pain felt right. 'Yes.' I pounded my thigh again. 'YES.' Pound. 'I'm stupid.' Pound. 'I fucked up.' Pound. 'And there's a chance I could be pregnant. Fuck.'

'Okay, but before you go another ten rounds on yourself, let me get a blood sample so that we know *for sure* what we're dealing with and then we can talk about your options.'

Options. I work in a woman's clinic. I know what 'options' is code for. Pregnant. How I've always hated that word. It always sounded so ugly to me. I watched Dr. Drake collect his blood drawing supplies and get my arm ready for invasion. Was he actually humming? Or was that sound of my brain cells frying, like over cooked bacon? I couldn't tell.

The puking and the tiredness and not being able to eat made sense now. Stupid. Stupid. Stupid. Linc. There was no one but Linc. There hadn't been anyone but Linc in almost a year, hence there had been Linc, or at least that was the story I told myself. The truth was I was 29, alone and being with Linc rolled time back ten years to when we had first gotten together as EMT-B newbs working the 12 hour shit shifts out of the shittiest office in the shittiest part of town. It was crazy and terrifying and absolutely the best damn time of my life and by trying to relive it, I may have fucked up a shitload of lives.

After Dr. Drake filled his vials with my red stuff, he insisted I lay down on the couch in his private office, behind a recessed door I hadn't even noticed until he led me through it. He told me to stay there until he got back with my test results. He wanted me to rest, but my head wanted to spin off my neck and hurl itself through the third floor window. My body's compromise was to shut down to that grey, foggy numbness where I had started this day from hell.

Minutes, hours, days later, for all I knew, I felt a hand gently shaking my shoulder. I swam to the surface and it was Dr. Drake, smiling sadly and holding a paper cup of something out to me. I struggled to a sitting position and accepted the cup without even asking what was in it.

'I thought you could use some tea.'

'That bad, huh?'

'Well, that's for you to decide. The test shows that you *are* pregnant, about four to six weeks along.'

'Is everything normal? I mean, after the accident and all?'

'With the exception of you having a fairly rare blood type, the tests don't show any abnormalities, but I'd have to do a pelvic exam to be sure.'

I dropped my head and stared into the tea like the muddy brown water held the meaning of life inside of it.

'I put cream and sugar in it, I hope that's okay. Tea always seems more comforting to me that way.'

I nodded and took a sip, more out of a need to please this man who was being kind to me rather than because I was thirsty. 'Just like mother used to make,' I said, fighting to keep the earthy tasting stuff down.

'Really? I'm glad to hear it. This tea is a special blend and a favorite of mine. It's kind of like chamomile, don't you think?'

I took a second, larger mouthful and swallowed it as quickly as possible. 'I'm sorry...I'm not really much of a tea drinker. It's kind of...kind of...'

Drake reached forward and neatly plucked the cup from my hand just before my body collapsed and I fell sideways across the couch. My eyes were open and I could feel my mouth opening and closing like a beached fish, but I couldn't move the rest of my body or make a sound.

'It's just a few deep sea...herbs let's call them, my dear.' Drake whispered in my ear. 'And I only gave you a smidgeon, just enough to get you downstairs without any fuss. Don't worry, the effects will wear off in a little while and it's nothing that will harm you or the baby. Believe me, the last thing we'd want to do is taint that exotic and delicious blood supply of yours.'

Delicious? Did he just say *delicious*? My brain was half way to fuck-you-I'm-out-of-here territory and my body was

Jan Kozlowski

right behind it. This was impossible. This was not happening. Maybe *I* was the one in the irreversible coma, or maybe I was dead and this was my personal hell, being stuck in some sort of bad horror movie for all eternity.

It sure felt real though. Even through the fog, I could feel hands on me, moving me, strapping me into a wheelchair, rolling me through an open wall panel and into a small, private elevator. Drake was jammed in beside me, so there must be someone else driving the chair.

I tried to force my brain back online. We were in the old hospital building. Sure, the medical group behind the clinic had renovated it before they moved in, but it was essentially the same building Linc & I were based out of back when we started at Capital City EMS.

Linc. His undamaged face materialized in my mind smiling that slow, lopsided grin that charmed every female it was directed at, myself in particular. Then, as I watched, the image began to fade away like Alice's Cheshire cat until the only thing left was that small, pencil-point scar on the right side of his bottom lip. The one I loved to flick at with my tongue. The one I *had* loved…

The sound of the elevator chime rocked me back to the present. *Focus Joss! Focus or you're dead…or maybe worse.* The clinic was on the third floor. Ding. Ding. Ding. The claustrophobic box slowed to a stop and the doors whooshed open. We had landed in the basement.

Drake stepped out and my invisible driver propelled me down what I recognized as the main hallway that led to the morgue. Despite the building's repurposing, what I could see of the lay out was virtually the same as I remembered it. Back in the day, our company office had been stuffed down here with the other behind-the-scenes departments like shipping and receiving, housekeeping, laundry and an old operating room amphitheater that, since the opening of the new surgical wing, was used mainly for storage.

Linc and I had worked the 7pm to 7am shift back then, three days off, three days on. It was a busy office, but we still managed to find enough down time for the two things we loved best, fucking or looking for unusual places to fuck. Over the year we had been stationed down here we learned every mother-humping inch of this place including some very cool hidey holes, forgotten closets and a set of narrow, poorly blocked off tunnels that, back in the first half of the 1900's, had been used by student nurses and interns so they could travel back and forth between their dorms and the different buildings on campus quickly and safely.

We had had a lot of fun and were truly sorry when we 'earned' a spot in a better office, in a safer, saner part of the city. Not long after that Linc and I had gone our separate ways, personally and professionally but I had always held a soft spot for this old place, even stealing a private, unauthorized last tour before the hospital's big move to the new building a couple of years ago.

The wheelchair slowed while Drake strode on ahead. He stepped up to the heavy steel bank vault door and danced his fingers over the keypad until a green light and a loud metallic click signaled that we were allowed to enter. Drake grabbed the door and swung it wide, holding it open for me and my driver. 'Welcome to my winery, Ms. Kane!' he said, motioning us inward with a grin and a flourish, like a charming host ushering me into his fabulous party.

The word 'winery' rattled around in my Swiss cheese brain for a minute, the images of grape vines, clinking glasses and orderly rows of gracefully curved bottles didn't jibe with the nightmare in front of me. This was definitely the old morgue all right. Structurally, the room stood almost exactly as I had remembered it. Four stainless steel tables, complete with drains and spray arms, sat along one side of the long, open room. On the other side of the tile floor stood the bank of eight refrigerated drawers, with counters, storage cupboards and cabinets filling in the rest of the wall space.

What was different, what I had never seen, even during the worst mass casualty situations, was what I was looking at now. Every table and every drawer was occupied, not by dead bodies, but by live, naked women in various stages of pregnancy and, from the sound of it, varying degrees of pain and sanity. Moans and muffled screams, litanies of curses and nonsensical babbling flowed over me like a tsunami wave.

Everywhere I looked, wild-eyed women struggled and writhed against their restraints and the tubes that wound into, out of, and in some cases, through their bodies, carrying various colored fluids to and from the different machines stationed around the room. Attending the machines, and all but ignoring the women were, what I can only describe as vaguely human-shaped creatures clicking and nattering to each other, as oblivious to the terror and pain around them as we were to a burning anthill.

Drake stopped to communicate with a couple of the workers, pointing toward the heavily pregnant young woman on the table closest to me. I could see that before she had come here, she had been what my grandmother had called 'an Irish beauty', with long dark hair, bright blue eyes and what probably had been a porcelain complexion. Unlike the others, she didn't struggle or fight against her restraints. She lay there limply, head turned toward me, eyes glassy, lips moving quietly, as if in prayer. I scanned her body, her belly was huge, the skin seemingly strained to the breaking point, and then I saw it, the muscle contractions flitting across her stretched abdomen; she was in active labor.

The workers, presumably at Drake's direction, descended on her and began to disconnect her from the cat's cradle of plastic tubing in preparation for transfer to the stretcher they were rolling over. Drake materialized at my side and continued to snap out what sounded like orders in that strange, unrecognizable series of guttural sounds.

'Ms. Kane, we'll have your table ready in just a few moments,' he said with a chuckle, probably realizing he sounded more like a maitre de than a respected surgeon at that moment. 'Unfortunately, Illysa took her sweet time going into labor and now we must not only rush to salvage her harvest, but also to get you settled in and ready for production.'

I tried to speak, to yell, to tell him he was making no

sense, but my vocal cords still weren't functioning and all that came out were a series of ga-ga-ga sounds.

'Oh, Ms. Kane, you might not understand now, but you will and more thoroughly than you could ever imagine. I want you to know exactly what I've built here and what will be your very important contribution to it.

'In a nutshell, what it comes down to is that while humans have enjoyed the taste of fermented grapes for thousands of years, my species has enjoyed the taste of fermented humans for as long as *your* species has existed.'

He paused and glanced at me, perhaps expecting another outburst, but I was too busy trying to process the enormity of what he was saying, so he continued his Wine 101 tutorial.

'We have always known, just as with the kind of fruit-based wines your species is accustomed to, that the type of product you use, how it's grown, picked, fermented and augmented determines the final taste. My winery here caters to those of my kind who enjoy the bouquet and flavor of HCG-Human Growth hormone, estrogen and progesterone, which basically translates into what we've come to call a pregnancy-related preference palette.

'Picking up on this trend years ago, I began experimenting with the medical waste from the clinic, bottling it and sharing it with friends and, I'm proud to say, my little hobby has since turned into quite the profitable business. Of course before long I got to the point where I needed more than what I could accumulate from a few days worth of abortions and D&C's, so I began collecting my 'mothers'. Now I realize that's a word more accurately used in vinegar production, but you'll excuse me if I find the irony of it is just too delightful to ignore.

'Anyway, after only a few years, I was able to afford this new facility and now, with my acquisition of you and your lovely AB negative blood, bursting with pregnancy hormones, I can build a whole signature vintage around you and your output.'

I tried to scream, but nothing came out. I sagged back in the chair but Drake lifted my head and pointed as the stretcher bearing Illysa began to move toward a large machine tucked in the far corner of the room. It was tough to see in the low light, but from here it reminded me of one of the old iron lungs they used to use to treat polio patients.

'I want you to watch Illysa's final harvesting, I think it will be instructive for you. First, the crushing...'

Two worker creatures opened the contraption's casket-like lid while another pair lifted Illysa's body off the stretcher. It took all four of them, but they stuffed her now struggling body, kicking and flailing, down into the metal cylinder. It could have been my imagination, but just before she slipped inside, I thought I saw the baby's head poking out from between her blood-spattered thighs.

I tried to turn my head, but Drake wouldn't let me look away. The workers slammed the lid shut, trapping Illysa and her baby inside. They took their time diddling with gauges and buttons, tightening valves and checking temperatures accompanied by the faint sound of Illysa's pounding and screaming. Finally satisfied with all their preparations, they turned to Drake for his approval. He nodded and the one on the right pushed a series of buttons that brought the machine to a rumbling, pulsing life. I could feel the vibrations as they radiated up through the floor, through the wheels of my chair and reverberated through my body.

'That's the rough chopping cycle,' Drake said, continuing his bloviation. 'It separates the product into manageable, uniform chunks so that by the time we get to the pressing cycle we get a nice even compression, which gives us a good, thorough squeezing.

See the lovely color of the juice running through the lines underneath the main chamber there?' he said, pointing to the tubing coiled underneath the tank like a nest of giant snakes. 'Illysa always gave us such a beautiful clarity and brilliance, not to mention an exquisite bouquet. It's a shame to bring her vintage to an end, but room must be made for new discoveries, right Ms. Kane?'

'Buh-buh-buh-buuuuuuh.' I shook my head and tried to fight my way out of the chair. I was getting some muscle control back, but not enough to do more than wiggle against the straps and throw hair in my eyes. A worker passing near Drake noticed my agitation, grabbed a syringe from a nearby instrument tray and stepped toward me. Drake knocked the needle out of his hand and clicked at him loudly.

'My apologies Ms. Kane. They're used to sedating the mothers when they get feisty. Even though it's another one of our organic herbal medicines like the tea I gave you, I refuse to take the chance of contaminating your natural taste any further. As it is, we'll probably have to wait at least twelve hours and perform a flush to make sure any taint from the tea has been negated. It's a shame too, I'm hosting our monthly tasting and auction here tonight and I so wanted to be able to have a few sample drops to share with my more ardent sanguinophiles.'

The machine, which had been chugging along like a clothes dryer full of combat boots, suddenly ground to a halt. A flurry of clicking erupted from the two operators and Drake stalked over to investigate. The effects of the tea were beginning to wear off and I could feel the strength return-ing to my arms and legs, as well as a noticeable lifting of the mental cloud.

I stole a glance at the women around me, trying to gauge their reaction to Illysa's fate, but most were caught up in their own thousand yard stares, either too drugged or too deep in shock to respond to what was going on around them. I wondered if I could get out of here, and if I did, what would happen to them?

The answer was a no-brainer. If I escaped, Drake would kill them and wipe this place clean before I could even get anyone at 911 to take me seriously. And even if I did manage to get away, what then? He had mentioned his cabal of sanguinophiles, rich and powerful entities who, like Drake himself, were successfully blending in among the human cattle, so even if I survived, chances were I was fucked.

Of course, the truth of the matter was my life was fucked six ways to Sunday even without this latest Lovecraftian twist. I had spent the last ten years of my life trying to be one of the good guys, saving lives and doing the bad ones, as the old EMS saying went, but all anyone was going to remember about me was how I cocked it all up.

I took a long look around the room, eleven women, more dead than alive, eleven human fermentation tanks...and one free table waiting for me. I can't let this be the way I go out. I may never make it back out to the world again, but if I die here, I'm going to take as many of these motherfuckers with me as possible.

Focus. Think. Drake was a chatty little douche nozzle and he had been info-dumping since we rolled off the elevator. He must have said something useful. I turned my head to check on Drake's whereabouts when I caught a glint of something shiny on the floor under one of the rolling instrument trays. It was the syringe Drake had slapped out of that troll's hands. It looked intact. I tried one more time to wriggle my hands out of the Velcro straps that held me to the chair, but I was cinched down too tight. Shit. All right, if I couldn't get to it now, it'll at least be something to keep in mind for later.

Later. Drake had said he was disappointed that he wouldn't have a taste of my blood to share with his crew at the auction and tasting that was happening *here later* tonight. The mental light bulb popped on and the bare bones of a plan began to knit itself together in what was left of my grey matter, just as Drake oozed his way back to me.

'My apologies for the delay, Ms. Kane. I believe your table is now ready. Let's get you settled into your new accommodations.'

Drake made a motion with his hands and his workers closed in around me. It was my first up close and personal look at them and I was shocked at how startlingly human some looked, only a slight squashing of their features gave any indication that there was anything off about them. There were some though, ones that hovered in the background supervising, that weren't as well integrated, reminding me of things that might have squirmed out of a deep-sea hydrothermal vent.

Several cool, moist appendages...I refuse to call them

hands, grabbed different parts of my body, undid my restraints and forced me to a standing position. In seconds, they ripped away my clothes and positioned me on the cold, steel table, legs pulled apart and strapped into stirrups, arms stretched straight out and taped down to crucifix boards.

My first instinct while this was happening was to struggle and fight, to try to punch or kick my way through their slimy, gelatinous bodies, but knowing an escape attempt at this point would be stupid, I played possum instead. I laid there still and quiet, allowing them to pull and bend and move my body into whatever positions they wanted, even when they moved between my legs and stabbed at my urethra with the catheter.

When the activity died down and most of the crowd had moved on, Drake drifted back in to my field of vision looking pleased with what he observed. 'There we are now, Ms. Kane. I believe you're all set. We're going to run a couple of bags of Ringer's through your IV and monitor your urine output until we're sure it's clear of contamination. That should take 6-8 hours, then we'll be able to get you hooked up to the production line.' He glanced down at his TAG Heuer AquaRacer.

'My goodness, how time flies when you're doing something you enjoy! I'm afraid I'm going to have to leave you in the very capable care of my staff, but don't worry I'll be right down the hall if there's an emergency and I'll stop back after the auction to see you.'

Not if I see you first, Dick Bag. There were no visible clocks in the room, so I had no idea what time of day it was, or how long I had been down here. If Drake was leaving to prepare for the auction though it must be getting on towards evening and soon his little party animals would be gathering…evidently right down the hall. I allowed myself a smile as the rest of the plan fell into place.

First things first though, I needed to get be able to get off of this table when the time was right. I started by moving my right wrist as surreptitiously as possible, stretching the tape and giving myself some wiggle room. It took me a lot longer than I thought it would, but finally, thanks to a leaky IV placement and non-waterproof tape, I was able to work my whole arm free. Once that was done, I inched my hand down to the leather thigh strap, unbuckled it and then laid it back in place so nothing looked amiss.

While I was working on freeing myself, I also kept a close eye on Drake's minions who, like their boss, slid around the room almost noiselessly, startling the shit out of me more than once. Luckily none of them had caught me working the tape, but still, it was unnerving. And speaking of them, I began to notice that the later it got, the fewer of them seemed to be around. Perhaps Drake wasn't the only one knocking off work to attend tonight's festivities? I could only hope.

Once I had done all I could do to partially extricate myself, the only thing left was to wait for an opportunity to finish the job and get the hell out of here. I laid back and tried to relax, but my mind and body were already in hyper drive. What if I were too early? What if I were too late? What if they had bricked up the tunnels or cleaned out that ether stash? I had to cut this shit out before I 'what if'd' my way straight into paralysis by analysis.

I snapped my eyes open and checked the room for creepers. It looked like there was only one left and it was on the other side of the room dealing with what was left of Illysa. My right side was already free so I rolled to my left, ripped the tape off my arm and unbuckled my left leg. Now the only thing connecting me to the table was the damn catheter. I reached down and felt along the tube, searching for the release valve, but the fishy freak noticed something was up and started toward me.

Fuck it, I grabbed the tubing and yanked as hard as I could. The pain exploded out of me like a nuclear mushroom cloud, along with the inflated balloon and about a gallon of red tinged piss. It didn't matter though, nothing mattered but getting my ass out of this room.

Cthulhu's ugly cousin was still barreling toward me, so I rolled off the table and made a dive for the forgotten syringe, coming up with it just in time to jab it into the thing's body as it made a grab for my leg. I hit the plunger hard and held on as it bucked and writhed underneath me. A century later I felt it go limp and I scuttled back away from it. I didn't know if it was unconscious or dead and I didn't give a flying fuck in a rolling donut either way. The only thing I was afraid of was that it would wake up and alert the others, so I bolted across the room, slowing only to grab one of Drake's lab coats off a chair and shrug into it.

I knew I couldn't go out through the morgue's front door. Drake had armed the electronic security system when he had left and every worker bee that had left after him had to punch in a ten-digit code to be allowed out. Hopefully though, another option still existed.

Back when Linc and I had been bombing around down here, we had found a small door in the back of one of the supply closets that led down a short tunnel and eventually came out behind a set of morgue cabinets that looked built in, but were actually sitting on hidden casters. Linc and I had driven a couple of the morgue attendants crazy that summer, pranking them all to hell, leaving notes, moving their stuff and making them think the place was haunted.

Irony 1- it turned out the secret exit was actually built as an escape route, just in case the place *was* haunted, or so the senior janitor had told me one night after he 'cleaned up' a quart of Red Eye. His Granddaddy had been the building's first janitor and had told him about the hidden door and how it came to be. It seemed that the construction crew were a superstitious bunch of men who were deeply creeped out that they were building a place to store corpses. So, even though it wasn't in the official plans, they included an extra exit, just in case the dead ever rose up and attacked.

Irony #2- a bunch of turn of the century laborers might have understood more about the world and the monsters that inhabit it than we ever would. And, as I finally found the release button on the right bank of cabinets and felt the cool, musty air of the tunnel wash over me, I knew I was going to have to buy them all a drink at the afterlife bar.

I didn't have a flashlight and no lighter magically appeared in the pockets of Drake's lab coat so once I rolled the cabinets back in place I had to feel my way along the tunnel wall in complete darkness. It wasn't as terror invoking as what Drake had planned for me, but it was still pretty awful. I tried to move as quickly as possible, but my bare feet kept hitting slime and I swore I could feel spiders and other crawlies brushing up against me with every step. The tunnel is short, I kept telling myself, no more than 15 or 20 paces, if I recalled correctly. It would dead-end in a smallish door that would take me into what used to be an old storage space in the back of the old operating room amphitheater.

I ran into the door, or at least my nose did, at step 17. As it turned out, finding the door was a hell of a lot easier than getting it open, but after pounding most of the rust and dirt off the latch and hinges, I was able to pry it open and squeeze my battered body through to the other side.

The closet was pretty much the way I remembered it-narrow, dank and filled with piles of ancient, crumbling boxes and canisters. Thanks to the light leaking in around the door frame, I was able to see clearly enough to pick my way around the mess and find what I was looking for relatively quickly. The boxes of ether tins were still stacked along the back wall, probably in the exact same spot some under-paid, over-worked operating room tech had carefully placed them 50 years or more ago. As an anesthesia, ether fell out of favor in the 1960's, replaced by nitrous oxide and other drugs that were easier to control and a lot less likely to go boom. It was the go-boom property that interested me now though.

Ether is fairly unstable, but *old* ether, particularly ones in screw top cans like these, were particularly volatile. After we had stumbled across this cache ten years ago, Linc had done a little research and found out that back in the 1980's the federal government had actually issued a Hazard Awareness Alert on a bunch of ether that had been included in Civil Defense Hospital Kits distributed back in the 60's and 70's. The EPA had their panties in a twist because they felt that cans 'presented an explosive and toxic hazard'. Why the hospital had never gotten rid of the ether wasn't clear, but Linc and I figured it had something to do with finances. It always came down to the green stuff when you were dealing with administrative pencil pushers of any variety.

Regardless of the reasoning though, right now I could kiss every one of those little penny pinching dicks for passing the buck year after year and leaving me the perfect holocaust delivery system for Drake and his kind. I knew it was too much to hope that I would get them all, but this would make a dent in their numbers, and more importantly, I'd be able to look straight into Drake's eyes as I sent him to oblivion.

I walked over to the door and pressed my ear against it. Besides the light, there were the sounds of their clicking, low sounds like murmuring and the unmistakable sound of glass and silver ware clanking. I put my hand on the doorknob and slowly turned it, praying it wasn't as difficult to open as the one from the tunnel had been. This time though, the handle turned smoothly and I was able to crack the door open enough to see what was going on in the amphitheater. From the looks of things, the party was in full swing, a hundred or more of the things, again all in different states of human-ishness drifted around the room, sipping wine and clicking and clacking animatedly with each other. In other words, it looked like any cocktail party I'd ever had the misfortune of attending. I didn't lay eyes on Drake, but I knew he was there somewhere, probably taking orders for his new vintage while pouring glassfuls of the increasingly rare Illysa label.

I eased the door shut and moved back to the pile of boxes. The ether canisters themselves were small, about four inches tall and maybe two inches wide. I had to be careful to choose ones that were intact enough that they didn't blow when I picked them up, but not so stable that they wouldn't ignite when the friction of opening the screw cap met the oxygen and ether. I found three that looked promising so I carefully loaded two into my lab coat pockets and kept one in my hand. I was now, quite literally a walking time bomb.

What I was about to do washed over me as I turned back to the door and prepared to walk out into that crowded room. I thought about Linc of course, and the pregnancy. The faces of friends and co-workers sped past and even childhood pets and favorite apartments made appearances, but all I felt was a serene sort of distance, the first peace I can honestly say I'd felt in 17 days…no, even longer, since the day Linc and I first fell back together a few months ago and maybe even before that. This was the right thing to do, I had never been surer of anything before in my life.

I opened the door, spotted Drake in the middle of a knot of his brethren and rushed toward him. The formally attired crowd shrank away from me as I pushed through them, fear and disgust twisting across their soft, gummy faces. Drake turned as I approached, the arrogant grin sliding off of his lips as he recognized the ether canister in my hand and the reality of the situation sank in.

'Ms. Kane, stop! Think of the other women! Think of your baby!' he shouted, drops of bright red Illysa sloshing out the glass and splattering his white shirt cuffs.

'They're exactly who I *am* thinking of, Drake. If there's one thing I learned in all my years in EMS, it's what a loving and unselfish gift a quick death can be.'

Drake screamed as I brought my right hand up and twisted the cap, his sea green eyes blazing into fiery emeralds as the hot roar of nothingness enveloped me, cleansing me of my sins.

East of Écarté

Andrez Bergen

I hugged the curve of the desk, partially playing sham detective but more honestly hungover and bored out of my brain, when the dame came to call—unannounced, as the choice ones do.

Which is an intentional play on words. This woman had no choice.

The fact was my employer not only underpaid me but also refused to invest in a receptionist, and this accounted for the fact that our visitor wandered in with an addled expression stuck on her mush.

I sat up straight to wave before contemplating how stupid that looked.

If she noticed, the woman let me off the hook. She indicated the only chair on the other side of the bureau, her ironing board posture putting mine to shame.

'May I?'

'Sure.'

She was young, late teens sliding into early twenties, had long, golden-brown hair severely tied back in a way that framed a beautiful face with minimal makeup.

To balance this and likely buck any unwanted attention, the woman wore an abstract floral dress looking like it was painted in wild collusion by Claude Monet and Jackson Pollock.

'Are you Mister Miller?' she asked as my eyes adjusted to the glare.

'Sorry, he's out. I'm in.'

'I see. I'm Mocha Stockholm.'

'Course you are.'

The woman frowned, though on that face the expression barely made a dent. I noticed her eyes mugged the colour of cinnamon.

'You know me?' she asked.

'Nah. Just sounded like a quip Humphrey Bogart would've rolled out—with far more flair.'

'To which Lauren Bacall would lob back her own face-slapping wisecrack?'

'The devil, you say...?' I grinned. 'You know your classic Hollywood cinema.'

'A wee bit. My mum was a movie journalist, so I grew up force-fed on the stuff. She particularly loved her black-and-whites detective stories, Mister—'

'Scherer.'

'Mister Scherer.'

'Call me Roy.'

'Roy, then.' She smiled. We looked at each other for several seconds. 'Care to know why I've come today, Roy?'

'Oh, yeah, 'course—sorry.'

I grabbed a notebook, and the first biro I scribbled with refused to work. I rifled through a desk drawer searching for another.

'Would you mind if I smoke?' I heard the woman ask as I ransacked the bureau. What was her name? Mockba? Momo? Better to stick with Miss Stockholm.

'No worries, Miss Stockholm.'

'Mocha.'

'Mocha. Sure—so long as you don't mind sharing one of the cigarette's brothers. I'm out.'

Mocha pulled her chair closer.

As she renounced good deportment and reclined back into it, the woman crossed a pair of obscenely long, narrow legs. I hadn't noticed before the minimal length of her overwrought dress.

She conjured up an ostrich-skin covered cigarette case and slipped out two cigarettes.

'Help yourself.'

Case in hand, Mocha leaned over and I prised one free. I tried my urbane best to snap up the fag with style, but my mitt shook. That would be the excessive amount of cognac consumed the prior evening revealing itself.

The woman lit our cigarettes with a Zippo that had the slogan *La Chauve-souris* inscribed in a flowing font across its surface.

Settling back to enjoy the moment I sensed the return of a wayward backbone, and granted my guest a grateful smile. She'd earned the truth.

'I have a confession,' I said. 'I'm not really a detective, just hired help.'

'I suspected as much.'

Mocha held the cigarette between her teeth as she placed the case and lighter into a small purse, and then she took it in her left hand.

'There's only one name on the business card—Mister Miller's. You're also a little young.'

'No younger than you.'

She pursed her lips, but there was a smirk there. 'Too young to play the hardened, streetwise PI. You need to get out in the sun more often, weather-up the good-looks.'

'You're a better detective than me.'

'Something I've always aspired to. Let me guess: Part-time job?'

'Bingo. Pays the bills and saves me scabbing off my parents.'

'They object?'

'I do.'

The woman nodded but I noticed she was looking over at the tattered venetian blind I had closed to fend off an offensive midday sun.

'The odd-jobs you do here. Surveillance or that sort of thing?'

'Would be neat if true. Alas, no. Mostly paper shuffling and photocopy chores. I double-up as a cleaner and short order cook. I'm quite the whiz with an egg and a pot of boiling water. But I don't think Art trusts me enough at this point in the field, doing things like surveillance. Prob'ly never will.'

'Art would be Mister Miller?'

'Yep.'

With her free hand Mocha pulled at the hem of her dress,

which was riding too high on her thighs. I praised my lucky stars that Art had never invested in a wider desk.

'Speaking of whom,' the woman murmured, 'can I ask where he is? We had an appointment for twelve.'

'That so?'

Mocha gifted me a laugh. 'That *is* so.'

This was a potential problem.

Art had been on the receiving end of most of the cognac the night before—two bottles of Château de Plassac, an undeserved gift from a grateful client. I'd drunk maybe half of one of them, Art the rest. Plus a couple of lines of speed. Given the current state of my brain, I assessed he'd be sleeping the cocktail off right into the next week.

I pretended to check a desk calendar my boss never used. 'Stockholm,' I mused, feigning diligence. 'Named after the city?'

'No, silly—the city's named after me.'

'Right.' I looked up at the woman. 'He's—um—indisposed right now, out on a case, but give me all the details and I'll fill him in.'

'Have you found a pen that works?'

'Right here.'

I was holding aloft a gaudy pen with cute images of Minnie Mouse splashed all over the thing. Where the blazes had Art acquired that?

'Fine.' The woman gave me a pleasant enough smile—difficult to read. 'I think someone is trying to kill me.'

I'd just crossed the t in 'think'—shorthand wasn't my forté—when she finished talking. The comment hung in the air like a predatory slap about to happen. I looked at her under my brow.

'You think...?'

Mocha glanced at the pad beneath my pen. 'I think someone is trying to kill me.'

'I know—you said.'

'Well, you haven't finished writing.'

'I'm not sure I need to—easy enough to remember.'

I took a last drag on my cigarette, which was already burning at the filter. Damn.

'What I meant to ask is this: You think someone is trying to kill you, or you have actual proof of the matter?'

'I have these. See what you make of them.'

Mocha had popped open her handbag—it was a Prada, no idea if counterfeit or real—and she took out a handful of twice-folded beige envelopes that she placed on the desk within easy reach. I picked them up and counted. Five in all, no address or postage stamp—just Mocha's name typed on the front.

'They were slipped under the door of my apartment,' she said. 'Well, four were put there. The fifth I discovered in my locker at the theatre.'

'You're an actress?'

'Ballet dancer.'

The perfect comportment of her legs crossed my mind. I opened the flap of one of the envelopes and opened up an abnormally sized page.

Mocha leaned forward to place elbows on top of Art's ink blotter map of the world, her chin in her palms. 'It's U.S. Letter, eight-point-five by eleven inches.'

'You measured it?'

'Well, like you, obviously, I thought this was a weird size. I checked into it. Whereas we use the international standard A4, U.S. Letter is the standard in—'

'The U.S.?' I hazarded.

'Spot on.'

'Ta. Wasn't that difficult.'

I turned my attention to the contents.

'Let's see: 'YOU WILL DIE!!' ...To the point, all caps, double exclamation marks for effect—making the threat childish. Not so sure of him or herself, since 'WILL' is employed instead of 'GOING TO'. Wow. You're right. This is a threat.'

'Using a manual typewriter.'

'Manual?' I stared closer at the print. 'Old school. Scrub

the childish quip. And looks like the 'L' drops down lower than the other keys.'

Mocha narrowed her eyes as I showed the page. Straight after I had to shake my head to clear it of the vision. The woman's eyes were dazzling.

'I hadn't noticed that,' she was saying.

I flicked through other envelopes in my hands. 'All these letters are written with the same machine?'

'I'm fairly certain, yes.'

'Similar commentary?'

'Pretty much. Things like 'Die, bitch', 'Prepare to meet your maker'—et cetera, et cetera. I haven't learned all of them by rote.'

'Original content.'

'Requiring writerly skill and excessive imagination.'

'For sure. Any idea why some dipstick would want you bumped off?'

'I haven't the faintest.' Straight after she lifted her head from her hands. 'Actually, that's not exactly true. I was recently promoted to principal.'

'Of which school?'

Mocha rolled those mesmerizing cinnamon peepers. 'I'm nineteen. A little young to be a teacher let alone running a school. I mean principal dancer at the company—what the French call *étoile*.'

'Well, I'm glad we got that sorted out early,' I laughed.

She charitably joined me. 'That's true. Could have led to some disastrous misunderstandings.'

'Oh, yeah. Now, back to the manual typewriter.' Balancing the chair on its two back legs—which my boss hated me doing—I scratched my head. 'Prob'ly it's easy enough to find in this day and age. What a giveaway.'

'Then you'll take the case?'

'I'll have to run it by Art when he steps in. Guy's a busy man.'

'Not your Mister Miller—you. Will you take the case?'

I stared at her. 'Me?'

'I like the way you think, even while you're nursing what I can only imagine is the hangover from Hades.'

'You noticed.'

'Mmm. But I think we have something, a spark. I trust you, in spite of any—*er*—alcoholic tendencies.'

'Well, I'm not qualified anyway. I'm no detective. Art runs the show and he'd hit the roof.'

'I don't care. Qualifications are often a ruse or no help at all. I'll pay you well—and I'll throw in a few front-row tickets.'

'You have that kind of pull?' I guessed it must be a third rate affair, probably some amateur collective doing rehearsals in a dilapidated warehouse on a forgotten back alley in Richmond or Clifton Hill.

'Right now, I seem to.'

'Which company?'

'The national one.'

'Ah.' I seriously needed to reassess my detecting skills. 'The big time.'

'These days, with the world falling apart out there—I guess.'

'Sorry to say, I'm not such a ballet fan, so the tickets would be a wasted perk.'

'Any sisters?'

That made me twig. Art's kid Suzie.

I could imagine her killing for the tickets—or, better yet, strangling me if I passed up this kind of opportunity. A tough ten-year-old mad about ballet. I peered at my watch. God knows why. The old man wouldn't be back for days, and anyway he wouldn't notice I was MIA.

'Okay,' I decided. 'You're on.'

We entered the Arts Centre complex via a back door that reminded me of hidden panels used by ninja in old Japanese TV shows.

I didn't even see it there in the wall until Mocha stopped and swung it open. Just as I stepped forward, another skinny woman—coming from inside—whacked into my guide.

The glare this woman sent Mocha's way bookended the

intentional nature of the bump. I would have guessed her age as early thirties, with crow's feet around the eyes and a boyish body she didn't hide. Pretty woman, but washed out and agitated.

'I see you're replacing me in the part,' this woman said.

Mocha held her ground. 'It's just temporary.'

'Of course. Nobody here is a permanent fixture.'

After that, the woman waltzed down the street. I'll give her this much—she waltzed well.

'Who's grumpy bum?' I asked.

'Neve Ryan.'

'And the name is supposed to be meaningful to me, because...?'

'The darling of the company over the past decade—but she's being forced into retirement by our new director Murray Helpman.'

'Bound to make someone grumpy. Any chance you reckon she could be the author of your fan mail?'

'Well, she doesn't like me.'

'I don't like people, either—but that doesn't mean I send irate love letters or plan to knock them off.'

'True. C'mon.'

I followed the woman's lead along a narrow corridor wrapped in pale linoleum and very little else aside from intrusive fluorescent lighting above our heads.

'So this is ballet central?'

'The bowels of it.'

Near an open door a wiry-looking middle-aged man in a baggy chocolate-brown suit, boasting a beige cravat around the neck and thinning hair up on top, intercepted us. He had a somewhat magnetic ski-jump nose undercut by a lopsided sneer.

'Darling,' he purred, ignoring me as he washed bulging eyes over Mocha. 'Where on earth have you been?'

'Having lunch with my friend Roy here. Roy, this is Murray Helpman—the artistic director of the company.'

'Yes, yes, charmed,' Helpman crooned, allowing his gaze to flick my way for all of one five hundredth of a second.

'Now—' His attention had jumped back to Mocha '—I want to create, to make something big out of something little, to make a great dancer out of you. But first, I must ask you a question: What do you want from life? To eat?'

The man appeared genuinely disgusted at the thought.

'Don't worry, I threw down only a salad,' Mocha assured him.

'With a liberal dashing of Thousand Island dressing,' I added.

Helpman fairly swooned. Mincing with feeble, the man leaned against a wall, wiping his brow.

'Oh, my God! Insanity!'

'Roy's only kidding round,' Mocha said, granting me a look that was thirty-three percent annoyed and the other two-thirds mischief. 'No Thousand Island dressing, I swear.'

Another man, handsome, taller and far more powerful looking than Helpman, strode up to us in an overly tight pair of white tights and a loose black t-shirt with the word 'IF?' emblazoned across the chest.

'What is this I hear for Thousand Island dressing? I love the Thousand Island!'

'Oh, Bruno, shhh.'

Mocha seemed disproportionately annoyed now. It was a sad thing to see the mischief scarper.

'Roy, this is my dance partner, Bruno Lermentov. He's from Slobokia.'

'Is that a real country?'

'Ahh, of course, of course! Very nice to meet you, Mr. Roy,' Bruno said, all odd eastern European twang, shaking my hand with a surprisingly strong grip that made my bones creak. Then he leaned in close, glittery eyes beneath a brunette fringe. 'Am I not magnificent?'

'Sorry. It's a bit of a mad-house.'

We were in a reasonably large dressing room that Mocha had scored for herself. It even had her name on the door—my dream.

One wall was naked brickwork and opposite that a huge mirror sat above a dresser. Light bulbs surrounded the looking glass and a clothesline dangled across it just above head-height, holding an assortment of undergarments and jewellery.

Below, the dresser was jammed with powders, creams, rouge, lipsticks, brushes and other bric-à-brac I had no hope of recognizing.

'D'you mean it's a mad-house right here or the ballet company in general?'

'Both?' Mocha giggled.

I barely recognized the woman.

She'd changed into a sequinned leotard with a wide, frilly tutu, while on her face she'd slapped a thick layer of white greasepaint, black eyeliner and ridiculously long false lashes. An ostrich-feather headpiece up top set it all off. Her midriff above the tutu was bare—a narrow, muscled thing that had absolutely no excess puppy fat. This was difficult to keep my hands off.

At that particular moment Mocha was grinding her feet in a small wooden box on the ground.

'Kitty litter?' I asked from my crap fold-up captain's chair by the door.

'Ha-Ha. No. This is ballet rosin, a powder resin we rub our toes and heels in to avoid slippage.'

'Oh, I get it—a fancy version of the blue chalk we use on billiard cues for a game of pool.'

'Mmm.'

I wasn't sure what she meant by her tone there.

'Anyway, I have a performance. I've reserved a seat for you in the wings.' She stepped out of the tray and pushed a ticket into my hands. 'I'll see you after?'

'Sure. Might do a spot of snooping.'

'If you're hungry—well, you'll have to pop out for something. There's a half-decent restaurant next door called The Archers, so try that. None of the other dancers have anything decent except rabbit food, and since he took over I'm certain Murray is trying to starve us all to death.'

'How long's he been in charge?'

'Two months, ever since Pat Hingle's terrible accident.'

'In what way terrible?'

'She was found in the loo—disembowelled, stabbed multiple times, and hung from a doorframe with her own tights.'

'You call that an accident?'

'The police did. Anyway, I can't complain. Pat tended to ignore me, but once Murray took over he gave me the promotion.'

The woman placed her arms in an 'L' position—the left one out straight beside her, the right pointed my way, and then she pirouetted on one leg several times, so swiftly her body became a blur. When she finished the rotation she struck a pose with her arms crossed low in front and one foot forward.

'*Bras Croisé*,' she announced.

I couldn't help myself—I gave a healthy round of applause.

Mocha winked at me. 'Warm up.' Her gaze whipped over to a digital clock half hidden behind paraphernalia on that crowded dresser. 'Gotta go, Roy—duty calls. Ciao!'

About three hours later, after countless curtain calls and once the orchestra had packed up and the audience piled out, Mocha came to find me in the right wing seats. She was still dolled-up, but had wrapped herself in a bland cream woollen cardigan and had her ostrich feathers at a jaunty angle. Surprisingly her makeup had held together okay. She also looked sweaty, and the complete package was sexy.

'So—what did you think of *Le Corsaire*?' she asked as she flopped next to me and stuck her pointe shoes on the chair in front. 'I presumed you might enjoy it since there're pirates tucked away in the faintly ridiculous plot.'

I glanced at her. 'Honest answer?'

'Go on.'

'I dozed through most of it.'

'And I thought you were supposed to be keeping an eye on me.'

'I had my leftie half-open.'

'Does that count?'

'In my book, yep. Quite the struggle.'

'Did you find any typewriters?'

'Forgot to bring my magnifying glass. Bring me up to speed on the yarn behind the ballet.'

'There really isn't one. Remember I said it was faintly ridiculous?'

'You're kidding.'

'It's the performance that matters. Kind of.'

'Right.' I rubbed my face and peered around the empty auditorium. 'Big place. How many people does it hold?'

'A thousand at capacity.'

'How many were here today.'

'A thousand.'

Mocha stood then and took my hand, which surprised me. I allowed her to lead me away from the comfy chair to a small set of stairs, and then up onto the stage.

Some of the spots high above still glowed, but the arena and its ramshackle sets created a dark forest effect that looked vaguely menacing—in a wire clothes hanger and papi-er-mâché way.

'Don't you get stage-fright in front of all those gawking plebs out there?'

'Sometimes my heart is in my stomach. Other times, I don't care. They're going to be building a larger theatre next door—it's going to hold five times as many people, apparently. Scary.'

'Ballet is that popular?'

'I didn't think so, but I don't make these decisions. An audience of five thousand is too big—can you see the dancers at all from the back pews? Next up, they'll erect video screens in the rear for those people—which means they might as well save their money and enjoy the spectacle on a telly at home.'

I decided on the spot the girl was cute when she soap boxed.

'How long've you been prancing partners with Bruno the Magnificent?'

'Ouch.'

Mocha slid off the humdrum cardigan and watched it fall to the boards.

'You make us sound like some kind of glitzy ballroom

dancing duo. We've been together a month, since I was elevated to principal. Bruno was Neve's partner before that.'

'Bound to make waves.'

'A drop in the ocean.' Mocha smiled.

'So no death notes in your locker this afternoon?'

'Nothing. But we've only been here half a day. Rome wasn't built in twice that.'

'Neither was my attention span. How long *did* it take to build Rome?'

'I don't remember them teaching us—we learned only the idiom.'

'That figures.'

I gazed up at the pulleys and ropes, lights and wire several dozen metres above, at the same time that I stretched the muscles in my back.

'Before you became a principal dancer you were one of those background people?'

'A member of the *corps de ballet*? Yep.'

'What's the wire on them? Any grumpsters amongst that lot?'

'People annoyed by my promotion? I don't know. Haven't thought to take a survey.' Perhaps feeling guilty, the girl picked up her cardigan and hung it on a small faux rock.

'When were you upped to prima?'

'Five weeks ago.'

'When did the fan mail begin?'

'Five weeks ago.'

I looked at her. 'The same day you were promoted?'

'Yep—that was the night I received the one in the locker. After that they've been hand-delivered by the arsehole to my apartment.'

'Before or after the announcement?'

'Which one?' Mocha was confused.

'The announcement about your upgrade—promotion.'

'God, I don't know. It was ages ago.'

'Try to remember.'

Mocha frowned and her eyes darted about as she searched

her memory. It seemed to be a losing battle, but then the girl parted her cherry-red lips and stared at me.

'Before? Crap—yes. You're right. It *was* before. We had a matinée performance of *The Sleeping Beauty*. Neve was Aurora, Bruno the Prince and I was the Lilac Fairy. Neve was so beautiful, Roy. I'd never, ever seen anyone dance Aurora so—'

I cleared my throat. 'The letter, Mocha.'

'Hmm?'

'The letter in the locker.'

'Oh! Yes, sorry. After the performance ended I brushed out my hair, had a shower, got changed to go to the company fund-raiser upstairs that evening—that was where the announcement about my promotion was to be made. I found the letter beforehand, squeezed into my locker through the grille.'

'You weren't concerned?'

'I didn't take the thing seriously, wasn't sure if it was a joke or some silly stalker's handiwork. I didn't have the time to fret.'

'Who knew you were being promoted?'

I was thinking of either Bruno the Magnificent or Neve, the forced retiree.

Incriminating ballet shoes best fit the two of them. Frankly, nothing would make me happier than to pin the wrong number tag on the guy who'd crushed my fingers— they still ached.

'Did Bruno or Neve know about the promotion?' I added.

'No. Well, I'm pretty sure no. Even I didn't know until the announcement was made. I spotted Neve's face straight after—she was horrified, but she also looked shocked. The woman played a wonderful Aurora, but she's not that great an actress.'

'Bruno?'

'Off chasing tutu. He'd slipped out straight after the encore to catch a flight to Sydney. Some dancer up there he has his hands all over.'

I breathed out loudly and looked around us. We were

alone. I never realized a theatre would be so eerie when no one was in it.

'When is this place closed up for the night?'

'The theatre? They'll be switching off the lights in an hour or two.'

'Do they object to people hanging round like we are now?'

'Usually it's okay.'

'So security is lax. People come, people go.'

'I never gave it much thought. Yes.'

After testing its stability I sat down on a prop representing an anchor. 'The key is the typewriter, but I doubt we'll find that here. You'd hear a manual a mile off.'

'We can't exactly ransack people's homes.'

'Who says? Art does it all the time.'

'And you?'

'The only ransacking I ever did was my older brother's room, looking for his chocolate stash.'

I performed the usual head scratch.

'Let's go back a way. Who would have known before the announcement? Who decides these things? And had the time to whiz home, type up the note on their fancy antique typewriter that probably needed to be oiled down beforehand, and then get back here—all this before the party—to make a letter drop?'

We glanced at each other.

'Helpman.'

Straight after, I was seeing stars.

Something damnably hard had hammered me from behind across the back of my skull, knocked me right off the anchor, and I lay on my face on the stage. The pain was excruciating and I thought I'd pass out—but didn't. I held on for dear life, since I knew life was probably something give or take in that moment.

It took a while to pull myself to my hands and knees, idiotic notions of protecting Mocha flying bat-crazy across my senses. I had to wait longer still to clearly see anything.

When I finally did, there was a sprinkling of blood on the floorboards around me—mine? Mocha's?

Velveteen stage curtains hung nearby and I used them to pull myself to my feet. I felt woozy and things threatened to bank sideways but at least they'd stopped spinning.

Bruno the Magnificent stood a few metres away at the edge of the orchestra pit, a glassy look on his face as he watched me totter.

'You?' I said.

The dancer peered down at his right hand.

There was an iron weight there, something heavy enough to have been the object that whacked me—and, in fact, there was hair and a tuft of scalp attached to it, but the hair was the wrong colour.

It was black instead of my brown.

A thick trickle of blood from his hairline coursed down the Slobokian's face.

'It fell on my head, yet!' he declared of the metal weight, holding it aloft for conjecture, and then he collapsed sideways with a loud thud.

'A wonderful dancer, but in all other respects a cretin.'

The theatre director, Helpman, came around the corner of a towering prop of the pirate ship the anchor belonged to. This newcomer kicked Bruno's body, which remained still, and he smiled.

'All that gutter English and poorly pronounced nonsense. Perhaps I should have bludgeoned him earlier?'

'Then you're the one that slugged me.'

'Naturally.'

'Where's Mocha?'

My skull puttered as I again fell to my knees. Yes, concern had come to bat, and I also decided I had to play for time—weak sister I might've been, but at the current moment I was in no state to put up half-decent resistance.

Time. I needed time. For a miracle to happen.

'And a fine question that is,' Helpman nattered—like all good villains should, wasting precious seconds. 'I thought she would be with you. Where *has* the girl got to?'

The man glanced about, displaying a relatively minor sense of unease.

If she'd taken a powder, good for her. Lot less to worry about. But I still needed the time I talked up, and clarity—p'raps I could even convince him to tip his mitt, for all the good that'd do me. Curiosity always was my weak point.

'Can I ask you something?'

'This depends, does it not?'

'On what exactly?'

'On the question, of course.'

'Well, okay, whatever. Yeah.' I shook my head. My vision was blurring again, but I kept to the chase like Art used to tell me about. 'Anyway, d'you happen to have a manual typewriter?'

'Yes, I do.'

'Does it get stuck on its 'L's?'

'Ahh. I see where you're taking this, Roger.'

'Roy.'

'I don't think your name is something you need to worry about ever again.'

'Yeah, yeah, I get that. But one thing I don't get—you're the one who sent Mocha those crazy notes.'

'Hands up, guilty parties!' Helpman raised five fingers into the air and he laughed in a mad, unnerving kind of way.

'Funny. Why? You promoted her to principal ballerina.'

That killed the laughter.

'Dancer. Good Lord, nobody says 'ballerina' anymore.'

'Dancer. Same question.'

Helpman raised both arms now, outstretching them toward the empty seats of the theatre.

'Great agony of body and spirit can only be achieved by a great impression of simplicity!' he declared with a booming voice—either clearly insane or up for a bit of ham acting.

As I studied the palooka I also felt more than a little confused, and was pretty certain this wasn't concussion-related.

'I think you want to word that the other way round, mate,' I decided.

'And who, pray tell, is the artistic director here?'

'I doubt you are. You strike me as more a professional nut-job.'

'Oh, ho!' Helpman chuckled, without genuine mirth. 'Do get these giddy expressions off your chest, before I crack your head wide open.'

'No, I've got a better idea.'

'You do?'

Time was working its little magic. I could see better and my head didn't feel like it had quite so many trolls tap-dancing about.

'Yeah, I do—let's bite the bullet here and now. You're going to kill me, so let's be upfront. I'm Roy Scherer and I work for a detective agency. The training wheels still haven't been detached, but there you go. I live in a mate's apartment, sleeping on his couch, and I have no money in the bank. My sad story in a nutshell. But Art Miller, my boss, knows I'm here and you don't want to mess with him.'

I wiped the back of my head. It was wet. When I put my hand in front of my face, it was covered with sticky blood. I blinked a few times, feeling ill.

'Now you,' I muttered. 'What's your real name? I know Helpman is a sham.'

'And why should I bother going into such detail?'

'Why not?'

He smiled. 'Pathetic. My name is Ivan Boleslawsky.'

'Okay. Never remember that. And your caper?'

'If you're asking me what this is about, you ought to direct the question to Mocha's mother. Mocha?'

The man turned full circle on the stage.

'Where the devil has she got to? She can't escape. I've locked all the doors, and the keys are right here.' He tapped the breast pocket of his blazer.

I felt like I was going to pass out. Not yet. 'Go on,' I urged.

'Hmm?' The man stopped looking around. 'Oh yes, of course, the story! Well, many years ago, Mocha's mother—a hack journalist, I must say—wrote a review of one of my father's movies. Do you know the famous Ruritanian director Rudolf Boleslawsky?'

'Nup.'

'A great man. His cinema style was sublime, moving, and—'

'You talked up a review.'

'Oh, yes. Thank you. This film 'review' was first published in *The Age* newspaper here in Melbourne. That would have been damaging enough, but the harpy syndicated the piece to *The Independent* in England and *The New York Times* in America. It even appeared in the esteemed *Ruritanian Gazette*. That five hundred-word critique destroyed my father's career and broke his heart—a year later he tried to drown my mother in the kitchen sink and was then committed to a mental institution. I was sixteen years old. It was a humiliating experience.'

'For your dad, or for yourself?'

'Myself, of course.'

I yawned. 'Y'know, this yarn is about as interesting as the story behind *Le Corsaire*.'

'How dare you!'

Bole-whatever-his-name-was strode straight over to Bruno's corpse and snatched up the weight from the dead man's hand.

'Now I'm going to return the favour by killing not just that evil reviewer's only child, but her rude, highly-unprofessional prick of a bodyguard.'

'My bad.'

'Bad luck isn't brought by broken mirrors, but by broken shoes. Remember that.'

'What's the point? You're going to crown me anyway.'

'True.'

The kook stepped slowly toward me. I still held tightly to the curtains and couldn't raise my hands to defend myself.

'Modern man is so confused, Roy. It's much better to work in the theatre—than in the horror of a world out there.'

'Whatever.'

That was when all hell broke loose.

Something fast darted out of shadows of a mocked-up grotto to my right, moving so quickly I couldn't hope to keep up.

I don't know when I realized the wildly whirling dervish was Mocha.

She hummed something familiar as she zipped, twisted, did a cartwheel—what was that damned tune?—and finally she somersaulted, catapulted herself into a handstand, scissor-kicked around Helpman's neck, and stopped right there.

'*Pas de deux?*' she said, her cheeks flushed even under all the makeup.

Helpman's eyes bulged, his head pinioned between Mocha's calf muscles. I could see he was stuck, and she wasn't about to let him go.

'Mocha,' I warned, 'watch out for the weight of iron he has in his mitt.'

'Ta.'

The woman knocked the metal away across the floor. Then she leaned up close to her captive. The flexibility factor alone worried me—I had no hope of ever touching my toes.

'Ivan,' she murmured softly, fluttering her enormous false eyelashes, 'now I know your real name, let me tell the other part of the story, the bit you missed. I'm your harpy.'

'What?'

'It was me. I wrote the bad review. The hack who destroyed your father.'

'Preposterous! What nonsense is this? That would make you somewhere in the vicinity of sixty years of age! It was your mother!'

Mocha laughed.

'Oh, I've lived for a *very* long time. One reason my ballet is so good. Lots of practice. What you don't understand is that I've been doing this mother-daughter routine for centuries. Makes people less suspicious. By the way, I hate to be the bearer of bad tidings—but your father's movie really was awful.'

A second later the woman spun abruptly, pushing off the floor with her hands, and I heard a loud crack.

Helpman, or Boleslawsky, or whoever the fuck he was, fell down across Bruno the Magnificent. His neck was bent at an obscene angle, and spread-eagled together on the stage like that the two men looked like an arty religious icon thrown together for some exasperating stage-play.

'Jeez. The horror of the world is right in here, pal,' I muttered as I let go of the drapes and sagged.

Of course Mocha caught me. This woman, I realized, was capable of anything.

'Roy, are you all right?' she asked quickly. 'I heard everything. I'm so sorry I hid. I needed time to figure out my action.'

'Guessed as much. I'm a good time-waster. Besides, in the end there you more than made up for the faux pas.'

'I did?'

'Christ, did you ever.'

I leaned back against her shoulder and could feel the woman's warm breath on my neck.

'I have a question, though—what'd you use on the bastard? Some kind of mixed martial arts?'

'Secret.'

She eased us both down to the floor and I sat there on my backside, positioned between two sensational legs in white tights that I'd just seen kill a man.

That was when I remembered. 'Stockholm really was named after you.'

Mocha snuggled her face into my neck and granted me a kiss. 'It was. Seven hundred years ago. Now, let's get you to hospital.'

'Ominous. You may be an old lady, but you rock.'

I leaned over, grabbed the keys from a dead man's pocket, and then slowly stood up all by myself.

Three Kings

Carol Borden

Chapter 1
Love Carries a .38

I was taking in the view from my office window. The view $25 per week gets you. I looked at the electrical towers and the birds perched on the wires running between them and thought about lunch.

My ruminations were interrupted by a familiar poke in the middle of my back.

'Turn around,' she said. So I turned around. The lady showed a lot of leg, so much I didn't notice her revolver until it jabbed right into my chest. I'm no doctor, but if she planned to shoot me in the heart her aim was off target. She bit her lip as she decided what to do next.

'Are we going to stand here playing cops and robbers, or are you going to tell me what you want?'

She dropped her arm and started sobbing. I pulled the .38 from her limp hand and glanced at it—police issue—before slipping it into my desk drawer to keep my toe nail clippers and loose change company. The clippers have been awfully lonely lately.

I gestured to a chair in front of my desk. Not a very good chair, kind of shabby, faded plaid moth-bait, but sturdy nonetheless. She collapsed into it, still sobbing.

'You're not so hardboiled. I'd say you were barely poached.'

She ignored my crack. I can't blame her. I'd like to ignore it myself. 'Look, I'm sorry. I'm tired and hungry enough to eat an automat.'

I handed her my handkerchief and tried again, 'What can I do for you?'

She dabbed her eyes and uncurled. 'You are Mr. Godzilla?'

I started to crack wise again, but thought better of it. 'Yes, and you are?'

'Miss Mothra.'

'Is that from Mosura?'

'Oh.' Her mouth formed a perfect little O. O could get to be my favorite letter. 'You speak Japanese,' Miss Mosura finally said.

I didn't begrudge her the name change. We all make compromises. 'What is your name?' she asked.

I handed her my card. "Godzilla, King of the Monsters." She looked up 'I already know that, Mr. Godzilla. I meant your Japanese name.'

I shrugged. Like I said, compromises.

Miss Mosura pulled a fifty from her pocketbook. 'I need your help. You're the only one who can help me. I've something I need you to find.'

Chapter 6
Monkey Town

I strolled down to Monkey Town in search of a fellow named 'Kong.'

The city was changing and Monkey Town was not primates-only anymore, all part of the Mayor's urban renewal program, a central plank in his re-election campaign. But I wasn't here to ponder urban affairs, I was here to put the squeeze on a Sasquatch.

I found him leaning on the wall outside a bar. Just above him a broken neon sign flickered red, 'See No Evil.' In Monkey Town, the bar patrons do just that. Several simian Black Hole Aliens scurried by without making eye contact, the heavy odor of Havana cigars trailing behind them. When I turned my head to watch them pass, the Johnny pulled a sap and swung. I yanked the Sasquatch up by the scruff of his neck. 'Is that any way to say hello?'

'I don't want no trouble, mac.' His sap thumped softly on the sidewalk.

I lowered Johnny back down onto the pavement and he

began nervously grooming himself. I felt itchy just watching him pick through the fur on his arms.

'Tell me about a fellow by the name of, 'Kong."

'Hey, us primates got to stick together!'

'I might see my way to donating a fin to the cause of primate brotherhood.'

'We're all brothers under the skin,' Johnny grinned. 'Kong's been in town maybe 3 weeks. He's a Skull Island boy. Operates out of New York now. They call him 'King Kong."

'King Kong, eh? Where's he staying?'

'He's got a place up near Palo Alto. Can't miss him.'

Chapter 7
A Private Dance

As Johnny Sasquatch had said, finding Kong wasn't difficult. Kong didn't care if anyone was following him and that made me nervous. I don't like being nervous. It makes my tail twitch. I lit a cigarette while I thought, but Kong saved me the trouble of smoking or thinking.

'Private dick, huh?' He smacked me in the back of the head.

'Following me around, huh?' Smack.

'Happy you found me?' Smack.

I was starting to get the hang of this dance.

'Planning a little surprise party for ol' King Kong?' As he raised his arm again, I ducked under it and grabbed him around the waist. 'I'll lead,' I said.

Kong grunted his disapproval and slammed his forehead into mine. Never say I don't learn. I shut up and fought.

We slugged it out over Palo Alto. If I could've caught my breath, I would have given him the business. But every time I charged up, Kong would pop me right in the mouth. He must've seen my dorsal plates light. I'm not a pretty sight at the best of times. I was going to be a lot less pretty in the morning. Lights were bursting in my eyes like the Fourth of July. Their trails started to fade to black, not because Kong had hit me again, but because he had stopped.

He was looking down at his bloodied knuckles, deep in

thought. 'I've been meaning to moisturize,' I said, standing up. On second thought, maybe I don't learn. Kong glared at me. It was terrifying. I was too bruised and exhausted to care. Maybe he was, too, or maybe he did his best thinking while punching someone. He didn't slug me again.

I handed Kong my card. Kong thought a little more before taking it. Trying to figure my angle, I presume. 'Godzilla, King of the Monsters.' He glanced at me derisively. 'You're no king.'

'And you're pretty big for a monkey.'

'Ape. I'm an ape.'

'Primates aren't my strong point.'

'OK, pal, you're King of the Monsters,' Kong finally said, letting the card flutter to the ground, 'I'm the King of Skull Island. Everybody's a goddamn king.'

'What's that supposed to mean?'

'The guy you're looking for is Ghidorah—King Ghidorah.'

Chapter 10
Three Crowns

I was spinning. Only I wasn't spinning, it was the room and there were two grinning gold heads on long necks bobbing over me like every crazy idea I've ever had. The bobbing was starting to nauseate me. A breakfast of doped scotch was no match for all this motion.

'Ah, Mr. Godzilla, you are awake at last,' a quavering metallic voice said. I realized the voice belonged to the heads, and that they really wiggling around, barely under control. But I wasn't looking at those heads anymore. I was focused on one in the middle. Titanium, I thought.

'I see you're looking at my prosthesis. I lost the original in the war.'

'We all lost a lot in that damn war.'

He sighed as he poured a drink. 'The miracles of modern science have restored to me some small portion of what was taken.' He gestured modestly at his central head, then heaved up his massive body from behind his desk. He was monstrous, possibly twice my size.

'King Ghidorah, I presume?'

'Mecha King Ghidorah, to be precise. Since my transplant, I find I enjoy precision. Would you care for a drink? I would hardly mar this excellent scotch with a 'mickey.'' He said that last word as if it might stain his mouth.

Someone had deposited me neatly on a divan, as neatly as a hotel maid would place folded laundry, but with no more concern. Shaking my head, I sat up.

Ghidorah replaced the stopper on a crystal decanter without pouring himself a drink. 'Then to business.'

'Return the kid's egg and let her go back to her little life on Infant Island.'

'As in legitimate business, Mr. Godzilla, there are levels of bureaucracy even among more adventurous entrepreneurs. The left head does not always know what the right head is doing, so to speak.' He paused and tapped his claws on his desk.

'It is most regrettable that Miss Mosura has been the victim of red tape. Most regrettable, indeed, but such small tragedies are sadly unavoidable in all ambitious enterprises.'

I reared up and slammed my fists down on his desk. 'The hell she has. You make it sound like Miss Mosura was fined for filing an improper flight plan to Carmel! She's no threat to you—what she knows about the Mayor's campaign, the X Aliens' classified underwater base and your development contracts could fit in the palm of my hand. The kid's no match for your thugs or your lawyers.'

'You misunderstand me, Mr. Godzilla. I intend to rectify the situation. Let no one say Mecha King Ghidorah is unmoved by the plight of the unfortunate. Given my new situation and opportunities after the passing of my esteemed colleague, King Kong,' his other heads frowned slightly, 'I believe I can provide unity in enterprise, a unity that will prevent such unforeseen misfortunes from happening in the future. It will be a prosperous new future not only for Miss Mosura, but for us all.'

I slumped back into my seat. Miss Mosura deserved her little chance at happiness. Hell, we all did.

'You, Mr. Godzilla, present more of a problem.' His other two heads echoed the sentiment eerily. It was the first time I heard them speak. I hoped I never would again.

'Yes, a problem, indeed.'

We sat silently for a while, contemplating my future. Finally, I stood up. 'You know my office hours, Ghidorah, if you need me.'

Ghidorah laughed his weird laugh as I started towards the door. If I never wanted to hear his other heads speak again, I would gladly destroy my secondary brain before hearing that laugh again.

I opened his office door and walked. I kept walking, noting every little thing between that door and the window overlooking the electrical towers in my own office. I became a chronicler of parking meters and cracked pavement, downed power lines and smashed coupes. All I had left was 35 cents and my old nail clippers. I was right back where I started, but I was lucky too.

A Mark in Blue

Carol Borden

Chapter 1
A Very Bad Dream

My mouth tasted metallic, like money. A bad taste. I slid my hand down my side.

'Hell,' I muttered, glancing down. My side was a mess of rearranged gears and blue coolant wept from a broad gash. There was another smear of coolant on my chest, in the shape of the letter, 'M,' right over my heart. And next to me, one of my own cards sticky with oil, blood and God knew what else, 'Godzilla, King of the Monsters.'

I nursed myself up off the floor. No need to hurry. Gingerly rubbing a dent in my head, I looked around. I was in an empty airplane hanger. All I remembered was a nightmare in strobe images—Tokyo in flames, a fight, a robot sitting in rings of light, a cybernetic head, bones at the bottom of the sea, a man with a black leather glove.

'This doesn't make any sense,' I thought.

I waited a while and, when no one offered me a hand, I helped myself up, then hauled myself across the floor. Leaning on the hangar doors for a moment, I noticed a tuft of red hair glinting in the parking lot lights and, at my feet, a stubbed out Lucky Strike.

Chapter 2
The Kaiju Lounge

At home, I slept for nearly twenty hours. It was just after 1pm when I awoke. The trail was probably cold by now, but who was I to argue with the spins?

I had more nebulous dreams. I thought I heard a voice say, 'Here in Tokyo, time has been turned back two million years.'

I dragged myself to the bathroom and cleaned myself up

over the sink. The coolant had stopped leaking, but my side was still stiff. I ran some water over my head. There was a picture of Minya taped to my mirror. Minya was only a kid, but he fancied himself my sidekick. I took it down. I didn't remember taping it there.

An hour later I was at the Kaiju Lounge, a bar so far gone it was in danger of being taken out and shot. Minya sat at the bar sipping a Shirley Temple, as dainty as a bee at a buttercup. Minya had very round eyes in a very oval head. And his eyes got even rounder as I walked up to him. 'Mr. Godzilla, I was starting to worry! I've been looking for you everywhere.'

If Minya were at the Kaiju, he surely was looking everywhere.

'I'm fine, kid.' I looked over the scattered patrons. What a sorry lot, they were. I made a mental note not to become the class of person who frequents bars in the afternoon. 'You seen Caesar around here? Red-haired lion-god?'

'Gosh no, Mr. Godzilla. King Caesar's in Okinawa, everybody knows that.'

'I heard Caesar's been palling around with Titanosaurus. I heard they had a job together.' Rodan was perched at the bar on the other side of Minya. Rodan couldn't help repeating whatever he heard.

'That so? What kind of job?' I said, pushing the complimentary basket of pistachios over to Rodan.

'I don't know.' Rodan pecked the shells off the nuts. 'I do know that they're supposed to be working for a scientist specializes in robots, a Dr. Mafune.'

'Gee, Mr. Godzilla, I was just gonna say you should have Dr. Mafune give you a once over. He'll fix you up.' Minya chirped, 'He'll fix you good!'

Chapter 7
The Man with the Mechanical Hand

White light arced around me. I was strapped into a rig, Dr. Mafune's mechanical hand whirring near my ear as he pulled a knife switch and shut down his machine. Sliding his goggles back over his head, he said, 'It seems, Mr. Godzilla, that you have been altered.'

'Altered?' I said. I was coming down with a nasty case of déjà vu.

'Oh, come now, you must've realized that you're not exactly what you thought you were. I built you—Godzilla's skeletal structure, Godzilla's brain, yes, possibly even Godzilla's mind, King Ghidorah's cybernetic head, they brought me all that, yes, but the rest—the rest was mine! You are powered by a reactor of my design. Uranium, the only devil the modern world knows! And you were disguised as the real thing, using my technology, my genius! You are my second greatest creation!'

'Second?' I began to tear myself out of the machine. 'I'm hurt.'

'My daughter Katsura is my first. She's completely cybernetic. In my sunset years I have become sentimental. After the accident, I missed her so.' He sighed. 'But tell me, how could you have let yourself come to be in such wretched shape, dear boy?'

Pulling free of the last lines, I said, 'Not an inkling.' But I was starting to get one. I thought of the fragmentary images that have been haunting me and the mysterious M on my chest.

'No matter. There is no purpose to your further existence. Please do not damage yourself struggling. I planned to scavenge your components for an even greater creation!' Mafune pulled another lever. A curtain opened and revealed a woman. 'My daughter has other uses. Titanosaurus loves her most unconditionally. He calls her 'Big Sister'- she calls him, 'Moose.' Charming isn't it? Beauty and the beast, they have a most unusual mental attunement.' He turned to his daughter, 'You hate Mechagodzilla, don't you, my dear?'

Katsura glared at me, 'I hate you.'

'Charming...' I didn't get any more out because my attention was temporarily occupied by 30,000 tons of Moose's love. I elbowed him in the face and spun my head around to give him the business with my atomizing breath. Moose was already down, a softy with a glass jaw, a metal plate on the side of his head and bad lungs from a lifetime of Lucky Strikes. How he ever copped a heel on me in that warehouse, I'll never know.

I emptied one whole fistful of missiles on Dr. Mafune's machines. Hopefully, he'd never pull this on another poor sap.

'My work! You're destroying all my work! Murderer! Monster!'

'Mechagodzilla!' I told him. 'Didn't you know? M is for Mechagodzilla!' And I left him wailing his despair in the smoke and wreckage while Katsura sat down carefully beside her beast.

Chapter 12
Hero in Bronze

Caesar was waiting right where he said he'd be, on a bench beside the statue of Jet Jaguar in Tokusatsu Park.

'I thought you'd want to know that he is going to be all right.'

'Who? Moose?'

Caesar's mouth quirked into a little hook. It might've been amusement. 'You oughtn't call him that.'

'I thought all the beautiful people did.'

Caesar's smile was definitely professional.

'Tell you what,' I said. 'I'll render unto you what's yours and we'll see how the rest plays out.'

If that dig bothered Caesar, I couldn't tell. He was a fed. I don't know if feds are born with bland expressions or if they learn it in Kindergarten. At least Caesar was pleasantly bland.

'Okay, no more cute talk. Were you the one who painted the letter M on my chassis?' I asked him

'No.'

I believed him. He only lied for his country and even then he was bad at it.

Caesar decided to say what he had to say. 'I thought you were Godzilla and that Godzilla had played us for suckers. Cities were leveled. Citizens were panicking. Someone had to pay. You were made to sow discord and provide cover. The question is, why?'

'I'm the chump. Every good scheme needs one.' I admired the statuary in the park. Great men stood orating in bronze. Jet Jaguar reached for the heavens. Funny how bronze kills greatness.

'Alright,' he finally said. 'I won't interfere in whatever you do. You should know, though, that it's big. Godzilla's off the board. Someone got a hold of Mecha King Ghidorah's head. While I was staking out Dr. Mafune's office looking for you, he had visits from Interpol and envoys from both the UN and the Black Hole Aliens. If I were you, I'd go home, go to bed and stay there until you fossilize.' He stood. 'Oh, and call Minya. I saw him looking for you at Dr. Mafune's office, too. He must be worried.'

Caesar walked toward the park gates. 'I won't be another statue in this park, Caesar,' I said, just because I'd been waiting to say it.

I didn't know if I were real anymore, but I didn't much care if it were Godzilla's brain in my head, well, Mecha King Ghidorah's head, or his bones in my exoskeleton. I didn't care if my memories were my own or Godzilla's or even Ghidorah's. Someone had played us. Someone had used us all and now, hero or no, it was simple. Godzilla was dead and I was going to do something about it.

Chapter 15
Five Shots

I finally caught up with Minya at the Kaiju Lounge. He was nursing bourbon and blowing smoke rings in a corner booth. I slid in across from him. He goggled his big eyes at me.

'Someone rubbed out Godzilla and King Ghidorah,' I said.

'And here you are, living Godzilla's life and wearing King Ghidorah's head.'

'You leveled the city and I was tailor-made for the rap.'

'You're a funny guy. I hear the bulls on the Island like funny guys.'

'The feds are out of it. That leaves just you and me having a nice drink.' I poured myself some of his bourbon.

He blew a ring.

'I guess this is the part where I ask why you betrayed me after all I've ever done for you and you give me a sob story about how aliens made you do it or someone dropped you when you were in your egg.'

'I guess it is.'

'Let's pretend we had that conversation.'

'This is bigger than you and me, G. The UN. The Earth Defense Force. Interpol. The Black Hole Aliens.'

'I only care about you and me in this. If I leave a Mechagodzilla-sized hole in someone's nice neat plan, well, let's just say I won't meltdown over it.'

Minya gave up on talk. Next thing I knew, one of his radioactive smoke rings was floating around my neck. He was inhaling for another go when I let loose with my megablaster mouth ray. He slumped down in the booth, flames rising behind him. I stood up, a little wobbly from his radioactive breath, and raised my hand to wipe that silly smirk off Minya's face. I still had five shots loaded in the chambers.

'But can I … can I help it?' He shouted, his face desperate and pained. 'Haven't I got this curse inside me? The fire? The pain? Who knows what it feels like to be me?'

I heard a small sound, a gasp maybe. Dr. Mafune's greatest creation stood in the doorway to the bar.

'Please don't,' Katsura said in a voice so quiet I could barely hear it. 'I never wanted for this to happen. I only wanted...'

Freedom from her father's machinations? Revenge for the monster called Moose?

I looked from Katsura to Minya. So many people involved. So many desires.

'Aw, nuts.' I lowered my weapon. 'Tell me one thing, Minya, did you leave those clues around for me to find?'

'No.' Minya was staring at Katsura, unblinking; she was already walking toward him, handkerchief in hand.

I grabbed the bottle and poured myself last call. If Minya didn't paint the M on my chassis, that left only Godzilla or me. Had I done it myself, a somnambulist trying to save my own skin? Had I freed myself?

I drank, listening to the crackle of the flames and Minya's gasping sobs. They say bourbon's the drink of kings. I might not be Godzilla, King of the Monsters, anymore, but I am Mechagodzilla.

I put the glass down gently, without a sound, and went home.

Black Moon Rising

Paul D Brazill

Colonel Ivan Walker went into the kitchen, washed his hands and made a cup of death-black coffee. He gazed out of the window of General Hoffman's luxurious penthouse apartment and waited for the expected release. A release that never came.

A crimson sky bled into Golden City's blood-soaked streets. Spectres of black smoke drifted up from the cadavers of the cars and buses. The corpses of the jeeps and the tanks. The people.

Flames licked and consumed the buildings. Sirens screamed and rocket launchers roared. Machine guns cackled. Helicopters swooped through the skies, black as crows. The pentangle shaped scar on Walker's neck burned.

Something slammed against the front door and Walker turned to see Sergeant Duffy stagger into the room, pointing an AK-47. His acne scarred face glowed. Sweat dripped from him. His military fatigues were torn and splashed with blood.

He gasped and collapsed onto the black leather sofa, dropping his weapon beside him. He took off his back pack and looked up at General Hoffman's pallid, naked corpse, which had been attached to the bedroom door by a bayonet that skewered his throat.

'Looks like you didn't need my help then?' he said. He blew his nose on a pair of black, silk boxer shorts, used them to wipe the sweat from his brow and threw them over his shoulder.

'Luckily for me,' growled Walker. 'He was a little pre-occupied when I arrived.' He pointed a thumb toward the bedroom.

Duffy craned his neck and peered inside the darkened room. A blood-spattered blow-up doll, made to look like Marilyn Monroe, hung deflated from the corner of a four poster bed.

'Well, you could have told me. The lift's fucked now and it nearly killed me running up those bloody stairs.'

Walker sat in an armchair opposite Duffy. He laid his head back and closed his eyes.

Duffy looked around the room.

'Swanky, joint, eh?' he said.

'Paid for by the blood of how many good men and women?' said Walker, eyes still closed.

Duffy nodded. Deep in thought. A shiver sliced through him.

'Any decent gargle in here, by the way?' he said, licking his lips.

'I very much doubt it,' said Walker. 'You know the good General's views on that particular vice.'

'Maybe,' said Duffy, rising to his feet. 'But we all know that talk is cheap. Especially from these religious looneys. Ask any choirboy.'

Duffy walked over to the radiogram. Behind it were rows of pristine vinyl albums. He flicked through them and shook his head.

'Have you seen this?'

Walker kept his eyes closed. Made a humming sound that Duffy took be an affirmative.

'He deserved killing for that Genesis album alone,' said Duffy.

'Indeed.'

Duffy pulled out an album. Put it on the turntable. Delicately moved the arm of the needle.

Steely Dan sang the Deacon Blues as he wandered around the apartment. Walker opened his eyes and sat up. He returned his gaze outside. More and more helicopters were swarming across the skyline. Whole tenements had been demolished. 'Operation Desert Wave' had been a success. The war was almost over.

'Jackpot!' shouted Duffy. He walked into the room with two bottles of Glenfiddich. 'He's got a hell of a stash there. All quality stuff. Bloody hypocrite.'

Walker finished his coffee and passed the mug to Duffy.

'Fill her up,' he said.

Duffy did a comedy double-take.

'Are you sure? I've never seen you drink since God was a boy.'

'Just do it.'

Duffy poured the drinks. They drank in silence, listening to the music until a bullet hit the window, causing a spider-web crack and jolting them alert.

'Let's take that as our cue to piss off, then,' said Duffy, stuffing his back pack with bottles of whisky.

The dark days of the war collided with weeks, crashed into months, and then collapsed into the aching years of peace. But they still cast a long, dark shadow over Ivan Walker.

Jolted out of yet another troubled, fitful sleep he dressed and headed out into The City. The sharp morning air tasted like a razorblade and black clouds cluttered the grey sky like malignant tumours desperate to spread. Death was waiting. And Walker had work to do.

Apart from Benny Vane's corpse, the front room of Roman Dalton's flat looked exactly the same as it had when he'd left it the evening before. A shithole.

The coffee table was still littered with empty beer cans; the battered old fridge in the corner continued to make a high pitched whirring sound; the Bakelite radio was smashed over the threadbare carpet; there was a mountain of paperbacks on the wicker rocking chair; dirty laundry was strewn around the place and a stained and ragged paisley blanket was dangling over one of the arms of the brown corduroy sofa.

Benny, however, was as smart and immaculately turned out as he always was. Apart from the machete in his chest. And the patch of blood that had spread across the front of his pink Hugo Boss shirt. And the shape of a pentangle that had been burned onto his neck.

Roman really wasn't in the mood for this. He'd spent the night before on the prowl. His werewolf form had been unsuccessfully following the scent of The Missionary, a religious maniac who scoured the city killing those he considered corrupt - prostitutes, junkies, drunks. The poor, disabled. He was also a hit man with a 100% record.

Eventually, Dalton had woken up in a local park with his clothes ripped to shreds and a couple of skinheads pissing on him. The wolf must still have been inside him, though, because he'd quickly jumped up at one of the chrome domes and bit off one of his ears. The other one had pulled out a gun and had been ready to shoot but Dalton ripped the thug's arm off before he had a chance.

Back at his apartment, all Dalton had wanted was a shower, a drink and a real sleep.

But those plans were scuppered when he pushed the door open to find Benny Vane there. He sat on the sofa, poured a drink and phoned his former partner, Detective Ivan Walker.

'Doctor Gordon Tito left home just before nine yesterday morning and shortly after midnight his corpse was found stuffed in a wheelie-bin at the back of a The Pink Pussy,' said Detective Inspector Ivan Walker. He took a packet of Polo mints from his saggy raincoat pocket. Popped one into his mouth. Crunched it.

It was no good, though. His mouth still felt like something had died in it.

He looked at his squad: they were hanging on his every word. Bursting with enthusiasm. Full of energy. He'd picked them carefully. Since Roman had quit the force Ivan had been feeling the weight of the job.

The new blood were just what he needed. There were three in the team. All fresh from the academy and as keen as can be. Lara Christos, a quietly spoken albino, well over six-foot tall with black belts in a range of martial arts. Cormac Blue, a tall blue-eyed Australian with a smooth tongue and a penchant for designer clothes. Jake Hankson, the wild card with a quick temper but a freaky photographic memory.

'And the question I am asking you, pop pickers, is what the hell happened to him in-between?'

Walker's every word was like a pebble making ripples

He popped another mint into his mouth, crunched it and waited for the ripples to become waves.

'Here's a photo of the victim. Before and after,' said Lara.

Walker took the photo. The first one was of a respectable, grey-haired, middle-aged man. Completely unremarkable.

But the 'after' photo phased him. It wasn't seeing a photo of a dead body. He'd done that many times before. Seen the real thing more times than he could remember. The machete in Tito's chest had no effect on him. It was the burn mark on the corpse's neck. In the shape of a pentangle

'For fuck…'

'Sir? What is it?' said Lara.

And then Walker's phone rang.

A wisp of the evening remained and Duffy's bar was filling up with loud, young people in fancy dress, much to Roman Dalton's disgust.

'Jesus, Duffy, where can I go for a quiet drink if I can't come here?'

He moved his bar stool further into a dark and dingy corner, next to the Wurlitzer Jukebox.

'Glad you're so happy for my success,' said Duffy, passing a bottle of Pabst Blue Ribbon and a straw to a man in a grotesque mask.

Dalton just grunted. Sipped his pint of Guinness.

'So, when did Duffy's become the place to be? You haven't done anything with the décor since you took over the place, unless you count occasionally changing the beer mats,' said Walker. He poured a snowstorm of sugar into his black coffee.

'Since Otto Rhino bought the old cinema across the street. Everyone calls in here for a beer before the evening showing.'

'Otto got a taste for the arts, eh?' said Roman.

'That, and it's the only cinema in The City where you can smoke,' said Duffy. 'And I don't mean Lucky Strikes. And guess who the main supplier is?'

'Ah,' said Roman and Walker, simultaneously.

'What's on tonight?' said Walker.

'A double bill of *Dogboy* and *Mask*,' said Duffy.

There was a moment's silence. Billie Holliday sang 'Violets for My Furs.' Walker's fingers drummed on the bar. Dalton glared at him but he didn't notice.

'Same again?' said Duffy.

Dalton nodded.

'And give me a shot of Dark Valentine as a chaser.'

'Fill her up?' said Duffy, to Walker.

'No thanks. I'm wired enough as it is.'

Billie Holliday faded out and Led Zeppelin kicked in. Roman tapped Walker on the shoulder.

'So, you going to share a couple of war stories then, Ivan?' he said.

Walker looked at Duffy, who shrugged. 'Your call, Colonel'

Walker ran a hand through his long black hair and began.

'So, the war had been dragging on for far, far, too long. And it was costing the government a packet. Which is why 'Operation Desert Wind' was set up. A massive, 100 per cent clean-up of the region. Take no prisoners. Also, another problem was that one of the top brass had gone rogue. A religious nutter called General Hoffman had set up a weird cult and a small crack group of CIB agents were sent into the city to neutralise him. Duffy and I were part of that team.'

A young woman dressed as a witch tried to sit on a barstool, slipped and collapsed to the floor, much to the hilarity of her friends and Roman's disgust. He tapped his shot glass. Duffy poured and left the bottle of Dark Valentine on the bar.

'Go on, 'said Roman.

'Well,' said Ivan. 'To cut a long story short, as we got deep into the Golden City, which is where the General was holed up – a few of us were captured by General Hoffman and his crew.

Turned out that Hoffman was organising Gladiatorial matches in the local football stadium. Prisoner against prisoner. Fights to the death.

He was also into some weird type of voodoo or black magic rituals, which is why he branded me with this.'

Walker pointed at the pentangle scar.

'And he sent me off to take on some gigantic German guy with a buzz cut and a swastika tattoo on his forehead. We were ready to fight when a rocket hit the stadium. Blew the place to bits.

In the chaos, I got out, got into the General's Penthouse and took him out.'

'And I'm guessing that Billy Vane and Gordon Tito were also part of the CIB crew?' said Roman.

'Yep. And they were both killed and branded.'

'So, the General's ghost is back from the dead? Taking revenge on the CIB?' said Duffy. He shivered.

'Or someone is avenging him,' said Roman.

'Well, whoever it is, we'll be on his kill list, Colonel Walker,' said Duffy.

Walker picked up the bottle of Dark Valentine and topped up his coffee.

'Did he have any kids?' said Roman.

'I checked his military record today. He was survived by one person. A brother called Otto,' said Walker.

'Shit, shit and triple shit,' said Duffy.

Dalton howled as he leapt from the dome of the Basilica and onto the roof of the Playhouse. His shape silhouetted against the full moon and he howled again. One more jump and he smashed through the windows of the Inter- Euro Hotel crashing into the four poster bed where a large German with a buzz cut and a swastika tattoo humped a blow up doll dressed in military uniform.

As Roman leapt, Otto swung a machete at the wolfman's shoulder. It hurt and all Roman could see was red.

Walker paced Duffy's, unable to relax. He dialled Roman's number again.

'Still nothing?' said Duffy, who was wiping the wooden floor with a dirty mop.

'Not a thing,' said Walker.

'Ah, you know Roman. He could have woken up in a tree top in the park. Or in a cage in the zoo. Anything can happen when he's drunk on the moon.'

They sat drinking coffee. Watching an old black and white comedy film about a haunted fire station. As the credits rolled, Roman rushed into the bar.

He held up two fingers and Duffy poured him a drink.

'Well,' said Ivan.

'Yeah, no problem, 'said Roman. 'Piece of piss. Otto Hoffman was out of his league.'

'So, where were you?' said Walker. 'I've been ringing you all morning.'

'Stomach problem,' said Roman.' My guts are ripped up. Must have been someone I ate.'

The Darkness Cult

Jennifer Martin

The street lights were little oases of brightness in the darkness of the trash-littered sidewalks. Downtown was dismal and dirty, but it was the area within the city that held the good trolling clubs that catered to the latest fetishes. Passing the alleys on the way to the trending underground Goth club gave off permeating whiffs of urine, semen and blood. Yes, this was that part of town.

A pounding beat was emanating from within the bowels of the building he approached. Loud music was great for getting a girl to step outside with you since that was the only way to be able to 'talk'. Tonight he needed a girl. It had been too long.

The entrance was down a narrow cement stairway and had a wrought iron railing that was painted a putridly bright minty green. In creepy looking font was the name of the establishment 'The Darkness'. The glowing red plastic was made to look like blood dripping down the brick wall. People were crowded around the stairway just like the garbage bags were crowded around the street level doorways. Refuse, just waiting to be picked up. It was quite the eclectic bunch. There were leather and silver and piercings and tattoos galore.

'Weak.' He mumbled to no one as he pushed through the mob and sank down into the club. Humidity and sweat mixed in with the smells that were barraging his senses. He flashed his I.D. to the dog collared door guy whose mascara was running. It had apparently been smeared as well since a trail of it was almost to where it was bumping uglies with the trashy red lipstick he crayola'd over his mouth. Adrian thought that if he had to spend sweaty hours on that guy's face he would run screaming too.

As he moved past the melting guy and surveyed his environment he was clobbered from behind. She smelled like decaying flowers and clove cigarettes. Laughing, she apologized and continued her trek into the club. Adrian wondered why she had laughed. The usual patron of this type of place was depressed and suicidal with a splash of horny mixed in. She disappeared into the mass of bodies as he made his way toward the bar. The smell of her was still on him, so was the feel of each place she made contact with his body. She was the one.

Adrian counted himself as somewhat of a psychic, and his senses were tingling for that girl something fierce. Ordering a wicked witch off the specials menu let him cast his awareness out for the girl. She was not far. Standing at the end of the long bar with an untouched drink in front of her, she was shrugging off a large doe eyed boy who was clearly trying too hard. She was beautiful. Long dark hair hung down her petite frame. Little wispy bangs floated just above her striking green eyes. With a button nose and pouty lips she looked like a pixie. He imagined her with little wings sprouting out of her shoulder blades.

Looking up from the bar, she caught his gaze. Playing coy she ducked her head and spun around so that her back was to him. Pushing away from his spot he made up his mind to approach the girl. The music was groaning so that the ecstasy soaked bodies were writhing against each other and pushing in pulsing fashion against everyone. Adrian, though trying to move forward, was pushed further and further back. He ended up so far back that he was squished into the little hallway for the restrooms. A narrow unlit passage with a door to either side. The leather clad muscle men in front of him turned then.

The men had the look of feral dogs, and their intent was clearly malicious. The smaller one stood at the hallway's entrance and the other blocked his way and leaned in close.

Breathing in deeply with his eyes closed, his head moving from side to side he said, 'You stink, man.'

Adrian tried to assess the situation and look for an out. The guy was licking his lips. His unshaven face held mean eyes that glinted danger. Knowing no one would hear him yell for help Adrian's fight or flight kicked in and he balled up his fist and brought it up hard into the man's chin. A growl escaped the man's lips, otherwise he didn't move. His friend howled.

'Let's play then. You, with your wanna-be evil.' He laughed. His breath was hideously pungent, 'We'll see who the 'big dog' is here.'

His friend laughed at that too. Adrian braced himself for a fight.

'Excuse me!' Someone shouted behind the shaggy goon blocking the hallway.

'Get outta here girl, bathroom's out of service.' The dude turned and as he did his nose rankled. 'OH!' He yelped in disgust. 'Nasty!' He turned and walked away without another glance at his steroid enhanced friend.

The girl Adrian had been watching stood there with a sweet smile playing across her lips. The man in front of him coughed and straightened from his menacing pose and squirmed out of the little space as well.

'Out of order, huh?'

'Yeah, they're all flooded in there.' He responded, trying to regain his sly disposition. He was not used to being the hunted. A turn of events had led him from danger and put his prey right back within his grasp. 'You want me to walk you to the drug store down the street so you can use their restroom?'

'Nah, I was just going to check my make-up,' she winked. 'You wanna grab another drink with me?'

Smiling back at her, they went back to the bar and squeezed in at the end near the corner where the music wasn't quite as loud. He ordered two of the wicked witch specials, and with a grin she looked from him to the bartender and ordered two sex with an alligator shots.

'So,' he said, trying to ease into a conversation with this clearly underage girl, 'are you from here?' She was here seemingly alone, in a Goth bar, underage, drinking. This was most definitely looking to be like the perfect match for his needs.

'No, I'm from Nebraska. I grew up on a little farm out in the middle of nowhere.'

'What are you doing so far from home?'

She looked down, trying to cover her embarrassment and guilt. 'I'm trying to find a better life. I want to be an actress. I just don't know where to go or who to talk to here. It's been hard, being all alone.'

'Did you run away?'

'Yeah.'

Adrian's adrenaline was zinging inside him. This was perfect! He lied and said he was a runaway too. He looked young enough, so he passed himself off as just barely eighteen. He was actually twenty-four. He had a good job as an electrical engineer and a house already, but his baby face let him lie with ease. Her name was Amanda. They traded their stories as to why they left home. She had been abused by her uncle who helped run the family farm, and once she got brave enough she fled. Came running to the big city to get lost in anonymity. They did their shots and drank the drinks while she played right into his hands.

'Where are you staying Amanda? You have any friends here?'

'No, not yet. I stash my bag in the alley behind the dumpster, and I've slept in the park for the last couple of days. It sure would be nice to get a shower sometime soon, but I don't know what to do yet. I only have so much money left, and that's been going toward food.' She looked so small and helpless. He was craving the taste of her already. 'Where do you sleep?'

'There's this house not too far from here. I was sleeping in this alley and saw that the owners left for vacation, so I broke in. Their calendar was marked that they'd be gone for the rest of the month, so I just decided to house sit for them. I even have the dude's car. Pretty sweet luck.'

'Wow. That is lucky! Do you think...? Do you think maybe I could crash there with you tonight? Get a shower and a bed for change? Or, or even a couch? I'd do anything, please?' Her precious, hopeful little face was so angelic.

Dumb bitch. He would have her six ways from Sunday and then some. This was working out so much better than he'd hoped. So much better than the last time. Nodding at her, she flushed with excitement. Her green eyes twinkled with gratitude, and a promise of something more. He was tingling all over with anticipation. Waiting until his hard on went away enough to stand he smiled as boyishly as he could and said, 'Shall we?'

They made their way through the bumping bodies in the club. Their path led them past the two bullies from the hallway as they made their way to the door. As they walked by Amanda turned her head to them and mouthed the word 'mine' and stuck her tongue out. They turned and walked the opposite direction in a huff. Adrian had a fleeting thought that they might try to follow them, but let it go quickly as he planned in his head what he was going to do to this country bumpkin's body once he got her home.

At the parking garage they climbed into the fairly new Nissan sports car.

'Wow, this couple must have good jobs.' She said as she stroked the faux leather interior suggestively. 'All I ever rode in was a half broke down pick up. You know the kind with the braided ugly interior. Fuckin' redneck, I swear. I hate that shit!' As he pulled on to the street, she ran her hand down his leg and giggled.

He shifted in his seat. And put his hand on her thigh. She giggled again and pulled it up to the curve of her breast.

'I meant what I said, Adrian.' She said blushing and ducking her head so that her bangs swung in front of her eyes. 'I'll do *anything* to repay you.'

'Don't worry doll, we have all night.' Tapping the clock in the dash that read a mere twelve-thirty in the morning, he pulled into the driveway. 'I think you'll like what this house has to offer.'

The garage door shut behind them and as the ignition switched off he leaned over and kissed her soft little lips.

Inside he poured some wine for them. His hands were sweaty; he was nervous and ecstatic all at the same time. She was marveling at how clean and neat the house was and all the cool modern things as she rambled on about the farm house she grew up in. You'd think this girl was from the old plantation days with the awe she was exuding. Damn she was stupid. Just the way Adrian liked them. Dumb and untraceable.

Chugging the wine down, she slapped the glass on the counter top a little too hard. 'Oops!' Giggles rose in her throat again. Clearly the alcohol was getting to her now, along with the mild sedative he had slipped into her glass. 'So, can I take that shower now?'

Trying to walk seductively up to him she ran her hands along his chest and added, 'You wanna join me in that shower, baby?'

'I think you should take that shower and I will set up the room for when you are out of that shower.'

She looked at him curiously but muttered, 'K,' and ran her hand down the front of his pants before she turned and sauntered off to find the bathroom.

This was unbelievable. He wondered if he'd given her too much of the sedative. He wanted her conscious for what was to come, especially since the sex was better once the girl's adrenaline kicked in to full gear. The meds just kept them from getting too feisty.

He went down to the basement to make sure everything was all ready to go. The heavy padded door hung open so that he could hear if she were coming before he was done. Lighting enough candles so that he could leave off the harsh overhead lights gave the air a cinnamon spice scent. The hand cuffs were tucked under the pallet of blankets on the floor, and the metal braided cord that was attached to them was neatly wound out of sight. Meticulously he checked his little table along the wall in front of the blankets and made sure all his instruments and devices were in order.

He went back up the stairs and listened at the bathroom door to make sure she hadn't fallen asleep in the shower. He heard her singing to herself in what sounded like another language. The water was running and her voice was low. He wondered if they taught other languages in high schools that were in Podunk towns in Nebraska. Languages other than redneck to English translations anyway.

He wanted her to hurry up. Knocking on the door, he cracked it open and asked her if she had found towels. She had. He fidgeted trying to decide what to tell her to get her out of the bathroom. He wanted to get started, because he was going to take his time with this one. She was ripe and ready. He couldn't wait to hear her beg. The water shut off.

'Finally!' He mumbled. Patience never had been his strong point. He usually got over excited and ended it too quick.

She opened the door and smiled up at him with the towel wrapped around her. Towel dried hair still dripped at the ends. 'Do I bother getting dressed, my demon lover?'

A grin splayed across his face. She knew him for what he was. How? It didn't matter. 'No need young one.' He took her by the hand and led her to the basement door. He wondered if she truly thought he was a demon or if she was just playing into the Goth role. It didn't matter, in the end she would end up gutted like all the others. His master would soon see that he was worthy.

He opened the door and let her go down first so that she had no way out if she decided to chicken out and run. If she caught on to what was really going to happen, at this point it didn't matter. She was his now.

The towel was discarded at the bottom of the stairs and she seductively sank down to the blankets and rolled on to her back touching herself as she waited for him to join her. Locking the door he lay beside her and took her. The sex was intense. That part he couldn't slow down. He needed the release. She made noises like a porn star and scratched and bit as he had his way. Upon his climax she lay back with her hands over her head.

This was just too perfect he thought. It was like she was a willing sacrifice. He snapped the handcuffs on her wrists. She looked up at them startled and then looked him right in the eye and said, 'Oh good, I was hoping we weren't done yet,' and smiled wickedly.

Adrian bit her lip hard as he kissed her, then got up and pulled at the cord secured to the cuffs. He pulled her straight up to her tip toes and secured the end to a pre-drilled loop in the wall behind her.

She laughed. She actually laughed. 'Kinky!' She was getting off on this. Maybe she wanted to die. He took out his knives where she could see them. The laughter died on her lips, but she didn't scream. Until he cut her. He carved a pentagram into the flesh on her back and licked the blood from the blade. Her shrieks were loud, but she never asked him to stop.

She was panting. He took a fat flat blade and held it to the candles flame as he looked her over. Her body sagged. Her hair was draped over her shoulders covering her breasts. Her face was hidden as her head hung forward.

'Are we having fun love?' His words jarred her back to reality. She whimpered. He brought the blade close to the sensitive skin on her thigh, just enough for her to feel the heat and cringe from it. 'Answer me.'

Shuddering she looked up into his face, her eyes sparkling from tears. 'No, I'm not having fun.' She whined.

'Beg me to stop then.' He tapped the burning blade to her skin. She cried out but did not ask for mercy. Adrian continued on telling her to beg him, and burning her when she did not. A couple of times he thought he had killed her as she just stopped responding all together. He was growing restless.

'Why don't you tell me to stop hurting you?' He shouted. She did not answer. Her body was covered in blood from both cuts and burns. The scent of singed flesh mixed in with the cinnamon spice and her aroma of decayed flowers that had clung to her even after she showered.

He began to slash at her. His frustration overtook his reason. How dare she not beg. He was in control not her! She even had stopped screaming now. She still struggled and grunted pathetically with each new cut, but she was not doing as she was supposed to, and it was pissing him off! Blood was pouring out of the multiple wounds and she was headed toward bleeding out. He said his prayer to his demonic master and gathered her blood in a chalice. Painting an upside down cross on her forehead he began his speech in Latin. His prayer to his evil God. He finished by drinking some of her blood. Again the taste was acrid. The normal coppery metallic taste was tainted with something else. Maybe she didn't release all the chemicals normally associated with fear and imminent death. Maybe he had given her too much sedative for her body to respond right. He fucked her again for a last disgrace before she died, then he left her hanging and went to take his own shower.

He was disappointed. He had thought she was going to be perfect. Bitch wanted to die. Not even the pain brought out her fighting side. He decided to deal with her later. He went and lay down in his bed from the shower without even drying himself. He was exhausted. He mumbled a final prayer to his demon as he fell into slumber, and asked if he had sacrificed enough in his name yet to be invited into the fold. Sleep overtook him.

The next day Adrian went to work as normal. Waking up in the morning had given him a new outlook on the situation and he thought it a good sign. The master must be pleased with him since he felt so good. He had all confidence that the smell would be kept under wraps by the great care he had taken to seal up the basement from light, sound and smell. There would be no complaining from nosey neighbors. No one at work noticed anything different about him either. He had grown accustomed to hiding his elation after a kill.

That evening as he returned home he changed for the task of getting the bloody stinking corpse into the barrel that it would be dissolved in. She was small so he would probably not have to cut her up any more. She would fold.

He made his way down the stairs and flipped on the lights.

She twitched.

The smell of old blood was sickening. She had bled out all over the blankets. There was no way she had moved. His mind was playing tricks on him. He kept an eye on her as he made his way around to the front of her.

She sighed.

Jennifer Martin

No, it had to be gasses escaping from the body. He chuckled at the fact that this had spooked him. Then she twitched again.

'No fucking way.' He said out loud.

Not looking away for a second he picked up a long stick from the table and reaching out a shaking hand he poked her with it. Amanda's body swung slightly from the force of the jab.

'You gonna use that Adrian?'

He was frozen. Shock washed over him as a wave.

She lifted her head and looked at him. Her lips were dry and cracked and she was deathly pale, but those eyes were sparkling a green fire. Her ragged voice crackled as she emitted a chuckle.

'Are you done with me?'

Adrian stammered, but could not get words out. A wet spot began to form on the front of his pants as urine ran down his leg.

'Oh stop that,' she coughed out as she twisted the handcuffs beyond their breaking point. They jingled as they fell apart and she brought her arms down rubbing her wrists. 'I'm bored now, and hungry.' She was on him in a flash, and sank her teeth into his jugular. He thrashed as she pulled his blood deeply into her. His fear and disbelief were like a drug to her and she moaned softly as she drained him. Once she had taken enough for him to stop fighting her she pulled back and whispered, 'Where's your demon god now?' Then she sank her teeth back into him and emptied him completely.

Dumping his body on the floor, she surveyed the room. 'This dude was seriously fucked up,' she said to no one. She was glad she had gotten him. He was a lousy fuck, but there wasn't room for some human to be killing on her territory, taking the lives that should be hers to take. She went up the stairs and showered again. Her wounds had healed but she was still covered in the dried blood from the night before.

Once true night had fallen, she doused the house with flammable liquid found in the garage and tossed a match as she walked out the door.

152

Later that night she was back at The Darkness. She could go without eating for a few days, but she had a score to settle. Sitting at the bar she shrugged off fat lonely losers until she saw who she was looking for.

The were' and his companion came in surveying the club for their target.

'Fucking wolf.' She spat.

Once again they cornered some poor shmuck in the hallway for the restrooms. Once again she interrupted their little intimidation game.

The poor kid was probably seventeen. He ran past her when his chance came.

'Go hunt somewhere else, dog. This area is mine. And when I mark someone, you sure as hell better stay the fuck back. Or else there will be puppy stew on the menu. Are we clear?'

Identity Crisis

Katherine Tomlinson

The receptionist smiled at the cute guy with the red quiff of Tintin hair as he walked into the office with a big bag of Thai takeout.

'Conference room?' he asked with a smile.

She pointed him past her desk toward a short corridor.

'Thanks,' he said over his shoulder and caught her admiring his ass.

She blushed and touched the Uhuru device in her ear. 'Good afternoon, Principato, Heublin and Roarke,' she chirped as if getting a call but Ellis could see the little blue light on her telephone receiver wasn't glowing.

Everyone in the conference room looked up as Ellis entered and closed the door behind him.

Justin Roarke, sitting at the head of the rectangular table, looked confused.

'Who ordered lunch?' he asked, glowering at the others in the room.

Roarke didn't believe in providing food at his meetings, even when they took place at lunch time. He didn't like his people eating and talking. He felt it encouraged lack of focus.

Roarke sighed when he saw the sheepish looks being exchanged. *So no one's going to cop to it,* he thought. 'Don't just stand there with your thumb up your ass,' he barked at Ellis, 'just put it down on the credenza.'

Instead, Ellis drew a little gun from the pocket of his hoodie and shot Justin Roarke twice, double-tapping him before anyone else could even react. He shot Kroger from marketing next, then Limon from sales. Linette Kefauver made a break for it and Ellis shot her just as she got her hand on the door.

'Please don't shoot me,' said a guy from under the table.

'Sorry,' Ellis said, and he meant it. He never liked a lot

154

of collateral damage and killing Crenshaw from human resources shouldn't have been necessary. But it was.

Job done, Ellis pocketed the gun, pulled open the bag of takeout and removed the Styrofoam container on top, bringing it with him as he left the room.

A pretty secretary glanced at him as he passed her in the corridor but didn't say anything to him.

They don't like to be called secretaries these days, Ellis thought, and that was bad because it meant he was already starting to shift.

He hurried past the receptionist's desk, dropping the take-out container in front of her.

'Pad See Ew,' he said, 'there was extra.'

'Thanks,' she said, but he was already out the door and headed for the ladies room.

In the empty bathroom Ellis stripped off the hoodie to reveal the French-cut pink t-shirt beneath. It was already starting to stretch out as his body shaped. He balled the hoodie up and crammed it deep into the used paper towel bin.

Ellis stepped into a stall and locked it behind him.

He wiped the gun with a couple of tissue paper seat protectors and stuck it in the metal container provided for used tampons.

At the sink, Ellis waved his hands under the faucet to activate the water flow. When he looked into the mirror, he had shaped completely and Ella was there.

She nodded at her reflection, noting how the t-shirt pulled around her middle. She'd always loved the color pink but now that her hair was the color of pink zinfandel (*so much like Lucille Ball's* she always thought), she felt like a clown wearing the color. But that was good. If anyone saw her, they'd remember the old lady with the Pepto-pink shirt and not even remember her face.

She turned slightly to get a better view of her stomach.

It wasn't that she was so much heavier than Ellis but her weight was distributed differently. After menopause it had all gone to her stomach. Her doctor had tried to convince her to use hormone replacements but they'd interfered with the medication for her WAI so she'd stopped taking the pills after only a month.

With a sigh, Ella relaxed her stomach muscles and let it pooch out. In her line of work, it paid to look like just another middle-aged woman stuffing herself into her favorite pink t-shirt even if it was too tight.

Ella turned to go just as another woman entered the room. They nodded at each other in that vague way that passed for politeness.

By the time the dead bodies in the conference room had been discovered by one of the company's unpaid college interns who had ducked into the room to avoid his supervisor, Ella was back in her condo, soaking in her spa tub. The job hadn't been particularly strenuous but these days, the identity slipping was hard. It took more concentration to maintain. The recovery period was longer. She felt every one of her 64 years.

I'm getting too old for this shit, she thought.

She'd made her bones in the Goblin Wars of the Seventies, hiring out to both sides, shaping in between jobs so no one ever suspected. The Goblin Wars had made her rich but she'd blown through the money and more than forty years later, she still had to work. It wasn't like her WAI meds were covered by insurance.

Way too old, she thought, but she was supporting her mother in a care facility that cost twenty grand a month so retirement wasn't an option. *You'll take my gun when you peel it from my cold, dead hand,* she thought, a bumper sticker of an idea that she'd thought was hilarious when she'd first seen it pasted onto the back of a beat-to-shit Pinto belonging to an asshole of a client who'd wanted her to kill his wife and kids.

She'd done the wife a favor and firebombed the car with the asshole in it. Cops had thought it might not have been an accident but what with the bad press about exploding Pintos, the insurance company had paid the claim.

The wife and her kids had moved to Santa Fe where she'd hooked up with a zaftig silversmith. The two women had moved in together five months later and lived happily ever after, raising children and taking in stray dogs and filling their home with plants and art and music and love.

Ella liked to think about that job when the blues threatened to descend, which she found was happening more and more often lately. The wife's happiness represented the road not taken for Ella and as long as she and her partner were happy, Ella felt like she'd done some good in the world to balance out some of the bad.

The client was pleased with Ellis' work and sent him a bonus, which was nice, and offered a referral, which was even nicer. A pleased customer was money in the bank.

The only problem was that the new client wanted to meet.

Ella hated meeting F2F. It wasn't like the clients were going to be able to tell something about her personality from meeting her since she wore a different face for every client.

Some clients liked young and crazy; outlaw types they figured would go out shooting rather than be taken alive. Others preferred a more businesslike approach and appreciated subtlety and finesse. Ella had been told her client was a faeblin, so she decided to err on the side of respectability. The goblin part of him wouldn't care but the fairy side might.

Not that either goblins or fairies really gave a good goddamn about humans.

But then, Ella wasn't completely human herself.

Before the meeting, she shifted into Ali, the shape she privately called 'Black Ella.'

Black Ella was equal parts Condoleezza Rice and Angela Bassett, vaguely middle-aged with beautiful skin and good hair.

The client wanted to meet in a sports bar frequented by football players and stunt men, a place a faeblin could easily blend in.

The space was much too confined for Ali's taste and the noise level was past her comfort zone too.

What really unnerved her though, was that it took three circuits of the bar to identify her client, who sat slouched at a table with four empty beer bottles and a half-depleted plate of nachos in front of him. He'd smirked as she slid into a chair in front of him.

'Hey brown sugar,' he said.

Really? Ali thought and Ellis gave him a death stare which the faeblin read as flirtatious.

He leaned a little closer to her across the plate of congealing cheese and meat, his breath rank.

'Want something to drink?' he asked, and before she answered, he'd held up one meaty finger. A willowy waitress practically teleported to their table.

He must be a big tipper, Ali thought. *Or maybe she's heard the rumors about goblin girth and wants to see his fuck-stick for herself.*

Ali managed not to shudder. Ella had been raped by a goblin in college, a weight lifter headed for the Olympics. No one had wanted to hear Ella's accusations.

No one had even believed them.

'Come on Ella,' her dorm advisor had said. 'Guy like that? He gets all the girls he wants. What would he want with you?'

And Ella, who rarely shaped at the time, knew it was true. She didn't look like the pretty Tri-Delts who decorated his arm at frat parties.

She didn't look like the shapely model wannabes that hung around him at the dive bars just off campus, shooting pool in skin-tight jeans and high heels.

He was in her Ecology of Geology course, a class that was known as 'rocks for jocks' and every time she saw him grinning at her from across the room, she felt sick to her stomach with rage.

She went home for Christmas break and never went back.

He'd won a gold medal in Mexico City that summer. One of Ella's shapes had been at his celebration party, had gotten close enough to dump poison in his drink. Had stayed close enough to watch as he convulsed and died, his fellow partiers too stoned or drunk to be of much use.

Not that they could have stopped or even slowed the process. The poison had been a concoction Ella had designed specifically for the purpose of killing her rapist. She'd been a chemistry major and had planned on working in research. Instead, she'd found more lucrative work that vented her rage.

The Olympian had been her first kill.

The client ordered another beer for himself and Ali ordered a dirty martini that she wouldn't drink.

She would have preferred Diet Coke, actually, but had found that clients who were drinking were put off by abstinence and felt that they were being judged.

He snarfed the rest of his nachos with his beer, not offering to share, which was fine with Ali. Ellis was a vegan and these days, even when Ella wasn't him, she had a certain queasiness when she ate dairy.

She didn't bother to make small talk, the music was too loud. Finally he pushed the platter away and belched.

Classy, Ali thought. To cover the awkwardness, she pretended to check a text on her iPhone. Much to her dismay, she saw that her left hand was beginning to morph into Ella's wrinkled white hand. She forced it back into shape with a hard thought and then casually dropped her left hand into her lap, just in case.

'So?' she asked, anxious now to conclude their business so she could get home and call her doctor. She barely listened as the client gave her the particulars of the assignment. A hit on a business rival, he explained, an inconvenient investor.

Who could have predicted that? Ali thought.

'I want it splashy,' the client said. 'I want to send a message.'

'That will cost extra,' Ali said coolly.

'I'll pay,' he said.

Yes you will, she thought. 'I'll be in touch,' she said.

As soon as she was in her car, Ali phoned Dr. Scolarzi's office and made an appointment for the next morning. She was a long-time patient and knew the woman would fit her in before her regular patients arrived.

By the time Ali pulled into her parking garage, she had fully shaped back into Ella, benign, little old lady Ella, who didn't look like she'd hurt a fly.

'You know,' Dr. Scolarzi said when old Asian-American

Ellis walked into her office the next morning, 'this is a safe space. You don't have to shape here.'

Ellis just shrugged. It was a worn-out topic between them. It wasn't that he distrusted the doctor, but it was just force of habit to never show anyone too much. And Dr. Scolarzi knew a lot. She had first diagnosed Ellis' WAI Syndrome, a psychiatric disorder that only afflicted shape shifters carrying a particular gene mutation.

'I'm sorry,' she'd said when the tests came back. The odds had been with Ellis-WAI only affected about 20 percent of the shaper population.

'Luck of the draw,' Ellis had said and shrugged, affecting a nonchalance he didn't feel. In fact, he'd been terrified; they all had. WAI Syndrome was insidious and it was terminal.

Named after Dr. Benazir Wai, who'd discovered it, WAI Syndrome was commonly known as 'Who Am I' disease because of the symptoms, which included shape slippage and identity issues.

There were meds that helped but ultimately, it ended in something like Alzheimer's, a long, slow loss of identity and a physical wasting away.

'I think I need to adjust your medication,' Dr. Scolarzi said, sounding a bit worried.

'Fine,' Ellis said, sounding not worried in the least.

The new pills left Ella dry-mouthed. Self-conscious about bad breath, she started carrying breath mints because she despised chewing gum and hated the feeling of having something in her mouth all the time.

She made her arrangements with the new client and began researching the target. He was gay, which meant Ellis would be taking care of the job. Ellis always took care of the jobs when sex was the bait.

He could look like anyone's fantasy and he loved sex. Ella was always surprised that he'd dodged the AIDS bullet back in the polyandrous seventies when there had been so many beautiful boys and girls and so many delicious ways to enjoy them.

After the rape, Ella had had no interest in sex at all and left the physical stuff to Ellis. She knew he was looking forward to mixing business and pleasure on the upcoming job and was pleased she could offer him that extra reward.

When the target traveled to Los Angeles, he always rented a luxury hotel suite for him and his posse. Aware that being predictable could get him killed, he alternated hotels, sometimes staying at the Sunset Marquis, sometimes at Shutters on the Beach. That precaution amused Ella. It wasn't his choice of hotels that made him predictable, it was his choice in men.

He liked them young and pliable, preferably Hispanic. Ellis had a shape named Eliseo that had proved irresistible to a certain kind of guy in the past. Ella had no doubt that the target would find him acceptable.

She wasn't really worried about the bodyguards either. The mark always traveled with two of them, supplied by Etebari Industries, the world-wide were-owned security company that was headquartered in Southern California. Etebari operatives were good but vulnerable to wolf's bane. Also, they never went into the bedroom and after Eliseo finished his work, it would be easy enough to neutralize them long enough for Ellis to shape into a maid delivering linens or a fellow guest looking for ice.

The plan had unfolded beautifully.

Eliseo had checked into the hotel the day before the target and made sure the man noticed his eight-pack abs as he pulled himself out of the pool and shook the water off his body in a move he'd copied from a sports drink commercial.

One of the bodyguards had made the approach at dinner as Eliseo dined on seared Ahi tuna with chipotle-lime corn in the hotel's restaurant.

'I don't mind eating alone,' he'd told his target after he'd joined him at the table, 'but I find eating alone in a hotel room ineffably depressing.'

The bodyguards had, apologetically, patted Eliseo down before he entered the bedroom of the hotel suite.

That was fine with Eliseo. Posing as one of the target's bodyguards, he'd insisted on searching the room before his 'boss' arrived and had planted weapons all over the place. The mark liked his sex loud and dirty and when Eliseo cut his throat, his death gurgles were quiet in comparison and didn't carry past the door.

Leaving the man spouting blood like the fountain show at the Vegas Bellagio, Eliseo slipped out of the bedroom with a smile.

'He's sleeping now,' he said and spritzed both men in the eyes with aerosolized wolfs bane in what they had assumed was a breath spray atomizer.

The larger of the two men started clawing at his eyes but the other guy just looked at Eliseo for a moment and said, 'What the fuck?'

Eliseo hadn't known that Etebari was an equal-opportunity employer who sometimes hired humans.

And that's when the plan went to shit.

As the human body guard pulled his weapon, Ellis reached for the gun Eliseo had retrieved from underneath an overstuffed chair and shoved into the waistband of his unconstructed linen pants.

He had positioned the Glock so left-handed Ellis could draw it cross-body. But the hand that closed on the gun was Ella's, and she was right-handed, so what she grabbed was the smooth, polymer barrel.

The confusion was fatal.

The bodyguard shot three times in quick succession, a double tap and a spare.

By the time hotel security arrived, the were bodyguard had recovered from the wolf's bane spray, although his eyes were red-rimmed and leaking pus.

The hotel detective took one look at the corpse on the floor.

'Who shot the old lady?' he asked, looking down at Ella, her frail body nearly shredded by the three shots at close range.

'That,' said the human bodyguard, 'is a long story.'

'I got all the time in the world,' the detective said, hoping like hell that he wasn't going to see his crime scene splashed all over TMZ by the next morning.

A Diabolical Liberty

Jason Michel

'Get'n th' fucking car, Mr Adamson.'

The tall skinny redhead stiffened at the banlieue-accented French voice as something metallic dug into his spinal column.

Dammit! It had been such a pleasant day, thought Adamson as he instinctively raised his arms, scratching the scar over his eye protectively as his ginger goatee-chinned jaw dropped. The Smith & Wesson 9mm nudged deeper into his vertebrae as he pushed against it, eyes all shifty, darting left and right. Looking for an exit that was not there.

His gaze settled on the purring black BMW strolling along the road in front of him. In the mirrored-windows, he caught a glimpse of the muscled coquin promising to send him on an aller-simple to spastic-ville. An unimaginative goon he was too. Shaved head, earring, footballer-bling and an air of undeserved arrogance. All swagger, no smarts. Undoubtedly violent and unhinged, but no true leader. A blunt tool. A glutton for nose-candy and immigrant prostitutes. The most aggressive peasant on the graffiti shit-pile. Scrambling for shiny crumbs thrown from His Master's table.

Adamson remembered the halcyon days of *Jacques Mesrine* – The Man of a Hundred Faces. Criminals had class and imagination then. Not like this monkey.

What was it *Jacques* had said to him just two weeks before he died in a hail of bullets in a gold BMW at Porte De Clignancourt?

Oh yes, 'I am th' last one, Adamson. There are no more.'

He was right.

His Master.

Who could it be?

The car door was flung open and the nudge became a shove. No smell of brimstone billowed from the automobile, just some Cuban cigar smoke and designer eau-de-toilette. A gaunt scowling face and a comb-over. What a disappointment.

Henri Lacroix, that weasel.

'Please *get in*, Mr Adamson. Let's not 'ave a fuss.'

Adamson nodded in resignation and ducked himself head-long into the parked vehicle. The angry bald evolved-monkey pushed in behind him and the door slammed itself shut. The car glided down the evening streets of Paris as the dying sun turned blood red in celebration of the murders committed that day

Adamson turned to face his kidnapper. A small leering man. He stunk of the fear of all those in the grip of mortality with something to lose. The death behind clenched teeth. Next to him was some young dead-eyed Maghrebian cooze in a tight, curvaceous white dress that left nothing to the imagination. The dark roots of her bleached hair poked out from her mane that sat upon the pout to end all pouts. Adamson smiled at her like a satyr as she stared dispassionately, sniffing her white-lined life away. She just seemed to stare nonchalantly at the scar on his forehead.

'Henri, what *can* I do for you?', spoke Adamson, his eyes still drinking the wench in deeply.

Lacroix shuffled in his seat, his cool momentarily blown by Adamson's intrusive interest in his property. Then he settled and spoke, his voice a touch higher and louder than before.

'Now, now, Mr Adamson. *Don't* look so surprised.'

The bloody French, thought Adamson, as slippery as silk toilet paper.

As cruel and ostentatious as a guillotine.

Every game a seduction.

'I really don't know quite what you're getting at, Lacroix and my patience for guessing games is short-lived. So, please tell me, *by Satan's fiery bowels!*'

The threat of a false smile appeared over Lacroix's lined

face. His eyes narrowed to malefic watery ovals. Nicotine stained teeth that gave Adamson the impression of glimpsing a urinal graveyard. The old bastard leaned in close and conspiratorially, as if even those who he grudgingly surrounded himself by were unworthy to hear the shit-smelling utterances oozing forth from his decaying-bone hole.

Then with a mere whisper his plans were unveiled.

'The *sword*, Mr Adamson. I mean to have the *sword*.'

And so we come to it.

The brass plaque screwed into Adamson's Parisian teak office door read, '*C.T. Adamson, Pourvoyeur D'Antiquités Exquises*'. In a country so obsessed with its own lost history, severed from time by the dropped blade of revolution, this led to inquiries from crestfallen aristocracy and nouveau riche chancers about Louis XIV bergere chairs and Baroque Gilt Brass mantel clocks. All of which were available for a view at the showroom in Saint-Ouen by appointment only, of course. Everyone hoping to touch the past and its secrets by buying something gaudy or beautiful.

Yet, while all antique shops and their owners seem to contain the hidden keys to lost knowledge, this shop contained something truly occult. Just behind a dark scarlet curtain that covered the back wall, through a door with thirteen locks, a downward passage once lit by candles, now by trailing electrical wires and lamps, led a certain knowledgeable and very select few to A Garden Of Macabre Delights.

This was Adamson's true passion.

Some have a penchant for instruments of torture and think themselves to be beyond the morality of crowds, while merely indulging in their flaccid sexual fantasies. Others collect ancient weapons, dreaming of a time where murder and rape was commonplace outside one's own door.

Adamson, too, dealt with instruments of pain and unique assassination.

Ever wondered what became of the gun that really fired the bullet that sped from the grassy knoll and shattered the back of JFK's thick Irish skull?

The quill with which Napoleon signed the order for the Marquis De Sade's imprisonment?

The metal case that once contained two pills of cyanide (*one still left unswallowed*) in Berlin on 30th of April, 1945?

The knife that castrated Rasputin?

The three nails that tore through the hands and feet of a certain Jewish preacher at Golgotha as the weight of the human body stretched the stigmatic wounds?

Torquemada's own personal thumbscrews?

A very old jawbone of an ass?

The objects were scattered respectfully around the crypt museum, each wooden and glass case a focus point for those with enough will to absorb the echoes and consequences of the powers that lay within.

Hanging there as a main centrepiece, and shot from above by a spotlight, was a single intricate sword.

The light crackled and spat around it.

The metal around the hilt seemed to liquefy then solidify into wondrous and terrible shapes, casting kaleidoscopic colours onto the cavern's floor.

The floor beneath was littered with the corpses of flies of all kinds.

The tiny disease-ridden intruders had been drawn to the pulse of humming energy.

The sword waited

It was patient.

'How is the delightful *Annabel,* by the way?', smirked Adamson as he lasciviously licked his top lip, feeling his tongue dabbing the smooth flesh.

'Out of the *hospital,* yet?'

Eyebrows raised. Mock concern.

Lacroix's smile dropped a thousand feet and he turned to face his guest, pressing nose-to-nose, like some passionate Inuit practice. Adamson winced as a foul waft of gum-rot and stale tobacco tickled at his nostrils. He felt the urge to recommend a good dentist to his captor, then thought better of it. He saw Lacroix bristling and sat waiting for the obligatory French insults. It was too easy.

'Do not *ever* mention 'er again in my presence or ...'

Ah, pride does indeed come before a fall.

The decaying cake-hole was simmering.

'Listen to me, you soiled lung, if you will go messing around with the *Goetia* ... Really, old man, what did you expect? *Instant power?* Poof! Just like that!' *clicks fingers* 'A rabbit outta a hat, eh? And in your infallible wisdom you use your own niece ... your own fucking flesh and blood as a vessel. *For the Goetia!* Not even someone with years of experience in The Art but your own messed up, sad, ex-cokehead, playing at prostitution, spoilt little rich girl niece who looks to her rich bad boy uncle for some kind of recognition of approval. I bet you've even entertained the thought of fucking her haven't you, you dirty old chap?'

Muscles tense around him.

'She's particularly good at sucking, I recall.'

'You son of a *thousand* whores!'

Wallop. A single backhand blow graced his cheek. It was louder than it felt. Lacroix was indeed getting old now.

'Now, now, ... she may have been a bit of an *original sinner*, but dear old *maman* was certainly no whore. Let me tell you.'

Adamson whistled and raised his eyebrows as his spine curved into the warm leatherette seat.

'Family, eh? We just do not have the facility for choice when it comes down to blood. It's a pity. I mean, you should have met my brother. An utter cu ...'

The car had stopped and all six eyes in the car were now on him and filled to the brim with malice. The old crook with a little dangerous knowledge that could turn into a nasty catastrophe. The goon turned in his seat and stared through his mirrored-shades panting for orders of violence like a hungry Rottweiler being shown a rabbit. The pistol tapped all relaxed against the leather seat-cover just spoiling for a reason to have its trigger pulled. Even the young soul-dead trophy whore mustered up enough flashing indignation that showed her to still be part-human. Adamson marveled at her acting skills. He doubted she even understood the heated exchange between him and her current owner. Her cum-face must be absolutely superb, he thought to himself.

Adamson turned his head nonchalantly and stared out of the window. Paris hustled and ran on in its own world-weary way. Young folks making their way to bars and heartbreak. Old folks hoping for just one more year to enjoy their retirement before some horrible disease took away their failed dreams. He knew that Lacroix wanted his blood. He also knew that Lacroix wanted that sword more and that he was the only way that the rotten bastard would get so much as a sniff.

If I have my way, he thought, not even a sniff for the power-mad vulture.

Not even a fucking glimpse.

The car moved on.

The grimy streets of Saint-Ouen were slowly emptying of people as the textile shops and cafés wound down and the bars around the corner shook themselves to life. Gangs of North Africans prowled the streets thinking of taboos. In the distance under a darkening sky council blocks hummed with the ever-present threat of a damn good riot, or at the very least, a car burning. The car cruised down to a creep outside the decaying shop-fronts.

Lacroix was nodding and smiling through his squinty eyes. A smile that spoke of victory and arrogance. Too much trust in one's own abilities and not enough in the casino dice-throw of life. The sin of hubris.

'Now you show me, eh?'

Adamson began to laugh, sending bouncing vibrations as his chest rose and fell.

'Oh, I'll … I'll show you alright.'

Lacroix stared bemused at him, then he too broke into a chuckle. The girl just stared vacantly. The old crook wagged his finger playfully at his captive. Adamson winked back at him and his head tilted back.

His hand was on his belt.

The stiletto was in his palm.

Leaning forward fast.

An elbow smashed into the old man's nose.

A gargle filled the car as the goon gripped the left side of his neck.

Adamson kept on stabbing like a piston.

Droplets of blood rained gently against the dashboard.

A random hand-print smeared the windscreen as the goon's right hand thundered into the glass, as if to steady himself against the oncoming wave of darkness.

Then he just let himself go with the inevitable tide.

The mean sweat-monkey slumped as all his vulgar memories escaped through his ear into the aether.

Grunting, Adamson sat way back on the seat and waved the knife in the direction of the shriveled bastard to his left. Lacroix's hand nursed his tender and cracked nose yet underneath the dyed comb-over, his eyes squinted with a inner venom. He was a tough aged brute, even Adamson had to agree with that.

'Now ...', croaked Adamson breathing deeply, 'I am going to exit this vehicle and you are *not* going to bother pursuing me like the kind of clichéd criminal that I know you to be. You are going to stay right there like a fucking statue until I get out, or I *am* going to cut out your eyes and I will piss in your sockets when I am finished. *Savvy?'*

Lacroix's face remained still and calm. The threat of repercussion subdued by hard intent and malice.

'I will wait, Monsieur Adamson. Do not think that just because you kill a single soldier in my army that I am scared.'

The blade slashed nimbly in front of the wounded man.

'Believe me, I have *a lot* more experience of this killing business than you give me credit for, Lacroix.'

Adamson probed with his fingers for the door handle behind him. His eyes never left the injured man in front of his face and once he had clicked the door open, he backed out of the vehicle slowly and sure. It was not a time to stumble or trip. The blade still glided serpentine in front of him and distance was being created, inch by single inch.

When he finally found that he could stand straight up, the redhead slammed the door shut with all his strength and con-

tinued to walk backwards for a metre or so. Palming the thin
blade then slipping it back into its sheath.

Adamson knew that the soggy ex-henchman possessed
a pistol on its cooling corpse. He also knew that if Lacroix
acted impulsively then the sword would be lost to him. It was
a risk, as Lacroix had the reputation of damaging people for a
moment's mild indiscretion, never mind a full dose of humil-
iation. Indeed, it was a risk but one worth taking. Through
the car windows, he could see the various bodies, dead and
alive, rearranging their positions inside. He took the opportunity to risk a glance both ways. No witnesses, no police,
the victim - probably a known felon in the car of a very well
known gangster. A thoroughly successful yet unnecessary
murder.

The sudden low hum of the sleek German machine broke
Adamson's train of thought and for a moment he felt to give
his one-time kidnapper a wave goodbye. He stopped himself.
Might just be the straw that broke the French psychopath's
back. Best not to chance it, he rationalised.

The car began to move. Finally, Adamson felt it safe
enough to turn and be on his own way.

'*Safe*'.

That was too funny.

Then he realised that the car had stopped moving.

Something was wrong.

Keep on walking.

'*Connasse!*'

From behind him came the raspy sharp voicing of insults
followed by the bang of a car door.

Tap tap.

Adamson spun around and it was his eye's turn to widen
in wonder.

'*Attendez!*'

An animalistic cry for help that stopped him in his tracks.

The Mahgrebian wrestled to put her high heels on in the
middle of the road.

A zombie-seraphim in white tottering towards him as
night fell.

*

'I just *knew* he would take it all out on me, the vicious cunt. He always does. I'm sick of it. No more. *That whore of shit!*

The dope-laced argot tumbled out of her in French as she sipped at her Italian coffee in Adamson's kitchen.

Adamson asked the stray her name.

'Hakima', she croaked.

'You have any *snow*?' she asked, sniffing hopefully. Tears had begun squeezing out of those big and dark eyes five minutes earlier and had continued in the finest Mediterranean fashion.

Adamson shook his head.

'I may have a tab of acid lying around here somewhere from the Seventies but I don't think that would prudent for you, eh?'

He watched Hakima's reactions very closely. Lacroix was a sneaky son-of-a-French-whore. A literal fact. He would not be surprised if the old fox had kicked her out of his wagon deliberately just to glean some information, or to leave the door ajar that night.

'Actually, I do believe I may have some … um … *kif-kif*, as you people say. Would you like a puff?'

The young lady looked up and nodded. Adamson noticed that he was seeing her smile for the first time. He was really in trouble now.

He brought her the tiny stash box and watched as she demolished one of her cigarettes to rebuild it into a new jollier form. She was certainly adept at this, he thought to himself as she lit the tail of the doobie.

'He'll be back very soon', she blurted out as Adamson took a deep drag.

'I know', he nodded, filling the room with a billow of smoke.

'Aren't you scared? What are you going to do?' she asked, raising her plucked eyebrows.

'Finish smoking this'

As the night shuffled on its stoned and rickety way, Hakima

fell asleep on the sofa. Her head rested on the pale redhead's lap as he gently stroked her bottle blond hair. Adamson had forgotten how soppy dope could make him feel when he smoked it around good-looking women who needed him for one reason or another. He remembered his wife, all those years ago. He looked down over the young curved body and dark sleeping beauty and hoped to all in Heaven that she was not part of Lacroix's plot.

Why had she not gone to wherever her home in that city was?

Was she really that lost that she would attach herself to anyone who treated her with a modicum of kindness?

Experience had taught him that some people needed other people to be.

Yet, she did not appear like just some parasite.

Lazily in a cloud of puff, she had told him that her father had been a deeply committed Sunni, and once she had gotten involved in the world of bars and bad boys he had turned all her family against her. Finally, she was shamefully disowned and exiled. At least she had not been murdered, she spoke matter-of-factly. It had happened to one of her friends when the girl's brother had found out. An 'honour' killing.

Adamson had gazed tenderly at her as she has spoken. He knew how being banished felt and how the loss of one's own family could be the greatest of all severances. Maybe that was why she was still there on his couch. Still resting on his knee.

And maybe this was the smartest move Lacroix had never thought to make.

Adamson rubbed the new moon-shaped mark over his right eye as he waited for his home to be invaded.

After all these years it never stopped hurting.

It was 03:07 AM when Adamson heard the first slide and crack of a crowbar forcing open the door to his shop below. The men shuffled into the wider-than-expected lobby of the antiques shop and their torches fluttered against the wall. They were searching for something. Grabbing his rattan cane, he headed towards the party.

Adamson smirked when he felt them freeze as he wound

his way down the metal spiral staircase that separated flat from shop. In the dark he could feel the weight of fingers on triggers and found that old excitement coming back. His fingers stretched and clenched over the metal head of his old cane. The head was in the shape of a horned devil grimacing with his tongue sticking out.

'You know, Lacroix, dear old *Jacques Mesrine* never respected you. He always suspected you of informing on him to Tillier. Said you had no balls. Said you were jealous.'

Lacroix was standing with that benign and indifferent smile that he tried to cultivate even though the light was barely enough to see his outline. He was leaning against a shelf. On it was perched a pair of 18th century Chinese Cracqule vases. He shrugged and one toppled to the floor. With a single smash it was worthless.

'Where is the girl?'

'How the fuck do I know? She didn't even get through the door. Now, please stop breaking my livelihood. It's the sword you're after. If you want to see it just be polite and ask.'

'Pardon?'

For the first time in the many years that Adamson had known Lacroix, the old crook genuinely looked perplexed.

'Ask me. Politely.'

Suspiciously, the old man cocked his head to the side.

'May I see the sword, please?'

Knight takes queen. Check.

'Well, seeing as you've come all this way, it'd be rude not to.'

Adamson sauntered past the four men and made his way to the back wall of the shop, flicking a switch and illuminating the room as he went. Pulling the heavy velvet curtain to one side, he revealed what seemed to be a solid metal door with keyholes scattered over it, seemingly at random. Reaching into his waistcoat pocket and he pulled out a chain and ring. Hanging on the ring were thirteen silver keys. Each descending in size. Each one bent, cut and sculpted into singularly odd-angled shapes. Each one a surreal object in itself.

Adamson unlocked the door methodically and intuitively.

When he had finished, the door opened inwards as if by itself. The redhead turned and gestured to his unwanted guests. His eyes glinted goat-like with some unwarranted mischief as he felt the push of metal into his ribs.

'After me it is, then'

The light from the passage lamps cast tortured shadows over the rough hewn granite wall. The interlopers crouched and stumbled on their descent. Fear had gripped them as a child fears the monster under his bed. Not one would ever dare let on, of course. They were the enemy of society, were they not? They were the ones who collected dues and broke fingers and shot kneecaps. They were the ones who lived life with true unashamed liberty. They were the ones who were now struggling not to piss themselves.

Only Lacroix with his lust for power seemed uncowed by it all.

His desire dulling his sensitivity.

A fool walking over the edge of a cliff.

Adamson waved his hand in the air and blew at particles of dust as they entered into the crypt. He turned, arms outstretched as the interlopers warily assembled.

'Welcome to my little den of iniquity, gentlemen', he spoke proudly.

It was the first time he had taken a good look at these hired guns. Loyalty bought, not earned. They all seemed to have been made in the same place. Thugs-R-Us. He watched them mulling around, as if in any old museum, reading the tags on his scattered exhibits. Only Lacroix's raised eyebrows showed any recognition of the dark atavistic power contained within each of the objects.

Their eyes met and Lacroix raised a finger telling him silently to wait.

Something was wrong.

One little injun. Two little injuns. Three little injuns. Four?

Somewhere up the passage there was an echo. High pitched. A lazy squeal.

Hakima.

No.

Adamson cursed himself for his error of judgement.

It was Lacroix's turn for smugness.

'Ah, … Adamson. What else have you lied to me about, eh?'

Adamson shrugged guiltily as his Adam's apple dropped in his throat.

' … your dog-fucking nigger hands off me!'

Behind him Adamson heard Hakima being dumped unceremoniously into the crypt. He turned to face her apologetically and she locked her gaze on him with her defiant tear-filled eyes.

Okay, he thought as he closed his eyes, inhaled and walked over to the centre of the room where the sword was already humming to itself with shadowed anticipation.

'Here', he gestured, barely able to raise his trembling arm.

'I can see. Give it to me', spat Lacroix.

Adamson stared directly into Lacroix's eyes and the Frenchman thought he noticed a dancing fire way down inside.

'No. You will leave now. I am giving you one last chance. You have seen it. You know it exists. Now, fuck off, … if it pleases you.'

The Frenchman's response was an arrogant and hollow sneer. He held his hands either side of the sword and giggling he watched the play of sparks and energy.

'I won't ask you again, Adamson. Or I will kill the girl and then kill you.'

'No …', Adamson grunted. 'Kill me first.'

'As you wish', Lacroix guffawed and he nodded to someone over the redhead's shoulder. Adamson drew in a sharp intake of breath as he heard a click just behind his ear. Hakima screeched something and a finger tightened on the trigger.

A bang rang and echoed deep beneath the earth.

Adamson fell down to his knees.

'Oh dear', he sang as his body began to grow and distort.

'Hakima, sweetheart. Go now, dear. Do not look back.'

The girl stamped on her black captor's foot and ran back

up the corridor. The man was too mesmerised by what was unfolding before him to care.

Adamson stood up and laughed as his eyes began to burn.

'Before you stands Cain, earthly son of Adam.'

Behind him the remaining intruders saw the flickering image of a goat's head.

'The first to usher death into this world.'

A flame was illuminated above the head.

'The bearer of the mark.'

Sombre wings were spread.

'Cursed by men and the pitiful man-god and his father to wander the earth.'

The room spun and danced like the death of a galaxy in the mouth of a serpent.

'Yet, my true father, Azazel of the Nephilim - bringer of the dark light to mankind - protects me still.'

Each man heard the voice within his head and despaired, even as they all began unloading the contents of their guns' magazines into the apparition's torso and head.

Cain gestured at the sword as pain tore through the men's heads bringing them down onto their knees.

'Whosoever slayeth Cain, vengeance shall be taken on him sevenfold'

The bullets embedded in his body began to squirm and mercurially move. With a wave of his hand the liquid metal was forced down the throats of his would-be executioners, filling their throats and then solidifying.

He grabbed at Lacroix's hair tearing, out a good proportion of it with the violence of the act. The musk of a thousand devoured corpses scented the creature's breath..

'You came searching for this sword, yet you know not truly what it is. The sword of Uriel. The Archangel who flung my father and beloved mother from paradise. With this sword I took the Seraphim's head and then his heart. It shall take the man-god's one day also!'

Cain leant forward and unhitched the sword.

'Would you like to taste him?'

Lacroix was unsure if the-creature-that-was-Cain was talking to him or to the sword.

As his head was severed from his body, he thought he saw *Mesrine* waving at him from some distant shore and one last thing crossed his mind – *What now?*

Evil and Life

Asher Wismer

The young lady who walked into my office that morning didn't stride out of any book; she was short, dumpy, not unattractive but not glamorous either. A human individual, just like any of us. She sat in the visitor chair and watched me watching her.

'How you doing,' I said.

'You investigate insurance fraud?' she said.

'I do.'

'Do you work for one of the corporations?'

'I'm freelance,' I said. 'That's rare but not unheard of. I get commission depending on how the case turns out, and whatever the client is willing to offer.'

'That's enough to live on?'

'Sometimes.'

She bowed her head and was silent. I watched.

'They're blaming my husband for a car accident. My insurance is refusing to cover their claims, and the court says I might end up having to pay. They said he...' she shuddered and covered her face. 'They said he was drinking on the job. He never had a drop of alcohol in his life.'

I slid the common form over my desk, with a pen; name, provider, etc.

'Fill this out,' I said. 'I have to have you on file as a client before I can listen to your case.'

The husband's name was Ralph Paxton, and he, like his wife Mildred, had been an ordinary person: a truck driver, working for one of the conglomerate shipping companies. She explained how he had died in the massive Main Street pileup; it had been in the news for two weeks, with fourteen casualties. Some folks were still in the hospital, their condition varying from almost-dead to mostly-alive. That was my first stop.

Typically, I'm allowed fifteen minutes with patients unless they refuse to see me. I've been involved with several high-profile insurance scams over the years, and the first guy seemed very excited to see me.

He had one leg raised in a cast, and another framing his shoulder and right arm. Despite this, he was lucid and alert: average height, blond, tanned. His face had several lines of stitching and a few staples, but otherwise looked unharmed.

'My name is Arvin Welch,' I said. 'I'm investigating the pileup that put you here.'

'John Freeman,' he said. 'Taxi services. Wrong place, I suppose.'

'How did the accident play out from your perspective?'

'Well,' he said, 'I had just let a fare off in front of the train station. Usually I hang around and see if anyone needs a ride, but my shift was almost over and I needed to gas up and get the rig back to the pit. Coming around Main corner, there were two trucks waiting for the light, and two more crossing. One of the crossing trucks just swerved out of its lane, smashed the other, and then came straight at me; I didn't see the rest.'

'Your statement says you tried to get out of the car.'

'Wasn't that the biggest mistake of my life... sixteen tons of truck coming at me and I didn't stay inside! The truck side-swiped me, and I got crushed in the door. The doctors say I'm the luckiest guy on the planet; I lost my spleen but everything else is going to heal up.'

'Did you see anything else?'

'Just some other cars behind the two trucks trying to get out of the way. I guess a lot of them didn't make it.'

'The second truck,' I said, 'over-corrected after getting hit. It rammed the waiting truck head on and they both tipped over.'

'Terrible things,' he said. His eyes were bright. 'What are you trying to find?'

'Relative of one of the victims thinks it might not have been an accident.'

'I don't know how anyone could have set that up,' he said. 'Not without a lot of planning.'

'The truck driver died instantly when the truck hit the building,' I said. 'They said he was drinking.'

'Maybe there was a bee in the cab,' Freeman said, grinning. 'Give him the benefit of the doubt.'

'Maybe so.'

'I'm actually surprised they didn't ask if I'd been drinking. Most hacks do these days.'

'Were you drinking?'

'Nope,' he said. 'I had a, ah, friend over that night and she stayed too late, but I was clearheaded all the way.'

'Hm,' I said. 'You're lucky your face isn't more badly damaged, what with the truck swiping you and all.'

'They have a great reconstructive surgeon on staff,' he said. 'Name's Kelp. He really fixed me up; says I'll have just a few light scars that will vanish with the right creams. I dunno, I think a scar or two will work great with the ladies.'

I couldn't argue with that logic.

Two other survivors gave more-or-less the same story. I spoke with three doctors; the wondrous Kelp was off-shift. Everyone seemed to corroborate with Freeman, who was listed to be released in a few days. He'd been average as far as injuries went; some of the others were in medically-induced comas until their bodies healed. Nobody involved with the accident knew Ralph, or had any idea what might have led him to swerve like that.

I talked to one of the orderlies who'd worked the ER that night, during her smoke break.

'Sure,' she said, 'I remember. That was a long night, lots of codes, lots of blood... I didn't know the accident was under investigation.'

'Private,' I said. 'For the insurance.'

'Oh, sure,' she said. We were standing outside the ER and I watched an ambulance pull in, lights silent.

'They all got banged up pretty good,' she said, pulling on

her cigarette. 'Bad luck for everyone. I don't know what else to tell you.'

'You didn't see Ralph Paxton?'

'He was dead at the scene. We only get the living ones, and the ones who are still under resuscitation. Bodies go straight to the morgue.'

'You didn't think anything was different about that night?'

'We get violent injuries all the time,' she said, and flicked the cigarette into a puddle. 'I barely even notice them anymore.'

I know three people at the morgue; sadly, my job takes me there more often than I'd like. The Director is a soft guy in his late forties; I avoid him as much as possible. The other two are doctors, both women: Sandy is my age, taller, but one of the friendliest people I've ever met; Cass is barely into her thirties, and one of those morbid people nobody gets along with.

I like Cass and dislike Sandy, so naturally I get attention from the wrong one.

Cass was on duty, and I stopped and made small talk. She hadn't been on duty the night of the accident.

'So I can't see the file?'

'Not without a court order,' she said. 'I don't get paid to throw private information around to any Tom, Dick, and Harry who says please.'

'How about dinner?'

'Has that ever worked?'

'Not yet.'

'Your hope springs...' she said, and sighed.'Come back tomorrow, when Sandy's here; she won't let you see it either, but she'll be kinder about it.'

'Do I need to get a court order?'

'Order, warrant, whatever. You're not official law so you might need to bring a cop with you.'

'I can do that.'

'So go do it,' she said, 'and get out of my hair.'

But she was smiling a little when she said it.

I called Mildred Paxton and we teleconferenced with a judge I know. He agreed to sign over an order for my official family-approved inspection of the autopsy report, and I walked back inside the morgue.

'Courier's coming with a court-order,' I said.

'You don't mess around,' Cass said. 'Sit over there.'

She doesn't mess around either; I walked to the bench and sat down. Shockingly, the morgue doesn't stock magazines for patron entertainment, not even the ancient periodicals that dentists love so much. I watched Cass instead; she almost looked over at me once or twice, and I interpreted that as a pledge of everlasting love.

The courier showed eventually. Cass grumped and got one of the other faceless body techs to cover the desk; she pulled the body out of its drawer and started explaining its various contusions in a deliberate monotone.

I stopped her when she got to the face and neck. Despite the general horribleness of dead bodies, his face looked mostly undamaged.

'Neck's broken,' she said. 'Just a simple separation of the vertebrae. It cut the spinal cord and broke connections with the brain; he died fast, probably never even knew it.'

'Do those big trucks have airbags?'

'Most of them do these days. Fed regs, you know. Anyway, I don't know if this truck did or not; if not, his face would have been all mangled from the steering wheel and column. I'm guessing yes.'

'How about an autopsy?'

'No autopsy scheduled,' she said, looking at the chart. 'His injuries are easily enough to have killed him.'

'Did they test his blood for alcohol?'

'Blood work's still in the lab,' she said. 'What, do you think he wasn't drinking?'

'Any chance,' I said, 'that you could copy the results for me? I'll need it to present my final case to the insurance company.'

Cass rolled her eyes at me, but scribbled a note on the chart.

The rest of the body was damaged in ways consistent with a high-speed truck collision. I asked Cass to say hi to Sandy for me, knowing she wouldn't, and went to visit the impound lot.

The truck wasn't there. Why would it be? The police investigation had shown no mechanical failure, and so the shipping company had taken their trucks back for refitting. I called their branch offices and got the roundabout for a while. Finally an engineer from their motor pool came on the line and answered questions patiently and clearly, which I appreciated.

As it turned out, the truck had no driver airbags installed; they were not entirely regulated on big rigs and this model had never been updated.

'Your guy,' the mechanic said, 'what was his name, Paxton? He should have been speared on the steering column if he drove straight into a wall.'

'His neck was broken,' I said.

'Really? That's rare, from what I've heard; usually the worst damage is in the face and the torso. You know, all that heavy dashboard shit getting shoved backwards. Sounds like your guy almost made it out alive.'

'Doesn't it,' I said. 'Thanks.'

I called the morgue and got some more information out of the redoubtable Cass. She agreed with the mechanic's opinion and added, 'They're all forensic detectives these days. I wish everyone in those TV shows would die in a fire.'

I nodded. 'That aside,' I said, 'is there any evidence that Ralph Paxton was killed before the accident?'

'No way to tell,' she said. 'I'd say he could have died anytime during that day. No major blood pooling that I saw, or rigor either.'

'But it's possible.'

'It's possible that I'll go out with you,' she said, 'but not likely. Why are you so interested in how he died?'

'Just a hunch,' I said.

The most important part of my job is research; I spend too

much of my time digging through old books and microfiche — yes, even in this day and age, not everything is in the computers. I burned through the newspaper archives until my eyes threatened to fall out.

Every patient, dead and alive, checked out. All legally in the country, all upstanding citizens, taxpayers, hard workers....

Except there was something wrong with one of the records. A duplicate name. That wasn't so strange; there are only so many names in the world and more babies born every day. In this case, though, every detail matched a child born in the 1920s, lived for six months, died of tuberculosis. Same middle name, same social.

I sat back and thought about it. Many people take on false identities, borrowing I.D. information from dead people; the system is so overworked that dupes get passed over unless someone — me — digs around. It's so common that nobody really pays attention without serious fraud — I mean, you can't ruin the credit rating of a dead person.

On the other hand, dead baby I.D. theft almost always focuses on a baby who died around the same time the thief was born; matching ages are so much more discreet. There was no real reason this patient would need to steal an identity from the 20s... he'd have to be over ninety.

And he very clearly was not.

I left a research order with the reference librarian and went home.

The next day, I returned to the hospital and talked to the front desk. The patient was still in recovery; the doctor, Kelp, was in surgery. He'd been on-shift all night; I asked for, and got, his posted hours, as well as a picture, and cautioned the staffer not to mention my name. Then I went back outside, got into my car, and listened to oldies for a long time.

Around noon, the doctor came out and walked to the parking lot. I watched him get into his fancy car and drive off. I followed in my own car, and trailed him to a reasonably expensive suburban home.

I waited a while, seeing lights and movement from inside,

and then walked up the short path and knocked at the door. The doctor answered.

'Welch,' I said by way of greeting. 'Insurance. Mind if I ask you a few questions about the accident victims from last week's pileup?'

The doctor, Andrew Kelp, was short and beady-eyed; the other employees at the hospital all said he was one of the best reconstructive surgeons in the business. He aimed those eyes on my face in a way that made me feel uncomfortable, but it's my business to be inscrutable, so I gazed back and didn't blink.

'I already talked to the cops,' he said at last.

'Not a cop,' I said. 'Insurance investigator. I need to ask you about the patients you treated that night.'

'Wasn't my shift,' he said. He was holding the door half-closed, as if I was going to try pushing past him; I made sure to lean forward a little, encouraging that possibility.

'I got called in for two patients,' Kelp continued, slowly. 'Both alive, both with mostly minor injuries. All the worse injuries were bodies or dead, and it only took a few hours.'

'You worked on John Freeman and Frank Davis?'

'I did.'

'You work on any bodies?'

'Not my department,' Kelp said. 'Morgue takes care of cosmetic stuff. I work on people with lives ahead of them.'

'How sympathetic,' I said. 'One last question: you deal with airbag injuries much?'

'It's common,' he said, appearing to think, 'but usually not severe. Sometimes there will be dislocated eyeballs, fractured bones in the skull from rebounding too hard, but mostly it's just broken noses and bad bruising. I work on worse problems.'

'Like teeth in the cheekbones?' I asked pleasantly.

'Are we done here?' he said. 'My family is waiting to serve dinner.'

I handed Kelp my card. 'If you think of anything else.'

He shut the door without another word.

Back in my car, I thought about facial injuries from air-bags; thought about stitches and staples.

I called Mildred Paxton from the car.

'Any luck?'

'It's only the second day, but I think I have something. You said Ralph never drank?'

'His parents both drank. He saw alcohol as a crutch.'

'So no history.'

'None.'

'Were you and your husband happy in your relationship?'

Silence.

'I have to ask.'

'I know. I'm sorry. We were fine, no real troubles.'

'Mildred, I have to ask you another question, and you won't like it.'

'...go ahead.'

'Did you or Ralph ever cheat?'

Silence again. I let it stretch; some things have to happen on their own.

Finally, she said, 'I don't know if Ralph ever cheated on me. I wouldn't have cared if he had.'

'Because....'

'Because I did,' she said. 'Sometimes. We were fine together, but that's all, just fine. I sometimes wanted more than fine.'

'Did he know?'

'If he knew, he didn't care, or never said anything. We were... fine... together. But I liked to go to bars; there's a certain type of younger man who likes to have an average woman once in a while. We fulfill some kind of fantasy.'

Silence.

'I just... liked to be treated well. Sometimes.'

'Did you go out the night before the accident?'

'...yes....'

'Do you think Ralph suspected? It's possible this was a suicide.'

'...no... he was happy... we had plans for Hawaii.'

'Thank you,' I said. 'If this doesn't have to come out, it

won't. But it gives me another clue; someone might have done this deliberately.'

She was crying.

'I'll call you again,' I said, and hung up.

Parts of this job, I truly hate.

Sandy was on duty.

'Arvin!'

I've learned, over the years, that the only way to deal with Sandy is to be aloof; not snotty and arrogant, but just a little detached.

'I came in yesterday,' I said, skipping a greeting. 'About Ralph Paxton? Something about his death doesn't add up.'

'Cass said something about you hanging around here,' she said. 'I'm just sorry you didn't wait until today.'

'How many car accident victims have you seen?'

'Pfft....' She thought about it. 'All of them, I guess. They pretty much follow a standard pattern; it's all due to angles and seat-belts.'

'And airbags?'

'Not so much these days.' Her professional side surfaced while she talked. 'There were so many accidents with detached retinas and the like that airbag manufacturers have been working overtime to make them safer. Facial injuries are mostly from broken glass, dashboard or window impact, and sometimes just general impact - you have to remember, car wrecks play out many different ways.'

'What would you expect from a big-rig that hit a brick wall between forty and fifty miles an hour?'

'Airbags or not?'

'Not.'

'Seat-belt?'

'I think the collarbone was broken.'

'So yes... it depends on how badly the dash and steering column were damaged. If they came loose, they could come up fast and pulp the face easily. There'd be very little to recognize; we'd need to go on wallet and teeth.'

'Have you looked at Paxton?'

'Nope.'

'Broken neck, face mostly unharmed.'

'He might have been thrown forward and then snapped back. It's possible.'

I sighed. 'Everything's 'possible.' Is it likely?'

'Not in my experience.' Sandy leaned forward over the desk. 'He should have had very severe facial damage.'

My phone rang. I held up a hand; Sandy grinned and started shuffling papers.

It was the reference librarian.

'Sixteen matches for your guy,' she said. 'All at the scenes of accidents.'

'As victim or witness?'

'About half-and-half. You should come by and pick up the copies.'

I hung up. 'Gotta go[,' I said to Sandy. ']Say hi to Cass for me,' knowing she would.

'Oh, before you leave....'

Sandy handed me a manila envelope. 'Blood work on your vic,' she said. 'All clean; no alcohol.'

'Thanks,' I said.

Not operating under the influence. That would push the insurance company back. Without proof that Ralph was at fault, they'd have to cover the claims and Mildred was in the clear. Technically, that was my job; I'd write up a full report, copies of both and all evidence to Mildred, her lawyer, and the insurance companies. They'd fold without a peep.

Something still nagged at me, though. I drove to the library and got the newspaper copies. They were all pretty conclusive; John Freeman, with most information matching, had been at the scene or involved with sixteen accidents across the country in the last... that couldn't be correct. In the last seventy years?

I made one more phone call.

I returned to the hospital later that day. John Freeman was sitting up on his bed, with the leg cast gone. His face was still stitched and stapled, but remarkably free of bruising.

'Hey, it's the snoop,' he said, grinning. 'Find anything?'

'Well,' I said, 'the truck driver wasn't drinking on the job.'

'Oh yeah?'

'Blood work came back clean,' I said, 'and everyone agrees that his face is too unharmed to have been in a head-on collision with a wall.'

'Oh, gosh,' Freeman said. His eyes were very, very bright.

'It took me a while,' I said. 'You're very good at this.'

'I've had a long time to practice. Too long.'

'You're immortal,' I said. 'Not invulnerable, because then you wouldn't have injuries, but you don't die of old age.'

'Two hundred some-odd years,' he said. 'It'll be three hundred in twenty years or so.'

'You've been setting up these accidents for your own amusement.'

'I get so bored,' Freeman said. 'Day after day... do you know how many people I've buried? Good people, better than anyone alive today. There's no point in pretending anyone is worth more than anyone else. I'm still alive and I deserve the right to entertain myself.'

'Not at the expense of human life,' I said. 'You should come quietly; I've got the records for a dead baby whose identity you stole in the 1920s. Forgot to update it recently?'

He paused. 'You have been busy. This was going to be my last prank under this name. I suppose I left it too long, but nobody pays any attention anymore....'

'I can prove you were in the cab, not Ralph.'

'Was that his name?'

I didn't respond.

'I watched those trucks drive through for months,' he said eventually. 'Tracked their routes, timing, everything. I got to know their families, spent time with their kids... spent so much money... but who needs money? As long as I'm careful, I can't die.'

'Did you kill him?'

'The driver?'

'Ralph.'

'Of course I did. He wasn't of any use. After the crash was finished, before the smoke cleared, I pulled him from the back, drenched with booze so it would look like he'd been drinking on the job.'

'And you got yourself injured when the truck hit the wall.'

'Gave me the best thrill I've had in decades. I heal fast; most of my face was better by the time the paramedic showed up. I was just able to crawl to my taxi. Kelp really did fix me up wonderfully; once these stitches are out, I'll look like new.'

Freeman's eyes were bright, just as they had been the first time I met him; it was only now, seeing his true self, that I could identify that brightness as an evil pleasure.

'You're coming in with me, regardless,' I said. 'Immortality doesn't give you godhood, and you don't get to decide who lives and who dies.'

Only the cracking of the cast saved me; I hurled myself to the side as he fired through the blanket. He had been just worried enough about ricochets to break the cast open before firing through it; his loss.

I hit the floor, rolled, and came up behind the next bed over. It would take at least two minutes for nurses and security to respond, and by that time I'd be dead; insurance investigators aren't like PIs, and we can only carry a gun with a permit and a clean record.

My record had been smudged for years.

'You're just a little person,' he shouted, standing. The cast around his upper body fell away; I decided that he could heal a little faster than most, and scooted backwards towards the door that separated this room from the hallway.

'Small people, small dreams,' he continued, stalking towards me. 'You're all just tiny minds in purposeless bodies. What is the point of anything if we die in the end? I live forever and I have no point except for the one I make! How could you be any more important, you creatures who die after only seventy years!'

I stopped scooting and slowly stood. He aimed the gun at me; it was a little one, four or five shots at the most, but plenty for me and I could just see him practicing for a hundred years to be really good at shooting.

'So you planned on getting away with it?' I said. 'Framed Paxton, walk off and plan your next accident?'

'I have for a long time,' he said. 'I switched from base-jumping at the turn of the century; parachutes were getting too good to give me my thrills.'

'A long time,' I said. 'About a hundred years? And you were involved at so many accidents.'

Still no response from outside. I raised my voice, just a little.

'You can come in now.'

Freeman took a step back; I could see his confusion.

Mildred Paxton walked in from the other room. She stood there, in a loose triangle with myself and Freeman, clutching her purse. She was so small.

'Millie,' Freeman said.

'Is it true?'

'He's lying.'

'You killed Ralph? We had so much fun together but I thought you were leaving the city. Why would you kill my husband?'

'It's what he does,' I said to Mildred, ' instead of going to Hawaii. He sets up these elaborate accidents and lets people die. Sometimes he participates in them, sometimes he just watches. He's been doing it for a long time.'

'Shut up,' Freeman growled. He aimed the gun back and forth.

'He killed Ralph,' I said. 'He broke his bones, made it look like he'd been in an accident, but he forgot about the face and the steering column. By the time he recovered enough to get out of the truck, he wasn't thinking about it.'

'Why would you do it?' she said. 'I don't understand. Why would you destroy our lives like this?'

Freeman aimed the gun firmly at Mildred. 'Because it's fun,' he said, and fired.

I was already in the air. I'm not a very athletic guy, but dire straits call for dire measures and I'd started my running leap as soon as Freeman had committed. I didn't have time to think about Mildred, didn't have time to think about myself or the strength of an immortal, I just leaped.

We collided as Freeman started to point his gun back at me. No choreographed martial arts here; we struggled for the gun, and I had perhaps enough sense to fight dirtier than he did. Still, he was very strong and very, very angry.

The only thing that saved me, I think, was that Freeman hadn't quite healed. As I kept his gun pointed away from me, it went off again and suddenly his leg gave way. I pushed forward; Freeman overbalanced, and I stomped on his leg as hard as I could.

Then hospital security finally arrived. Freeman, in pain, hid his face as the three burly guards pinned him, and I raised my hands and waited.

They arrested all of us.

Mildred had been shot in the shoulder. Freeman had started to pull away before firing, and so his kill shot had missed. She was recovering in the hospital, they were paying her bills (partly to cover for allowing a patient to acquire a gun), and the insurance company had accepted my evidence.

I saw John Freeman once more, behind bars.

'They can't hold me,' he said.

'Sure they can,' I said. 'With Mildred's testimony and mine, and the evidence I found, there's no way you're getting out of there.'

'I've escaped prison before.'

'In this century?'

He didn't answer.

'You were gifted,' I said. 'Something created an immortal human, and you chose to live your life at the expense of others. I can't feel sorry for you, no matter how big your existential crisis might be.'

'You have no right,' he said. 'I'm the next evolution of humanity. I am a god among you children. Do you have any idea what I've seen? I've watched kings rise and fall, I've watched the world crush people with the greatest dreams. Nothing has ever mattered; all of recorded history is just cavemen scribbling on rocks. I will continue long after you've turned to dust and been forgotten.'

'Sound good to me,' I said. 'But you'll live on in here. Besides, I'm sure after you've been tried and convicted, medical science will take an interest in your longevity. If you don't die... well, they can do all sorts of tests.'

Before I turned to leave, I saw what might have been fear behind those gleaming, evil eyes.

Some jobs I hate. This, I decided, was one of those jobs. Freeman had had a long time to develop his twisted ideology, but it was so nihilistic that I couldn't find merit in it. The only thing that made sense was his plea for life to mean something, and even that was worthless since his meaning came from destruction.

We are little people, and we can't do anything about the big problems in the world. We can, however, call someone we like and ask them to dinner, and so that's exactly what I did.

And she said 'Yes.'

Gus Weatherbourne

Michael S. Chong

To start with, I look like anyone else if I wear my gloves. No one would even look twice at me when I'm walking by unless it's too hot out to be wearing gloves.

Without gloves, that's another story. My left hand looks like a crab claw and my right hand is made of lightning. These unique attributes are due to my mixed parentage. My father was a sea creature, the kind that looks different depending on who perceives him, and my mother was a storm nymph. No corporeal form other than a lone cloud or a low hanging fog.

My mother raised me in the mountains, but I never got a chance to meet my father before he passed on. I have lived on my own for quite a long time now but my mother is never too far away, the lonely cloud or the late morning fog.

My mother taught me many lessons. She showed me how to grow vegetables, knit mittens and make bolts shoot from my right hand. It isn't easy to do it. It's like shaking a kink out of your elbow. Sometimes it's easier and only like an ache in your wrist, you have to flick. After it got easy to conjure, I got lots of practice. I'm still not a sharpshooter but I can knock a leaf off a tree if it needs doing.

My left hand, the claw to those that can see it, is extremely strong, able to crush a street pole as I found out once on a dare by my Uncle Charlie. Uncle Charlie is one of those Creatures from the Black Lagoon only in a large Panama hat. Uncle Charlie hit the road quite a long time ago and has yet to come back though his humour remains with me. I still laugh when I remember him, chewing his prey with his mouth open, saying 'See food.'

When I first came to the big city, I was taken in by a

couple of brothers of Greek descent who ran a diner. Chris and Peter taught me how to properly fry an egg, drink Ouzo and hide my differences. Peter first caught me without my gloves on. He said 'You should see the birthmark on my back,' and never mentioned it again.

Roy, their waiter, who lived on tips, had found me first in the alley behind the restaurant. I'd been around a little bit but I still could barely tie my shoelaces, having left the mountain a long time ago but staying away from others and mostly keeping to myself. He never looked at my hands and just offered me some food. The English I got from the cartoons and sit-coms got me a pork skewer and some garlic bread. I never left. They let me sleep on a cot in the storage room which I shared with a mouse I named Max.

Roy's pride was his belt buckle given to him by Hulk Hogan, a dragon wrapped in upon itself. No one ever believed it but we all wanted it to be true. He died of liver cirrhosis awhile back. A few months later a daughter he'd never met came looking for him. Chris gave her the belt buckle.

After Roy died, we tried a few wait staff that never seemed to fit the diner family, until one day Deena walked in, not noticing a run in her stocking, until later while sitting on a stool then trying to cover it with her hand as she was interviewed by Chris and Peter. By the counting of years, I was definitely older than her but emotionally she probably walked out of the womb an adult. We found out a little later she had to take care of her drunken father until he had died while she was still in grade school. She had worked in a cafeteria before she walked into the diner or so she told us.

Deena was the most beautiful human I had ever seen and she was nice to me. Not that Chris, Peter and the others were bad to me. When Deena spoke to me she made me feel special even though I was basically the lowly helper. I did whatever needed to be done around the diner. I washed dishes, peeled potatoes and chopped onions, tomatoes and beef for the chili and stew. No one bossed me around but when Deena spoke to me, she made me feel like the most important person in the world.

When it wasn't too busy on her shift, Deena would come and read to me from the newspaper. She saw me trying to read with a dictionary Peter had found for me. While I hand-formed ground beef into home burger patties, Deena would explain words and situations from current events to me. I never spoke of my life or the past, but from what I could piece together from the little details she let loose; Deena lived alone and did not keep in touch with her remaining family wherever they were. She did mention an ex-boyfriend occasionally but it seemed she spent her time off reading. She liked to read what she called trash, but from the look of the covers she tucked into her purse, they looked like romances with beautiful women being held and kissed by handsome men.

After awhile, Deena asked me why I wore the gloves and I answered with the Chris-prepared answer of 'skin condition.' She started calling me 'Gussie' and I liked that.

One afternoon while I was in the kitchen mashing potatoes for the night's hot roast beef dinner special, I heard Deena's scream then a racket from out front. Running out there with my claw and lightning fisted and ready, Deena stood over a fat slob she had pulled out of his seat and punched after he grabbed her backside. With me watching from the kitchen door, Peter and Chris ushered him out, throwing him on his backside into the rain. Deena apologized but the brothers told her she did the right thing. The fat slob was lucky she dealt with it before I could squeeze and shock.

After Roy passed, it took a while for the diner to feel like a home again but after a few months with Deena, I knew she fit right in with the family. Some nights after close, Deena would stay behind and watch late-night movies with me on the small set that Chris and Peter usually had on sports games for themselves more than the customers. One movie we watched together made me think of the relationship with Deena. It was about a regular guy like me and a beautiful girl like Deena who were just friends then an evil man tried his best to harm the girl and after the regular guy rescued her from the bad guy, they fell in love and lived happily ever after.

While we sat next to each other in the booth watching the film, feeling her body warmth near me, I knew that would be the only way a woman like Deena could ever fall in love with a guy like me.

The time went on like that. My life was full of cooking, family and love. Without a remembered birthday, Chris and Peter chose the day I was discovered by Roy to celebrate. That first anniversary, Chris and Peter got me my own apron with the name Gus written on it. Deena baked me a chocolate cake.

As my mother used to whisper to me as she cradled me in her mist, family comes first. So the first troubles for my diner family began that I had to help fix. Peter, the younger brother, had a gambling problem, or at least that's what Chris called it. Peter said he was just having some tough luck recently. Peter liked to play cards and bet on the ponies. From the way Peter spoke of it, he had made real money in the past. Peter said he was just going through a bad streak of luck and was due for a big win to make up and wipe out the small losses that had been plaguing him. Chris said he was wasting his money and would be better 'ripping up your money and throwing it into the wind.'

I had watched Peter going over the racing form at the diner counter and calling his bookie to put down bets. To me, it seemed that Peter had made a study of horse racing. Every bet was like a scientific calculation. Still, it seemed he was quite in debt to his bookie from all the calls he was getting.

One night before closing, a couple of large gentlemen came in and politely asked Peter for the money that he owed them. They never mentioned a sum but did say that Peter could take out a mortgage on the diner. Peter told them he was good for the money, gave them an envelope and they left. That night after locking the door, turning over the sign and shutting the lights, Peter came to me.

'Gus,' he said, 'we've been good to you, no?'

Yes, I told him, you took me in and treated me like family.

'Well, this family needs your help now.'

After Peter gave me the address of the bookie and some

directions, I went over there that night. The big house was about ten blocks from the diner. Breaking into a basement window, I made my way upstairs and found the bookie in his bed beside a woman I assumed was his wife. I took off my right glove, touched his chest as he snored on his side and gently shocked his heart until it stopped. He never woke up and neither did his wife. I was glad I didn't have to end her life too. She was probably a good person with no idea how her husband threatened my family.

When I got back to the diner, Peter was waiting up for me, nursing a coffee. After he saw me enter, he came to me with his arms open. As he hugged me, we cried. It had been a long time since I had taken a life but this was for family and Peter made sure I felt his gratitude. From then on, Peter called me son more than anything else and let me do some cooking which was usually Chris's or Peter's job. Peter even named a sandwich after me: deep-fried battered fish on a toasted Kaiser bun. It made me feel a little better about what I had to do to keep the family safe.

My mother used to say that troubles like birds came in flocks. The next family problem came not too long after the death of the bookie.

When Deena's ex-boyfriend Jack showed up one afternoon at the diner, I wanted to dislike him but he seemed like a nice guy. Deena was out running an errand during her shift and he spoke to me for a little while. He said he'd been looking for Deena for a long time.

When Deena showed up, she shook her head and said 'You shouldn't be here.' Jack had brought flowers with him but Deena still did not seem pleased. They sat in a corner booth with Deena's back to me as I watched from the peek-through. He was smiling as he talked and Deena hung her head low; so low that from my perspective she looked almost headless.

Jack left, smiling and waving to me, leaving Deena crying at the booth. I went to her, putting a gloved hand on her shoulder.

'Are you okay?' I asked.

She just wiped her face and said 'I'm fine.' Deena then

walked to the washroom and came out a few minutes later more like her usual self. The rest of the evening passed quickly and Deena was flittering about like a hummingbird, highly energetic and speaking faster than ever. I thought the return of Jack had brought some new joy into her life.

After work that night, Deena kissed me on the cheek, left and did not return for her next day's shift. Chris and Peter tried calling her but she never answered the calls or the messages left, asking her to call back and let them know she was alright.

I gave it a few days since I thought she may have gotten together with Jack again and lost track of time. Their renewed love may have caused Deena to forget about her diner family which hurt me, but she had a right to find love like almost everyone else did except me.

A week after Deena stopped coming, I found her address on her application and after closing went over to her place to make sure she was okay. Her apartment was way across town and in a fairly upscale neighbourhood or at least on the edge of it. Trying the intercom, there was no answer. Taking off the glove from my right hand while looking around and making sure there were no witnesses, I modulated the electricity with my lightning hand on the locking mechanism until the front shared door buzzed open.

Walking the flights up to her apartment, I could smell the strange food aromas of many different ethnicities. At her door, I put my ear against it and listened. I could hear either a TV or a radio just above a hush; the way people use them to ward away loneliness.

I knocked on the door, saying 'Deena, it's Gussie.' She eventually answered the door and Deena looked like she hadn't slept since I last saw her, despite the fact she was wearing a robe.

'What are you doing here?' she asked. She looked at me from under her greasy bangs with red eyes.

'We were worried about you. You haven't answered the phone or returned any messages. We thought you might be in trouble.'

'Yeah, well, I'm fine,' she said, turning away from the door and walking back into the apartment. I followed her into an apartment that was messier than I thought a person like Deena would have. There were clothes everywhere. It looked like she would just take them off and leave them wherever she was. 'Sorry, the place is a mess,' she said.

She sat down at a coffee table covered in magazines. On one of the magazines were a few lines of cocaine with a rolled-up bill besides it which she picked up and with head bent snorted up a line.

'You shouldn't have come here,' she said, plucking her nostrils and breathing in through them in two quick spurts.

'Why are you doing this?' I said. 'This stuff will kill you. Come back to work at the diner. We all miss you.'

'I've been busy.'

'Yeah, I can see that.'

She bent her head down and did another line. Her head up, she seemed dazed, eyes unfocussed, grinding her jaw. 'I have some other shit on the go now...'

Sitting on the couch beside her, I reached out and grabbed her shoulder. 'What happened? This is not like you. Did that Jack guy get you on this?'

'I owe Jack.'

'What do you owe him?'

'Gussie, you'd never understand.'

'Maybe,' I said, 'if you could explain it. I'm not the loser you think I am'

She turned to me at that and said 'Gussie, you're not a loser. Listen, you don't know my life before I came to the diner.'

'You don't know my life before the diner. You probably wouldn't even believe it.' With that, I took off my gloves and let her see my hands. When she saw them, she squeezed her eyes shut then opened them wide. 'What the hell happened to your hands?'

I told her about my past, about my mother and my father and the mountain. She took the claw in her hands and kept stroking it. She tried taking the lightning hand into her hands a few times but the small shocks that emitted from it stopped her from doing anything more.

'I always knew you were special,' she said. We talked about me and my past for a long time and she never did another line until she fell asleep hours later with her head on my lap, clutching my claw like a teddy bear.

Before she awoke, I was able to slip out from under her and make her breakfast from the limited supplies in her kitchen. As I was frying the potatoes into home fries, she came into the kitchen. I poured her a coffee and while she ate she told me about Jack and her debt to him.

Jack had first met Deena while she was working at a department store. She was a counter girl selling perfume and cheap jewellery to single moms pushing strollers and he was a plainclothes security guard usually catching suburban teen-aged shoplifting video games. Jack, Deena later discovered, had many side jobs. He dealt drugs and ran a string of girls and boys.

Jack and Deena started dating like any other couple but then Jack introduced Deena to cocaine. The coke made everything better for awhile but especially the sex. Deena got hooked and then Jack ran out of money for the cocaine. Jack got Deena some dates to pay for the coke and then one day Deena woke up a drug addict and a hooker. She met the others who Jack pimped. They were all quite young and all had similar stories that Deena had. Deena got really tight with another girl named Laura. They shared a love of cocaine and romance novels. They would sit up late on off nights doing lines and reading lines from the latest tearjerker.

They even did clients together, 'the ones wanting to watch more than participate,' she called them. Even back then, during the real throes of coke binges and anonymous busi-ness transactions, Deena said she had moments of clarity but the drugs and aching would cycle themselves into being all that mattered. The need for drugs, the use of drugs, the need for drugs, it just went on and on.

Then one client who liked it rough, took it a bit far with Deena and Laura. Having tied Deena to the bedposts, he started to choke a barely conscious Laura with his belt around her neck. Deena freaked out, scraping the skin off her wrist to free herself, then picked up a lamp beside the bed and beat the john to death with it. Laura was unconscious until Jack showed up later prompted by a hysterical call from Deena.

Jack somehow made everything go away. Deena left, holding Laura up on her unsteady feet. Together they took a cab away from it.

After a few more bad tricks, Deena weaned herself off the blow and tried to get Laura to do the same. Laura said she would but died of an overdose after a brutal attack by a sadistic john. Jack left Laura in a rolled-up carpet in an alley.

The next night, Deena took off and was away from Jack until he showed up in the diner a week ago.

'Now,' Deena said, 'I don't know what the fuck to do.'

'Well, first, you should stop the cocaine.'

'Yeah, I know,' she said, 'but I still owe Jack.'

'What do you owe him?'

'He wants me to pay off the debt of the dead john. He told me he had to pay off a lot to make sure it all disappeared. Turns out, according to Jack, who's a total bullshit artist, the dead john was a connected man which cost a mint.'

'So how much?'

'Jack told me he would let me know when I was near.'

'Sounds like lies to me,' I said. 'I'll talk to him.'

'I don't know if that'll do any good,' she said. 'Maybe you could wring his neck and electrocute him. Whatever did happen to that bookie Peter owed large?'

'I made him leave Peter alone.'

'Jack is a piece of shit. He deserves to die.'

'Maybe I can scare him or pay him off…'

'I doubt it,' she said. 'Jack'll probably be by soon.'

'I'll be back soon,' I said. 'I need to get back to the diner but I'll be back. Don't go anywhere and don't do any more coke.'

I left her there, sleeping in her bed after I tucked her in and kissed her on the cheek.

When I got back to the diner, I found Peter smoking a cigarette in the alley. I told him everything.

'Gus, I had problems with cocaine myself,' Peter said. 'You can't trust anyone on that stuff. They'll lie to you even when telling the truth would do them better.'

'Yeah, but it's our Deena.'

'Not our Deena when she does that shit. When I was into it, I would've sold my mother for another line.'

'Well, I'll just make Jack go away then.'

'You probably could,' Peter said, 'but could you get away with it?'

'I don't know,' I said and went to my morning's duties.

All the while I was prepping food, all I could think of was Deena. Was she asking me to kill Jack like Peter got me to kill the bookie?

While walking back to Deena's apartment after the lunch rush, a deep, lush fog surrounded me but when I spoke to it, it did not answer as my mother would. At Deena's apartment's door, I followed in a resident, holding it open for them as they pulled in their grocery cart.

At her door, I knocked and no one answered. Putting my ear to the door, I could hear loud music, and flesh-slapping flesh with grunting and growls.

Deena was either having sex or being raped. I ripped through the door with my claw. The room was filled with smoke. Jack was fucking Deena on the couch with his hands around her neck.

Jack turned as I put the claw to his neck, sliced it in half then with the next pinch, cut off his head. It took a second for Deena to feel the blood and look up, then screaming at me. She picked up a beer bottle as the headless torso slumped at the side of the couch and struck me full against the head. I heard a sudden ringing, my eyes filled with blood. I thought perhaps she really loved Jack and I tried to fling the thought and her away.

The bolt of lightning from my hand tore her apart while singeing and cauterizing the pieces, blasting the glass out of the patio door window.

The fog crept in and enveloped me. 'Son,' my mother said, 'it's time you left.'

She picked me up in her billows and floated me on currents of air out the broken window and back to the mountain. She put me in our cave and I went to sleep right away. I don't know exactly how long it was but when I got up the trees were taller and thicker and the season was different.

It took me a long time to understand where I was, but that last image of Deena was forever etched in my head. I went back to the diner to make sense of it all. Chris was still around but Peter had died while I was asleep. Chris, now an elderly man, was so happy to see me but a little confused as to why I had not seemed to age at all. He filled me in on the death and mystery of Deena and I tried to let him know the truth or at least what I thought the truth was.

I slept that night in the storage room on my old cot. I woke up and poor, old Chris had died in his sleep in his bed above the diner. The last of my earthbound family gone, I felt lost. Looking out the small window of the storage room, all I saw were blue skies. When the thoughts of Deena got too much for me, I had the claw around my throat and the lightning to my temple, knowing either would kill me but trying to figure out which would hurt the most.

Wonder Woman Walks Into A Bar

Leeyanne Moore

Wonder Woman walks into a bar.

'What's your name, Dracula?' She says to the bartender, taking a seat on the stool.

'Stan,' he says, pulling out his lighter for her cigarette. She settles her distended tan purse at her feet near her red plat-form boots. While the gold lighter is employed she stares at his Adam's apple. Leaning forward, she inhales. The wrinkled ties of his cheap nylon cape have slipped up to his throat, and there is a permanent crease in the cape's high black collar that reaches up along the back of his head.

She knows his name is Stan. She's heard others call him that. She's been there lots, left hefty tips for him too, but it hasn't helped him remember her. She gets the same absent-minded flirtation he gives all the female customers. He's elusive, going through the routine, his mind elsewhere. Like now: he walks down to the end of the bar toward the tel-evision. What's that on the boob tube? She thinks. Oh. It's President Ford, tilting his block head to say something to a reporter. Stan adjusts the volume a smidge. Is this an excuse not to look at her? Then he starts walking back. He stops. Now he's making himself a drink. She slumps, tired. Her large boobs sag forward between the square ended gold eagles of her strapless outfit.

'I'd like a grasshopper,' Wonder Woman says. Now he remembers her. Always some fancy-ass thing, he thinks.

'Fuck's that?' he asks.

She shoots out a long line of smoke straight up into the air.

'Didn't they teach you anything in Bartending School?'

'Taught me how to make a real drink.'

'How 'bout a pink lady?'

He picks up a shriveled tiny wad of fossilized gum from the flat golden aluminum ashtray and it looks like a little gray brain between his fingers.

'Snatch the pebble from my hand,' he says, putting the gum on the flat of his right hand. She snorts without laughing, her elbow on the bar, her cigarette sticking up from her plump closed fist like a 'fuck-you' middle finger,

'Snatch the pepple from my hand grass-hoppah,' he says in a rotten Chinese accent. 'Bourbon and coke,' he suggests.

'Deal.'

He tosses out a coaster, boarded with a blue band that says 'Drink at Al's Hideaway'.

She has dimples, but little else about her resembles Linda Carter. She has a small, cheap, blue tattoo of a butterfly on a spot that would normally be covered by a bra strap. He pours out a bourbon and coke, placing it on the cardboard coaster in front of her.

'On the house,' he says, rapping the bar with his knuckles and then he walks away into the gloom, his black cape a silken swirl behind him. He's not impressed; they all think they're bad girls.

Today she was indeed bad. Her supervisor sent her home from the bank for inappropriate dress, though every customer who walked up to her cage saw her and beamed. Obviously they loved it.

'You're talking back again, Fran,' The supervisor said.

Wonder Woman raised her left eyebrow.

'Okay, I'm writing you up.'

Wonder Woman switched, now raising her right eyebrow. The supervisor made a lemon lips expression back at Wonder Woman. 'This is going into your permanent file.'

'Your permanent file,' Wonder Woman said under her breath, her voice very soft, but screeching with mockery. The supervisor returned a look of blistering wrath. Thus Wonder Woman lost the battle, hands down. But what the hey—she's Wonder Woman, so she left work early.

Driving home she started wondering if maybe the vampire was at the bar. Usually he worked at night. She drove by the bar. It was hard to say from the outside if he was there or not, since the bar had no windows and she didn't know what kind of car he drove. She tapped her fingernails on her teeth, hesitating because she had places to be and left reluctantly. Later, on her way home she took a detour and drove into the strip-mall parking lot to look at the bar again. It was still light out, the never ending gray of a California twilight. It's early; she rationalized to herself, hands still on the steering wheel. Walking into the eternal night of the bar, she saw that he was there. She felt like she'd won a hand at blackjack.

Now she wants to double down, and hopes the bar stays empty enough that she can get a little conversation rolling. Addicted to hope, she sips at her drink and the weariness of her work-a-day life slowly starts washing out of her system.

'Sexy cape,' she says to him.

'They all say that,' he replies. His hair is strawberry blond, really pink, like an inbred cracker boy from Podunk she thinks. She stops herself going down the path of ridicule, and changes her mind. His hair is red, like the flicker of her desire mixing around in the bourbon of her bloodstream. He pulls out a cigarette for himself, his chalky skin accentuated by the big black framed glasses he wears—the kind they give out in the army to the four-eyed nerds.

'You in the war?' She asks.

'Yup,' he says, his lips holding onto the corner of the cigarette, which is dangling. A saggy business salesman type comes into the bar and sits next to her, wanting in on the company, in on her action. Stan opens his mouth asking the guy what he wants to drink and the cigarette stays stuck to his lower lip, like magic.

'How old were you when you signed up, twelve?' she says. He has no lines on his face.

'Old enough. Went to Australia after that.'

'What's in Australia?'

'Kangaroos,' the guy sitting next to her says. She ignores him, which is not good bar etiquette, but Emily Post can take a flying fuck, she thinks. This guy asks Stan for a double martini and a cyanide capsule to go with it.

'Fresh out,' Stan says. The guy bitches about his day. Penicillin, Stan thinks, that was in Australia. He caught the clap in Thailand going to brothels at night for a little fuck and suck. He went to Perth to see a doctor an Aussie tourist recommended, but the place hadn't agreed with him. Stayed for two years at a buddy's place, wandering around in the dim tea-stained afternoons, the rattan blinds always drawn. Came home with a taxidermied Koala bear under his arm and a box of ugly wooden sculptures. Dark. Aboriginal. All banana tits and boners.

'Too sunny in Australia,' he says to her. Three women from one of the back booths get up and leave, tootling their goodbyes. He says nothing but smiles sleepily. Like her, he has bad eyes. He smiles with his eyes almost shut. He smiles blind.

Seeing this, she melts like a rainbow colored snow cone, her nostrils quivering, dimples showing. A musk of sweat, cigarettes, and Halston perfume arises from her body, while a sheen of flop sweat appears across her torso. She sees herself grimacing in the mirror; it's a habit she has from simultaneously showing her dimples and hiding her teeth, which are gray-green and ugly.

In five minutes the bar goes from sluggish to full, a group of office workers come in blinking from the lack of light. One by one they all instantly pull back to get a look at her as she finishes her cigarette. Stan goes to feed the jukebox quarters and the music ties a pretty bow on the happy hour. The volume of conversation rises, and the little bowls of peanuts along the bar begin to empty out.

'Who you 'sposed to be?' The guy on the stool next to her says over the music.

'Wonder Woman.'

'You?' His dubiousness emanates from him like a gust of bad breath.

She turns and sees Dracula lighting his own cigarette down the bar a few feet away. He catches her staring and winks. Her heart does a double back somersault with a half twist and nails the landing. She doesn't care any more about anything, her vision becomes a tunnel that ends at the yellow polyester shirt and black cape.

'Smart ass,' she says to the slumping sales-type.

'Wonder Woman?' the asshole says. 'What? Like Wonder Bread?' he projects loudly. The people sitting on the other side of him smile at this. He stretches his neck at them in the mirror, enjoying his own joke.

'So what's so wonderful about you?' the guy says, turning away from his fan club.

'Wondrous.'

'Yeah what's so wondrous about you? Can you do anything amazing?' He raises his voice so that all eyes near them go onto her and stick.

'I've got three jobs and a kid.'

'That all?'

'I catch bullets in my teeth.'

'Bullshit,' he says.

'You wanna see?'

'Sure.'

'You got a gun?' she asks him.

'No.'

She pauses, looking down at his crotch pointedly. 'I didn't think so,' she says. He slinks off to the men's room, and she savors the contemptuous smiles of everyone he passes.

A little while later, happy hour slides off the stool and unsteadily walks out to the parking lot. People leave blinking in the comparative brightness of outside. The place empties, with only the seriously aspirational staying to drink their dinner one slow course at a time.

'Got kids?' she asks him the next time he passes her way to put empty glasses in the plastic tub.

'Nope. You?'

'One.' She's already pulled the picture out of her wallet, lying in wait for him. She tries handing Stan the little square of a school photo. However the guy on the barstool next to her is back, and takes it from her first, chuckling over it sentimentally.

'She's beautiful,' the guy says.

'Thanks.'

'Doesn't take after you,' he adds. 'You know, she'd be more beautiful if she didn't smile an' show that missing tooth,' He held onto the photo delicately in his stubby fingers, 'Kid, why'd you smile like that—ruin yer face?' She glares at the guy.

The guy pushes the photo over to Stan. Stan takes the photo and looks. Seeing the small face with a delicate chin that tilts to the left, and the golden curls wrapped in a thick white yarn bow, he pauses.

Not because he wants to. Stan operates under a curse. This ancient curse so old even the crumbling illuminations of monk's manuscripts have not captured it. It's such an old curse, and it's affected him for so long, he's actually forgotten about it. It happens this way a lot more than people think. That's part of what makes it so curse-y.

This particular ancient curse is called to life the moment he sets eyes on the picture of the little girl. The little girl is not just a little girl. She is the reincarnated soul of his long lost love from way back in the fumes of his past. For him it's so far back, so far buried under the pile of memories he's stacked on top of it that he doesn't remember her. The curse makes him remember his one true love and forget her at the same time.

So now, seeing the reincarnated face, he is cast back in time against his will. Cast back to a different era. His memory suddenly roams the streets of the Gilded Age. Like locks tumbled into the right position by a thief, he lives again the final moments of his last encounter with this same delicate chin, this same face tilting to the left. Her face comes up before his eyes, but not with a yarn bow. This time she is much older for when she was his lover, she was an adult. Well, almost. The memories of her two years with him zips past, a blur.

He can only catch onto the faintest smell and evocation of her soul firing through his nervous system. Yet one solid picture from the past comes up and frames itself behind his vacant eyes for just an instant. It is a picture of her in

the languorous heat and ennui of a stifling July. Her deca-
dent crimson velvet dress cinches her into her sordid fate in
this age of the fin de siècle. She is sitting at her vanity. The
smell of the magnolia trees that line the boulevard comes in
through the open window.

He remembers one last taste of her tongue upon his, like
sugar melting in a small chartreuse pool of pure absinthe.
Under this curse he is mute, incapable of thought or
awareness of anything else going on in the bar while these
impressions stomp around his brain.

The obsessive curse still upon him, he places the picture in
his yellow shirt pocket and walks away.

'Hey! He took my picture—' Wonder Woman says, not
specifically to the guy next to her, but in protest nevertheless.

While the curse slowly lifts and fades he is unaware of his
own actions. Clinks and voices come back into his ears. The
smell of magnolias in the heat is lost. He's crumbled a blue
cocktail napkin in his hand. This is an inbetween moment
where his feelings are wrenched.

The moment recedes finally and Stan comes to himself. He
looks down, he is drying a glass with his towel, unaware that
anything occurred. He's lost time again while above his head
Barbara Walters talks about this thing called Watergate.

Later, Fran beckons Stan over.

'Another?' Stan asks her.

'Depends,' she says. 'Who's paying for it?'

'Your old man,' Stan suggests.

'No such creature,' she replies. In response to this, Stan
puts in his plastic monster teeth, which gleam and glow along
with his yellow shirt under the dim track lighting. He throws
away her second knotted cherry stem.

'That's an agile tongue,' Stan says.

She raises her left eyebrow in agreement.

'Bar's closing ladies and gentlemen!' he says loudly, joking.
A few heads go up in alarm in the distant booths, but they
know it's not closing time.

She sings with the juke box, 'Early one mornin'...makin'

the rounds...took a shot of cocaine and shot my woman down...'

'I like a girl who knows her Johnny Cash,' he says. She looks up a little drunkenly at the clock behind the bar and at the glowing blue hands that circle round the chrome rim.

'My little girl's in the car,' she says. 'I should probably,' she picks up her purse and leaving a ten on the bar for a tip, goes out the door. Two minutes later she comes back in and sits down again, the stool seat still warm. 'She's sleeping,' she whispers.

In response to this, he hauls out a spiral bound bartender's recipe book from beneath the bar, and flops it open to the table of contents.

Ten minutes later, sitting with the Pink Lady in front of her she puts her elbow up on the bar.

'You gotta place?'

'Live with my folks,' he says.

'Oh yeah? In a coffin—in their basement?'

'Garage. They don't have a basement.'

She nods. 'It's dark at least,' she says. 'Dungeon-like?'

'A little.' He puts his mouth up to sip the drink he made himself.

It wasn't dungeon-like at all, it was hot. Grey cinder block and his mother had put up ruffled curtains to cover the side windows.

'It's got whips,' he says.

'Her dad went to Vietnam,' she says, pointing with a finger to the photo in his shirt pocket. He glances down but can't see more than the outline of the photo.

'He come back?'

'Unfortunately.' She says slurring the word. It's her tiredness that makes her drunk, not the drinks.

Meanwhile, he remembers becoming Government Issue, how the army put three years of his life in their back pocket, and walked away without even saying thank you. They stuffed some bad juju up his nose on his way out, making him forget things he ought to remember.

'You try any strange foods while you were there?' She asks.

He knows he crushed skulls and drank blood from headless bodies; but he couldn't summon up any of the specifics, only bad dreams, explosions, and memories that he hadn't even had—the byproduct of juju still reeling through his brain.

'Tiger. Everyone eats snake. I had some tiger.'

Later...much later...2:30 am. Tiredness had reached out and caught her again despite her judicious, slow imbibing. All her propulsive energy is carefully nursed. She has to keep moving, she thinks. She doesn't want the weariness to eat up all the anticipation that's been building.

He's been talking to her, he's been making her drinks, he's been smiling at her sweetly. Standing outside the door of the bar as he locks it, she sees he's only slightly taller than her in her heels. He walks her to her car, the lone faded green pinto under the blaze of the orange parking lot lamp. He's pushing her up against the door of the car, raising the wings of his cape with his hands quickly. It's only for form's sake, and she gives a feeble chuckle in response. Then he leans into her and finally sinks his teeth into her throat. He does so surprisingly hard, and she struggles for a bit, her ankle twisting out from under her, until she regains her balance, hoping her blood doesn't reek of bourbon in an unpleasant way.

He drains her blood while she caresses the back of his head, thinking about how early she has to get up the next morning, go to the bank. Then there's her second job transcribing psych reports at a mental hospital on the weekends. She keeps turning her head trying to see the back seat, causing her neck tendon to block his access to her carotid.

'What are you doing?' he says finally, exasperated.

'Just making sure—is she still sleeping?' she asks.

'Sure, don't worry about it,' he says without looking, but she persuades him to move over to the hood of the car. They rock the pinto, her blood flow never ceasing, but it slows down and then slows down even more. He starts pulling on her neck harder and harder, at the same time pressing his full weight down on her. There's a range of different little tricks he's learned over the years.

She feels like she's sinking into herself. It is almost pleas-

214

ant under the orange parking lot lights, the feeling of being on the edge of something so obliviating. It's nice. But there's never a day off. She starts thinking about the laundry, she doesn't have any clean nylons. She pushes against his chest. 'Hey, hey, come on, I don't want to wear a turtleneck to work tomorrow.'

Withdrawing his teeth for a moment, he puts her fingers up to her neck. 'Too late,' he whispers into the ragged hole he's made. For some reason this makes her giggle. He wraps her legs up around his waist, making sure her feet are higher than her head and sinks back in, the hood of the car rocking even faster. After a while he gives up and stands straight, feeling wet and cool on his mouth, feeling engorged.

Looking through the windshield into the back seat, he can just make out the pale hand of a child clenched tight and flung out. Then he ducks a little and sees the girl's face. Her head is back, eyes closed, her delicate chin titled to the left. The face and the fist are both pink and tender. Seeing the little girl thrusts him once more back into the ancient curse.

He loses all sense of where he is. His eyes flutter back in his head. He is thrust back in time, back to a moment when he saw her a hundred years before, her face reflected in an oval spotted mirror of the vanity. Not even knowing he's suffering from a curse, he is not in the present, he watches with his eyes as the gold earring in her heavy earlobe dangles about while she places perfume on her collarbone. His eyes rip through the dark to focus on her bare shoulder emerging from her corset, her skin silky with a lavender powder he'd bought her. The room is heavy with the smell of ambergris.

In his trance, his head drops over his untucked yellow shirt, getting blood splotches on it. Fran is still on her back as he walks away from the Pinto, unaware of what he's doing. His fingers grope through his pocket for the small square photo there, feeling the edges.

She thought he was just going off to pee or something, but then gradually realizes he's gone. She slowly sits up, hoists her golden eagle wings back into place, and walks around to where her purse lies on the worn asphalt near the car door.

She reaches down grabs it, and fumbles for her car keys. She is so tired she cannot find the key in the vast cave of her purse. Her fingers move over the wallet, balled up tissues, lipstick, check book, and back again. She is so tired, so exhausted, she could cry. She tries again to find the key, whimpering, and opening her purse wide so it's inner depths are illuminated in the harsh orange light, which suddenly goes out. She looks around and realizes that it's already tomorrow.

Weariness hits her again like a heavy sledgehammer just as her fingers scrape across the keys. She plucks them up, raising the fat jangle of metal in her hand, triumphant. She'll come back to the bar tomorrow and see Stan again. She holds them up in the darkness, greedy with the hope that he likes her, while she tries to find the key that opens the car door.

Charred Kraken with Plum Butter

Christopher L. Irvin

Frank pushed through the rotted saloon doors, shuffling into the back room of McGuthrie's Emporium. His left eye was blood-shot and twice as large as his right. His mother hadn't earned enough credits to buy purified water when she was pregnant and had settled for the rad-tainted stuff. A situation all too common in the Underbelly. Frank got off easy though; purely cosmetic, with all ten fingers and toes and smart as a whip for a young teenager. Frank's right eye twitched; his left scanned the room, lidless. Empty crates lined the back wall from the morning's delivery, smelling of blood and spice. Refrigerators hummed, struggling to protect their contents from the oppressive humidity. A wide growth of orange mold collected along the brick wall in the near corner. Frank made a mental note to scrape it next week and grind it into a powder. The shop was almost out of sherbet. His eye settled on Miles who was in the middle of filleting the skin off a sparkle fish. It crackled with electricity as Miles worked his knife along, his hands gloved in rubber, pinning down its flank.

'Miles,' Frank called out over the slapping of the fish. (You had to take the skin while the fish was still alive. Cruel by some measures, but delectable with a hint of electrical charge when properly prepared.)

'What is it, son?' The fish's tail arced high off the table, barely missing his cheek. 'I'm in the middle of something.'

'We've got another one,' said Frank.

Miles slipped the knife through the last strip of skin and laid it on the table. Then in a flash he whipped a cleaver from his belt and brought it down hard. The fish's head bounced on the floor, buzzing with life before it died.

'Another one, huh?' Miles stripped off his gloves and rubbed the dark stubble on his cheek. *I need a shave*, he thought.

'Third this week,' said Frank.

'And it's only Tuesday,' said Miles. 'He wouldn't take the discount on the cricket jelly?'

'No, and I offered it twice like you said.' Frank appeared anxious. Miles could tell the kid's nerves were acting up when his right eye twitched. Miles felt a pain in his heart. He'd done his best to raise Frank, to make him strong. A life spent in the Underbelly was hard, one that sapped the strength from most men, turning them into hopeless zombies. The store gave Miles a purpose, kept him alive longer than any third generation resident of the Underbelly had a right to. A purpose that he hoped to pass on to Frank.

A young woman left Frank in the Emporium when he was a baby, swaddled next to the register. Miles was restocking shelves and caught a glimpse of her silhouette as she ran out. She had Topside features—a slim figure with a slender nose and auburn curls that hid the rest of her face. Her lemonberry scent lingered behind, a fragrance which was thought to smell like the Sun and only available in the summer months when the Emporium received smuggled shipments from above. At first Miles thought she was a thief. Foreigners who found themselves lost in the Underbelly, whether from kidnapping, banishment or other means often turned to crime to survive. But then Miles heard the baby cry out. The boy was small, barely registering on the meat scale. To Miles' dismay, the baby had been underfed, and he couldn't stomach negotiating over a sick baby with the freaks who would come in looking to make a purchase. Miles didn't deal in skin but everyone was trying to make a buck in the Underbelly and Miles was no exception.

McGuthrie's catered to all walks of life: pluggers looking for an untraceable poison, ferrymen in need of smack to keep them awake on long river trips, unlicensed docs desperate for medical supplies to stay in business. But when Miles bent to hoist the baby off the scale and the baby curled his fingers around Miles' thumb, Miles felt his chest bloom. For the remainder of the day, he couldn't keep his hands off the kid, carrying him around the shop, showing off the glow bait for fishermen who worked deep in the flood mines, and two top-dwellers stopping in for a 'cultural experience.' Miles named the boy Frank after a wild old man who was missing his nose and one ear, but was one hell of a raconteur and had entertained Miles for months on end when he worked on a river barge as a pup. Miles overhauled the shop, did away with the weapons and the drugs. He liked to think of his shop as the top shelf of the black market. A delicatessen, where a customer could take his time, sample the Underbelly's finest mud pies, the Topside's most delicious wines (smuggled, of course.) But with its new reputation came attention, and soon Miles found the Emporium under constant strain from drifting vagabonds and gangs of ill-tempered young men who were upset with the lack of inventory. Frank had taken more than his share of knuckles on the chin, so when the kid was nervous, Miles was bothered.

'Bag these up and—', said Miles. The overhead lights winked out mid-sentence. Miles groped along the back wall for the orange emergency handle. With a greasy hand he pulled down and the basement generator hummed to life, sucking up oil reserves. *Perfect, another outage*, thought Miles. They had become increasingly frequent and the generator expense was cutting into his bottom line.

'Bag up these skins,' he said, wiping his hands on his stained apron. 'I'll handle this.' Miles sheathed the knives on his belt and walked to the front of the shop. The doors squeaked as he passed through. *You're getting soft, pal*, he thought. Once new—as 'new' as a place could be in the Underbelly—the emporium had fallen on hard times. A lack of customers was threatening to put him and the shop in the ground. The place was falling down around him and he'd taken on debts that he was no longer confident he could repay. He let out a sigh and squinted in the dim light.

The first thing to hit him was the stench, and it wasn't the dried long-stalk fickle 'shrooms hanging from the ceiling. It smelled like someone had smashed a jug of bog water and let it seep through the foundation. He should know. That had happened once and Miles had to tear up half the floor boards to find the problem. He carried a scar from the clothes pin he'd kept clamped on his nose for over a month afterward.

'Nothing to worry about, folks,' he called out to the few customers browsing the aisles. 'Just another dip in the grid.' He tried to smile but the smell made him wrinkle his nose, turning the grin into an awkward sneer. He turned his attention to the customer standing at the counter and realized he'd found the source.

The patron was dressed in a similar style to the previous two, a faded black trench coat, buttoned to the neck and a gray fedora with a pinch-front, tear-drop shaped crown. He looked like a detective in those ancient films Miles' father used to watch late into the night. Trends had come and gone. No one dressed like that anymore, not even police, and they rarely ventured to the Underbelly anyway. The stranger's skin was dark and hidden in the shadow of his cap. Miles scratched his neck. He dealt with a host of bad characters every week, but something about these men felt wrong, made his skin tingle with uncertainty. He put on his best shit-eating grin.

'How can I help you, sir?' said Miles.

The stranger clicked his tongue. Miles knew why the man was in his shop, but he decided to let it play out. The stranger raised an arm and pointed to the chalkboard hanging from the ceiling behind the counter. His arm was hidden inside the sleeve, but the way the coat hung slack on the appendage, Miles could tell it was slender and misshapen. Miles glanced back at the board, partially obscured by strands of hydroponic sour berry. It read, 'NEW! KRAKEN TENTACLES. EXTREMELY RARE. 97.50 CR/LB.' Miles' mouth watered, as it did every time he read the board. He'd only had a small taste of the delicacy, charred with plum butter, but it was the most delicious thing he'd ever had. So when he'd heard the rumors of another legendary find he put his entire savings into the purchase and filled his inventory. It was expensive, even for black market standards, but he'd almost sold out in a week and the flurry of customers had, for the time being, saved his shop. He even made the protection payments to the Pennywhistle Mob on time. He looked into the refrigerated glass case under the counter. One last piece of tentacle lay on a bed of plastic show-greens. It was very small by kraken standards, about a foot long and no thicker than his wrist. The initial shipment had only consisted of two tentacles, both longer than a mud snake and thicker than a river eel. They had taken over the back room and he had used Frank as a post to coil them in stacks.

He looked up at the foul-smelling customer. 'I've got just a small bit left, maybe two pounds?' Miles told himself he'd take it in back and grill it if it didn't sell by the end of the day, recipes turning in his mind. The previous trench coat twins had spoken, but this one just clicked his tongue again. It sounded like a drop of water hitting the sink. He whipped an appendage up from below the counter, clutching an item with a bunch of the coat. Miles threw up a hand to defend himself from the quick movement but refrained going for a knife. The stranger revealed a small card the size of a coaster and dropped it on the counter in front of Miles. The card was filthy and covered in mucous-like slime. Miles flipped it over with his index finger, avoiding the slime as best he could. In thick ink, barely legible scrawl, it read, STOP SELLING KRAKEN. FINAL WARNING. The same message as the previous trench coats. Miles had dealt with eco-extremists before, and he had six ruined rat dog pelts as a lesson on how not to make a scene. Miles played it by the book, pretending the card didn't exist.

'Can I interest you in our finest cricket jelly?' said Miles, gesturing to the back. 'Pressed in house.'

The man rapped an appendage hard on the card. *No one for cricket jelly anymore*, thought Miles with a frown. It was his childhood favorite when smeared on salt biscuits. The stranger clicked his tongue several times and rapped again.

Miles felt his face burn. There were others who had protested the sale of rare delicacies in the past, but never with such persistence.

Miles jabbed a finger into the stranger's chest. It felt soft like rubber. 'Like I told your ugly friends, the kraken is here to stay.' Miles stared down the shadowed face. 'Now get the hell out of my shop before I add you to the menu.' Miles drew a knife from his belt and ran it along the edge of the counter. The stranger seemed to get the picture and turned, clicking, to leave. Miles watched him as he exited the shop. He had the same awkward gait as the previous two; his feet angled out to the side and he limped like something was wrong with his knees. Miles had seen every kind of rad-born abnormality but it was curious to see such similar afflictions. The stench dissipated and Miles was left standing in an empty store. He stormed to the back. Frank had finished packaging the sparkle fish skins and was wiping down the butcher's block. Miles shook his head and entered his office. The kid had a thing for cleanliness that he couldn't understand. Once dirty, nothing ever got clean in the Underbelly.

Miles pulled a ceramic jug out of a cabinet and uncorked it. He poured two fingers of a murky brown liquid into a cloudy glass. It came out thin and then thick. He stirred it with his pinky finger and took a healthy gulp. His mouth twisted and puckered but he held it down as it warmed his belly and cleared his mind. *Can't handle the hard stuff like I used to*, he thought. *Can't do a lot of things like I used to.* Ten years ago he would have gutted the stranger and hung him from the second floor balcony overlooking the shop. The people who mattered in the Underbelly knew he meant business and left him alone—Hell, they were his best customers. Now he was getting pinched for protection by a local gang. Times had surely gone south. Miles had told the Pennywhistles roaming his block about the strange men in the trench coats, but they'd just laughed and walked on. Who was he kidding? He was paying them less for protection and more for *not* beating him up and smashing his store. He swallowed the last of the drink and slammed down the glass.

Sometimes when you need it done right, you do it yourself. He hefted a long bag off the wall and slung it over his shoulder.

'You're on point, Franky,' he said as he crossed the back room, heading for the front.

'Heading out, Pop?' said Frank, still scrubbing the table.

Miles untied his apron and draped it over a chair. He retained his knife belt. 'Things to set straight,' he said as he pinched a crispy petalfish fin and hurried out of the shop.

It was always dark to some extent in the Underbelly but the power fluctuations had zapped the juice from the street lanterns, shrouding the blocks around the Emporium in shadow. The star lights embedded in the rock ceiling twinkled high overhead. Installed as a morale booster, the stars became much more than cosmetic, forming a rudimentary navigation system akin to their cousins above. The area outside the Emporium was quiet. There were rumors that the Pennywhistles had engaged in a turf war. Miles had yet to see proof but as rumors are wont to do, it kept people off the streets and shut in their homes. Those who had no choice, the working men, were out milling around the city. A group of miners had turned on their headlamps, casting beams of light that swiveled, illuminating the mix of mud and rock that formed what passed for a road beneath their feet. Other dwellers carried cages full of moon slugs that glowed brighter than wax candles. Miles kicked himself. He thought moon slugs were a disgusting fad brought on by the outages and refused to carry them in the Emporium. Now a year had passed and every home seemed to glow with them. Miles broke off a bit of the crispy fin and crunched on it while looking around. The stranger couldn't have gotten far. Miles knew his corner of the Underbelly like the aisles of his shop. He'd lived there his entire life, knew its secrets. He'd endured far longer than a shopkeeper ought to. With no sign of the stranger he turned right and jogged down the main street. Several regulars waved as he passed. One thing he knew for sure was the man wasn't a neighbor. Another block and he caught sight of a gray hat. The man was *slow*. He'd barely made it five blocks from the shop. Miles backed off, took a seat on a rusted bench and finished the fin. As bizarre as his antique garb and walk, no one else seemed to notice the man. The street was getting more congested and yet no one turned for a second glance. Miles blamed it on the darkness. If they'd seen what he'd seen in his shop, they'd be as upset as he was. After what he measured to be a safe distance, Miles stood and continued pursuit. The stranger never wavered, strolling forward along the side of the street.

An alarm bell rang in a large decrepit brick building, startling Miles. A flood of children with ragtag outfits and greasy hair poured out of the front doors. Miles hunched over, clutching his knife belt and wallet as he waded through. *Stinking thieves*, he thought, but a bittersweet grin grew on his face. He missed the kids. He missed them in his shop. Now they just went straight to the gangs to become 'men.' Miles pulled Frank out of school to help with the shop when he turned ten. The teachers were rubbish and classes full of bullies with no future. Three years later Frank was a skilled apprentice, able to take the seeds out of a marmabulb in a minute flat—and he wasn't half bad with the money books either. Frank was becoming a less salty version of Miles in record time. In the chaos he almost missed the gray hat slip into a side alley. Miles fell in behind. The alley was pitch black, shutting out all light from the kids and their purring moon slugs. Miles shivered. *Moon slugs, goddamn it*. He kicked himself again. The stranger shuffled ahead. Miles ran a hand along brick wall of the alley and followed. After several careful steps, the alley turned in an elbow to the left. Miles peeked around the corner and saw the silhouette of the stranger, and another man dressed in similar fashion, long coat and a short brimmed top hat. They clicked their tongues back and forth, the top hat in short bursts and the stranger from the store responding in a much more animated fashion, waving his arms. He looked desperate, like he was failing to convey something important. The arguing continued until the man wearing the top hat took out a long blade and pressed it against the chest of the other who wrapped his coat arms around it and nodded as if he understood. Miles felt his bladder tighten as the men parted ways. He'd witnessed similar events before, hell, even been in the same position. The boss telling his boy he'd messed up big. This was his chance to clean up the mess, puff out his chest and show them he was the real deal. He clenched the bag on his back. A silhouette ambled back his direction with the weapon. *Franky*, thought Miles. *Shit, he's heading for the store*. Miles kept a grip on the corner of the alley and backed into the darkness in a crouch. His legs shook and he wiped his right palm on his pant leg. Scraping feet neared the turn. Miles held his breath to avoid the stink. Rage built in his chest along with the need for air. With a start Miles drew a long butcher's knife from its sheath and leapt, driving the blade deep into the man's chest. Hot liquid sprayed Miles as he held the rubbery body against the wall, grunting as he punched the blade in again and again until his shoulders burned. The man slumped to the ground without so much as a click. Miles' heart thumped against his ribcage. He wiped the blade on the back of the man's trench coat and sheathed it in his belt. The alley was quiet. He bolted in the direction of the second man, took a deep breath at the opening to the street and strolled out. Miles' adrenaline was still pumping hard when he spotted the second man in the distance. He felt twenty years younger and had to stop himself from charging down the street. A series of deep breaths calmed him as he blended into the busy avenue, crowds coming and going from a nearby market. Another block and Miles could hear the river.

It was always loud at the docks amidst the traffic and the river itself. As wide as two city blocks, the river was the subterranean thoroughfare that connected the wards of the Underbelly. The river kept the Underbelly alive, providing the only efficient method of transporting goods and people. Miles had split his early years between fishing and barge work, dangerous stuff when almost everything lurking below water wanted to eat you. He followed close behind the top hat. Two barges had recently docked and the area was full of activity. Miles slipped through the jungle of crates, halting at the edge of the pier. Below, the man stood in a small gondola.

He flicked a switch on a lamp hanging on the front of the craft and shoved off the docks. Miles dropped down after him and whistled to a group of ferrymen who ran the taxi service.

'Hey, I need a ride,' Miles shouted. The men were slow to break up their group. When they did, they laughed at the sight of their caller.

'Wha'? You get inna fight with a juicer?' asked one man.

'I've never seen such a green juice,' said another.

Miles glanced down at his chest. In the light of the docks he could see he was covered chin to belly in green ooze. The stranger's blood. *Fuck me*, he thought.

'Right, green,' said Miles, searching for resolve. *Blood disorder? I've never heard of such a thing*, he thought. His mind scrambled for words. 'That man wrecked my shop!' He pointed out to the man in the top hat coasting down the river and dug into his pocket for some coins. 'Now who's gonna chase him down with me?'

The men looked uninspired, doing their best to stall until one spoke up. Finally, a tall young man with shriveled limbs stepped forward. The docks had stolen more than his youth. He moved off toward a gondola only slightly larger than the top hat's boat. Miles followed him in. The size made Miles nervous. He couldn't see his reflection in the dark water.

'Relax, old man,' said the ferryman in an odd, high-pitch voice. He tossed Miles a dirty towel. 'It's not as dangerous as it used to be.'

Kids, thought Miles as he wiped himself down, smearing the blood more than removing it. *They wouldn't know danger if it had teeth the size of children and could swallow the boat whole*. The ferryman grabbed a long oar and shoved off. The water in the vicinity of the dock was thick with vessels headed every which direction, each captain doubling as a personal traffic cop. Two self-propelling fan sailboats darted around a rust-colored barge carrying crates of caramel crystal stacked three-high. A river cruise puttered along, full of tan top-dwellers in loud multicolor attire. They shouted amongst each other, swollen fingers pointed with excitement, cameras flashed over and over, capturing everything the eye could see and more. Two women called after Miles, asking him to strike a pose. He hunched over and looked away, playing the uninterested caged animal who didn't understand their language. It was best that way; folk fingered by top-dwellers as threatening were quick to feel the heat from above.

A minute later Miles had the top hat in sight. 'Slow down,' said Miles.

'Don't you want to catch 'im?' asked the driver.

'I want to see where he goes,' said Miles. The ferryman flashed a grin of chipped and yellow teeth.

The stranger hugged the coast of the river into a tunnel where the ceiling dipped and then rowed into a branch where it dipped further still. He faced forward, alternating two easy strokes at a time on each side of the gondola, like clockwork. The ferryman glanced back at Miles, unsure of their next move.

'I can pay,' said Miles and the ferryman turned back. The river's system of tunnels was formed of thick layers of limestone and granite. But it all looked like charcoal in the dark. The tunnel was pitch black except for the top hat's light and torches the size of small bonfires set high into the walls to mark the way. Though as they moved on, the tunnels became smaller and the bonfires reduced to smoking husks. The river's arteries were a puzzle that Miles vaguely remembered. When the smell of decay hit him, he knew where they were headed. The air grew warm and humid but a chill lingered in his gut. The ferryman stopped the boat hard, jabbing his oar into the wall.

'Can't go any farther sir. Bog Harbor up ahead, that's where your man is headed,' said the ferryman.

'It's not as dangerous as it used to be,' said Miles with a smirk. Inside his guts rumbled and he rubbed the scar on his temple. The ferryman was right, it wasn't safe. But he'd come too far to turn back. Miles lifted the bag off his shoulder and placed it at his feet. Then he pulled out a harpoon gun and leveled it at the ferryman. 'Carry on now, boy.'

The ferryman looked at the weapon in disgust, like he'd been cheated. They were nowhere near land and the old man would put a spear through him before he could get halfway across the boat.

'It's not safe for a vessel this size, you know,' said the ferryman. Miles knew. He knew all too well. But he buried the memory and motioned the ferryman onward.

They entered a tunnel where the shaft hugged the gondola so close that Miles could touch the walls, could see its sweat gather in large droplets and drip down into the brackish water. The air smelled of rot. The ferryman's shirt clung tight to his body, soaked with nervous sweat. Miles' nerves were on edge. He'd never been this far off the main thrust of the river. He'd never heard of a passage so tight. The water frothed in places, bubbles raced to the surface and small waves rocked the boat from unseen creatures moving below. As they rounded a tight corner, the tunnel brightened and the ferryman slowed the gondola to a crawl. The top hat had pulled up alongside a small outcropping and was tying his gondola to a post. Two loops and a tug and he disappeared up a series of stone steps. Miles ushered the ferryman over to the dock. He pushed hard off the wall and coasted over to the stranger's boat. When they hit the side, Miles pulled out several coins—more than enough to cover the trip—and handed them to the ferryman.

'There'll be more upon my return,' he said, slipping the empty bag back over his shoulder. He actually didn't have any more coins but he had to say something and the kid wouldn't take kindly to threats, as Miles had already played that card. He lowered his gun and vaulted up onto the stone dock. The ferryman stood with the coins in his hand, contemplating the return trip. Miles figured his chances of the kid sticking around were slim, but the faster he was the less time the kid had to think about it.

He turned and made haste up the steps, taking them three at a time. The staircase and walls were smooth, carved with unparalleled precision as they curved upwards in a spiral. Soon there was light and he slowed, bringing the gun level with his hip. Large transparent shells in the shape of sand oysters and bog clams lined the walls, back-lit. Miles squeezed his finger in behind one of the shells. The glowing material was spongy and smelled of mildew. *Algae? This is incredible*, he thought. Miles had never seen such a thing. He made a mental note to stuff his satchel full of the stuff upon his exit. He had the perfect spot to grow it in-house, though Frank would be upset—they'd have to scratch the sherbet.

Miles continued up the steps. It was eerily quiet and his presence echoed with each guarded step. The stairs widened into an entryway of a grand cavern with a ceiling that seemed to continue on forever upward. Miles' jaw dropped. He'd never witnessed such a space. He was certain such a room, like the stairs, had been carved, but couldn't fathom how it was possible. It felt ancient. Two staircases, one on each side, curved up and into the rock wall behind. The floor was smooth tile that glimmered in the dim glow. Strange symbols and glyphs that he couldn't begin to understand covered the walls. Algae grew in patches, illuminating random sections of the immense room. His eyes lingered on the rear wall. He couldn't grasp the picture at first because it was so large and camouflaged in algae. Then he saw the gigantic eye and the outline of the bulbous head. The strange carvings formed a mural of a gigantic kraken, its body rising on the rear wall, tentacles stretched and coiled around the rest of the room. Miles felt a shiver creep up his spine. *No wonder they've got issues with me selling the beast*, he thought. Miles took another step into the room and slipped on a puddle of slime. His right hand shot out to catch himself and his fingers caught on something that felt like moldy skin. He cried out as he hit the ground and the thing covered him. He ripped it away. It was a trench coat like the men had been wearing. Along the entryway wall were a series of hooks with identical trench coats and hats. Miles' head spun, screamed at him to leave, to forget and go back to his simple life. *And suffer at the hands of these maniacs?* They were sure to come in groups now that he had killed one of them. With their clubs and knives they'd tear through the store. He had worked too hard to stay clean and raise Frank away from trouble. Now trouble had found him and he'd gone too far to turn back and hope they'd leave him alone.

His body tensed at the sound of footsteps. Shadows swayed at the top of the left staircase. Miles scrambled to his feet and hurried right and up the stairs. He reached the top without being seen. That's when he heard the chanting. Soft at first, but his ears picked it up as he moved down a short hallway. The stone walls were dusted in salt and a strong smell of brine replaced the rot of the previous passage. As he neared the end of the hallway the chanting grew louder and what before was buzzing static he now heard as a combination of guttural cries and clicks. The hallway opened into an even larger chamber than the last, overwhelming Miles. Thick marbled columns lined the inside of another staircase that curved up to a plateau that jutted out to a point over a mammoth body of blue water. Miles stumbled behind the first column. Water lapped over the walkway, soaking his feet. *Clear salt water?* He couldn't believe his eyes but confirmed his suspicions with a lick of his finger. He peered around the column at the chanting figures on the point. Five...*men? No. Some sort of bizarre creatures*, Miles convinced himself. They had blue-green skin and were covered in scales. Three of them had one or two tentacles that wriggled from the elbow in place of a hand. Their heads were curved and misshapen. *What the hell have you done, Miles?* He gripped the harpoon gun tight against his chest. There was still time, he could make it back to the boat.

Before he could move the chanting increased to a deafening scream and his mind went numb. The floor began to rumble beneath his feet. Dust and rock chips fell from the walls and the sea water churned. Miles felt faint. He backed away from the column, slumping against the wall. He clutched at his ears in an attempt to shut out the wail. Then the water exploded. Eight enormous tentacles sprang out of the sea, gripping and coiling around the marbled columns. The appendages were crimson in color and thicker than Miles' waist. The chamber shook as if it was going to collapse, crushing everyone inside.

KRAKEN.

Miles' mind cleared and he snapped back into the room. The chanting was replaced by screams equally loud and full of terror. He watched as four men, beaten and bloodied, were led to the edge of the point by more scaled creatures with barbed weapons. Thin tentacles slithered out of the water and upwards to the frightened group. The tentacles danced back and forth in front of their pale faces. Then on a silent cue they slipped into the quartet, wrapping around the limbs of a haggard old man and dragged him screaming into the water. The tentacles then returned, wriggling up the cliff face. Miles was no longer distracted. His full attention was devoted to the tentacle wrapped around the column in front of him, which alone could not only pay off his debts but bribe his way out of the Underbelly. *My word*, he thought. *We could start a franchise, bring the Underbelly Topside!* He couldn't take the beast himself; he was greedy, not suicidal. But he needed proof of such a find. He placed the harpoon gun on the ground and drew his cleaver. 'One nice slice should do the trick,' he said aloud.

Miles waited until the second of the men was dragged shrieking off the ledge. Then he put all of his strength into a downward angled chop. The blade sunk deep into the rubbery flesh. The tentacle tightened its grip on the column and the chamber shook. He ripped the cleaver out and swung it back hard at the opposite angle. Before the kraken could move he plunged both hands into the arm and popped out the slice like a piece of cake. The maimed tentacle released its grip and retreated into the water. He slipped the slimy mass into his satchel and retrieved the harpoon gun.

A deep moan sounded below the waves and the chamber shook hard, causing Miles to stumble into the open. One of the creatures pointed a barbed staff at him and a cry went up from those on the plateau. Miles bolted into the hallway but the stairs at the other end were blocked by more of the creatures. *Shit. Shit. Shit. There must be another way out.* He took a step backwards and felt the slime of a tentacle as it wrapped around his ankle. His feet were ripped out from beneath him and he was flung across the room, colliding with the terrified men on the point, knocking a short, blond man into the water. The last man tried to make a run for it and was impaled by a spear that whistled across the chamber. The room was a blur. Somehow he'd maintained hold of both the satchel and the harpoon gun. It was hard to breathe, the chamber suddenly a furnace. He turned over onto his back and the bright red image came into focus. The beast rested on the edge of the cliff, gigantic beak clacking, eyes monstrous half-moons on the sides of its head. The creatures whooped and clicked around the chamber as they converged on the plateau. With a mix of pure terror and adrenaline pumping through his veins, Miles pulled the trigger, burying a rusty harpoon in the side of the kraken's head. It bellowed and released its hold on Miles' leg. He struggled to his feet. The creatures had formed a chattering mob to his left, blocking his escape. Miles drew two blades from his belt and stood firm.

The kraken roared, blasting Miles with hot air. He licked his lips. With any luck, Frank would have flames roaring on the grill because he was famished.

Yao Jin

Joyce Chng

She hated the abattoir.

Her client knew it and still sent her on this merry jaunt. Perhaps he had never inhaled the smell of coagulating and frozen blood, still coppery, still rich, still with the hint of heartsblood. Perhaps he had never touched the cool skin of the formerly live animal and wanted to feed.

She cursed him to the Eighteenth Hell and padded down the stairs, mindful of her own urges. She didn't like to eat on the job. Trixie would have kept some in the fridge, just for her.

The creature was somewhere in the cold *dripping* bloody *delicious* meat factory.

Her shoulder brushed one of the hanging carcasses. It moved, as if it drew breath. Indeed, she heard its breathing, like a szzztszzztszzzt.

Bloody Eighteenth Hell!

Something dark and hateful and spiky with spite hit her.

This time, she responded by letting out her urges.

Trixie was mopping the floor when she limped in through the door. She had to stop. Trixie hated getting the floor dirty. And now she was mopping the tiled floor with the passion of a scourer, one of those god-bothering devotees. Trixie wasn't a scourer. Never professed having a religion or any form of spirituality.

'Feck!' Trixie swore, dropped her mop and rushed over to her. 'You are fecking injured.'

'Glad you noticed,' she replied. The creature got her across the chest, across her breasts. Which meant she had to loosen her binds and let Trixie treat the wound. Trixie was ex-medico.

'Feck, sit down, Amara, before you get the tiles bloody. Wait while I get the med bag.'

She eased herself on one of the rickety chairs. Once she get the damned money from her client, she was going shopping, damn it. And a new jacket. The creature had ruined it.

Trixie blustered out of the treatment room with her med bag. It was genuine leather, made from a bovine source and highly priced, not like the cheap humanaskin in the markets

'Feck,' Trixie muttered as she carefully peeled off the thin grey camisole, fresh red blood welling up from disturbed scabs. 'Feck, what didya do?'

'Fought a preta,' she winced. 'Hey, careful!'

'If you sit still,' Trixie still had the medico voice down pat. She started cleaning up the wounds with medical alcohol. 'Claws?'

'Long ones.'

'Feck. Ah Long asked you to do this?'

She nodded, comforted by the concern in Trixie's soft contralto.

'Was it worth all this?' Trixie gestured at the wounds, deep gouges that even her body would take some time to heal. 'All *this*?'

'I do what I am born to do.'

'Feckhell, don't give me that nonsense again.'

Trixie finished padding the wounds up with enough gauze and bandage, sternly warning Amara to take care when she showered. She always gave the same lecture. The same 'Don't this' and 'Don't that' since they started the preta-hunting agency. Trixie made sure she ate. She lost energy after hunting preta. And preta were growing more and more common in Nightshome, like an infestation of lice.

The cold slabs of meat – bovine and fresh from the killing market – went down her throat in a rich thick river of *bloodbloodblood*. She savored the copper, knowing that her wounds were knitting as the blood went into her body. She sighed out of sheer pleasure.

'You are showing your fangs,' Trixie said, and this time she was smiling.

The phone rang an hour before dawn. She knew, because her body was attuned to the dawn and the darkness between it. And on her off-day too. Beside her, Trixie stirred and murmured 'Feckoff' before going back to sleep.

It was Ah Long. She had never seen him. His voice was all she ever knew of his existence. He belonged to the upper clans. He gave assignments and paid on time.

'Apologies for waking you up on your rest day.'

Oh sure, bloody Eighteen Hell brat. 'Never mind, just give me the assignment.' Outside, she heard the city stirring, just as Trixie had stirred, waking up. Steeltrains rumbled on their rail tracks. People swore and spat. She smelled the breakfast trucks. Her mouth watered.

'There is a flesh forest found at the fringes of Nightshome. I think there is a preta or more of them there. The payment will be 1,000 skulls.'

1,000 skulls? Oh precious skies. We are rich.

Then her hearts sank. High pay usually meant an extremely difficult case.

She wasn't sure how she would tell Trixie. But Trixie was normal human and normal humans thought like normal humans. In flesh ways and in flesh terms. She had to keep them both fed and the agency going without tanking again.

She left Trixie still wrapped up in the blankets. She slipped out into the Nightshome morning, holding her ruined jacket close to her body. She was already shivering. Her urges were calling out to her.

Of course, she fed. She stopped by one of the meat trucks and ordered a string of hearts. She bit into the juicy organs, feeling herself grow stronger.

'Out hunting, dakini?' The seller asked. He was a familiar face.

She nodded. She couldn't resist ordering another string. They were always so sweet and delectable. She knew where he had gotten his supplies. Finishing the hearts, she turned to a beverage stall. As usual, she had her stim-tea, flavored with blood flakes. She sprinkled a liberal amount. She loved that particular spice.

Breakfast done, she began her hunt.

In the dream, she ran, clawed feet, running and flying.

In the dream, she was the hunter and she knew her prey was near.

She laughed and the whole universe laughed with her.

In one hand, she grabbed her vajira. In another hand, she held the skull bowl.

She supped deep of the skull bowl.

Her song filled the roiling skies.

Flesh forests grew regularly in Nightshome.

It wasn't Nightshome all the time. The realms changed frequently. It was the cycle of the Prayer Wheel. Soon, it would be another cycle. But that would take another hundred years or more.

Flesh forests grew, because humans died and left the corpses behind to seed the plains. The vulture-birds, the Cleaning Ones, were no longer alive. They had become extinct when Terra died. Even planets died and she had told Trixie of that truth before.

'I am no preta,' Trixie had said, her eyes clouding over. Her eyes were like cirque lakes. Even those were gone when Terra trembled in her death throes. 'I am... me.'

She didn't have the hearts to tell Trixie she had found her unconscious in a life-pod.

She had to focus. Preta were hard to kill, sticking to undead and Hungry life as they did when they lived. She hated flesh forests too. They were as triggery as abattoirs. Within her, her urges howled. They always howled before the hunt. They simmered like fire lakes beneath her skin. She wore this skin to live unharmed in Nightshome.

The flesh forest had the stench of rotting flesh and the hiss of a thousand flies. Her feet, sheathed at the moment, crunched on dry scalps. The swollen bodies in various sizes and shapes of putrefaction stood like the trees of old. One, still huge with a dead fetus, had outstretched arms like branches. It bore stranger fruits, boils the size of infested bolls along the gnarly sides.

Preta lurked in these forests.

She didn't have to wear her jacket. That too was an affectation like her name. She wasn't always Amara.

She opened her skin and let her urges, her real self out.

Trixie had seen her real self once before. There was before they founded the agency. Trixie didn't freak out. Her claim was that she had seen worse.

She had a wolf's head but with three luminous eyes. Her fur was blue, the blue of a bruise, and her claws were crescent-shaped. Her wolf's mouth was filled with dagger teeth, to shred preta and return them to truth. Her hair, the night-black hair, framed her wolf face.

Her vajira she held in her claws, its pommel a screaming dakini's head.

The preta didn't take long to emerge from the bodies. They hid there.

She slashed through them with her vajira, taking their heads off and biting into their necks. She had forgotten about her wounds inflicted by a preta now gone to its Final Death. She hoped it would reincarnate in a better world.

They kept coming, a loathsome walking phalanx.

'Would you… bring us… to nirvana?' One hissed, corpse-breath escaping from the slit on its face. 'Now? Now? Now? Would you? Would you?'

'Would you? Would you?' The rest echoed, a macabre choir.

Her vajira answered. Limbs littered the scalp-covered forest floor.

'Go to your Final Death!' She howled and the forest shook with her rage.

The killing took less than an hour. The limbs and heads piled up. She clutched their souls and flung them away, into the truth-light. They were different from the hate-thing which had slashed her the day before.

When she closed her skin, she realized she was cut and bruised everywhere. The flesh forest stank even stronger now. She hadn't fed. Flesh still lingered in her mouth and she spat it out.

Trixie was going to yell at her.

The payment pinged into her credit on time. She was surprised that Trixie didn't yell at her. Just looked at her with tired eyes.

'More cuts,' Trixie said. 'Aiyah.' She had removed her contacts and her real eye color was the color of dark chocolate. Chocolate was now rare in Nightshome. She saw gold in the darkness, like flashes of anger. 'You know what the stalls called you? Yao jin. Demon.'

'They can't differentiate between yao jin and dakini.'

'Feck, stay still. I don't like rotting nails digging into your already stressed flesh.'

The antiseptic tingled. She was grateful for Trixie's gentle touch.

'Trying living as human for once.'

That argument again. Trixie never gave up trying to convince her to live normally. She couldn't deny her urges.

'I am not human,' she reminded Trixie. 'Not once, never.'

'You wear human skin and behave like one.'

'I have to pass unnoticed.'

Their conversation tittered towards an argument, one long overdue.

'Amara, listen. I love the agency as much as you do. But you… you hurting yourself every day for it… isn't going to work in the long term. I don't like seeing you hurt.'

Ah. Human feelings. Human sentiments.

'Trixie.'

'Don't 'Trixie' me,' Trixie's eyes narrowed. 'Why did you take human form if you hated us so much?'

'I never hate you,' she said, shaking her head slowly.

Trixie muttered a long string of words. The words were familiar, so achingly familiar.

'I am…'

But Trixie had already turned around and left the room. The argument fizzled and stayed stale.

She fed on the bloody strips of meat savagely. She wanted to tell Trixie that she didn't mean to hurt her. She heard the door slam. Trixie had left the apartment.

The phone rang just when she was about to chase after Trixie. Nightshome at night was not a safe place. Not only would the preta appear, but murderers and thieves. Meat hunters. So much to salvage for the renderers and rags-and-bone men. The sky was already filled with dark clouds from the renders' factories, processing bodies, carcasses.

It was Ah Long. It was always Ah Long.

'Another assignment for you since the night is still young...'

She ignored the smooth voice, high-born and arrogant. She needed to find Trixie. She had to find Trixie.

'Payment is high. I want you to...'

'My partner is lost. I have to look for her,' she said flatly.

'The assignment is more important. Listen, you hunt preta. You don't need human attachments. The assignment will be at another abattoir.'

She growled.

'You are a beast, just like the ones you kill. You don't need human love. Go to your task. I will input the payment into your credit.'

Eighteenth Hell!

The windows shattered with her scream.

A dark shape hunted the streets of Nightshome, a shadow among shadows. The skies rained ash. The steeltrains roared, metal animals with passengers in their bellies, factory workers and renderers on their own secret missions. The night food trucks waited for customers. Figures in humanaskin robes waited in their corners. In dark streets, a flick of steel, a grunt – and a new body joined the harvest. Someone would get rich tonight.

The dark shape was a beast, clawed and fanged. Having discarded the human affectations, it was purely primal. A hunter led by smells and spool.

Trixie.

The wolf's head sniffed the air. Blood. Bone. Marrow.

Trixie.

The claws dug into mud and broken tiles.

Tiles!

Trixie.

The beast stood up on two legs.

It held a vajira.

She found Trixie at one of the meat stalls along the river. The smell of rotting fish filled the air. And many other things too.

The stall owners scattered as the wolf shape emerged from the inky darkness. 'Yao jin!' They screamed and abandoned their meat stalls in a burst of frantic action.

'Amara!' Trixie's eyes were huge. She had paused in the action of selecting a string of hearts. 'Feck, I was only out for a walk!'

'This place is not safe,' the wolf snapped furiously. 'Come back. Please.' The growl softened now, pleading, kinder.

'Amara, you are scaring everyone, including me.'

She closed her skin. The dakini form went back in.

'Oh feck!' Trixie hugged her impulsively, tightly.

Szztszztszzt.

Breathing.

Preta.

Something dark and unholy grabbed Trixie from her embrace. Trixie screamed and kicked the swirling darkness. It had multiple eyes and multiple limbs. Trixie fought like a lioness. A tendril strangled the air of her and she flopped down, limp.

'Trixie! TRIXIE!'

She crashed through walls, pursuing the darkness. She shed her jacket and ran nude. Halfway through the chase, she ignored the nudity and opened her skin.

The darkness led her on. Nightshome was a huge city, a maze with steel, factories and clusters of buildings. It moved like a black tornado, all spinning with…

She couldn't place the smell of it.

It was part-preta, part-something else.

But it took Trixie.

A sun burned within her chest. This must be pure rage, like the song of the universe when it came out from nothing.

Burning.

Burning.
Burning.

She ran, clawed feet, running and flying.

She was the hunter and she knew her prey was near.

She laughed and the whole universe laughed with her.

In one hand, she grabbed her vajira. In another hand, she held the skull bowl.

The skull bowl was deep with fresh crimson blood. They spilled like red tears. When they fell, they transformed into bloodstone.

Her song filled Nightshome and its citizens cried in their sleep. Yao jin, yao jin, yao jin.

She was none of those.

She pursued the darkness until it reached a renderer factory. The darkness was a sentient oil slick, flowing through the gaps and the holes, Trixie tucked within its tendrils. The chase was a game, a dance and a taunt.

'Just stop *moving*,' the creature named Amara growled deep in her throat. The darkness felt more just than a simple preta, a simple hungry ghost lost between the sleeping and non-sleeping lands. More feral-intelligent, a creature like her and yet not a dakini, a protector.

The renderer factory loomed before her like a sagging drunkard, its sides run down and the paint peeling off. It reeked of human and animal ash, the aftermath of a crematorium. She knew about the renderers and vice versa. They just kept their paths clear from crossing outright. They rendered human parts down to their component bits and sold them off to the traders of the plains who then sold the minerals and metals to other traders from the satellite cities. Not much was left after Earth's death.

She savored the taste in the air. The lingering meat and oil, burnt flesh and meat. Her eyes got the heat flashes of small animals. Rodents, feeders of detritus. In the dim light, her eyes burned like three suns and their fire roared like the song of raging galaxies.

There was no sound, no human or non-human noise.

The renderers had gone home for the night. Or the factory had been abandoned not so long ago. The ash was still fresh. The flesh carts were still parked in front of the steel doors. Someone had vomited there. Rancid meat and stomach acids. Congealed and half-digested meat.

Trixie.

She kicked open the doors. No subtlety there. The darkness took Trixie.

Something reverberated through the still air, a boom and a long ululation like crying or laughter. The racks of hooks rattled, touched by a passing breeze. The floor was metal, scrubbed and scuffed by multiple boots. Clusters of femurs and hip bones waited for the renderer's machine.

Amara went straight into a crouch. Her vajira screamed. Her focus narrowed. She smelled something.

'I am glad you are here, beast.'

The life pod was a metal tube nestled amongst the crumbling boulders. The sky still rained fire. She reached it as the ground hissed with liquid flame.

New into the world, a protector born from fire, she tapped the life pod with her front claws. The metal pinged. The sensation was oddly pleasurable and her bones sang with the song.

She opened to find a woman, a young woman, curled up in a fetal position. As if she was a child about to be birthed. She was clothed in white. Her hands held a brown box. Not a skull bowl. Not a vajira. She was not a protector.

It was then the young woman opened her eyes and they were the color of clear water.

She did not scream. Instead, she uttered this word.

'Oh, feck.'

They travelled a long distance before they reached the nascent Nightshome, still growing with the flood of refugees.

She took on human form, the weak limbed shape of the woman, tucking her urges in. She had black-night hair and pale skin.

'You look better,' the woman said with a grin. She called herself Trixie. It was probably a bastardization of her name:

Tri Xie. But she felt more like Trixie, all pink-haired and nutmeg skin. She was small for a human woman, but she moved fast. In the caravan they followed, she became the source of all healing, checking on wounds, giving advice for colds and infections. Coughs were common as abused lungs struggled to cope with the dying ash-filled air. Many developed sore eyes and one or two, bleeding pupils. Too complicated for Trixie to cope with and left to die. That was when the first few preta appeared and the creature named Amara heeded her original calling.

'You are not human,' Trixie told her one night when they rested, spooning against each other's warm skin, sated with warm flesh. 'I saw you in your... form. I don't think there were any three-eyed bipedal and blue-furred wolves running around.'

Amara made a deep purring sound in her throat.

'You remind me of the Bardo. Oh, *feck.*'

That was whispered in the dark, her breath a gentle warm tickle on bare skin.

'Something dark and primal – But, you've never harmed me once. That's good, isn't it?'

Then Trixie slept, stirring as her dreams disturbed her. Amara could see those dreams. Buildings falling, a child crying... and Trixie running running running. She had no power to stop those dreams.

Presently, her eyes focused on the figure standing before her. Male, obviously so, with musk and body fluids. He was clothed in an ironed grey shirt and starched beige pants, topped off with a long overcoat of black leather. In one gloved hand was a cane – an affectation, she realized, like her skin – and in another similarly gloved hand was a hat. His eyes were shadowed. The rest of him looked as if he was dipped in shadows.

Behind him was the darkness, curled around his figure like a protective cobra.

Behind the darkness hung Trixie, her hands tied, her legs limp. She was unconscious and unharmed.

'You.'

Recognition came like a clap of thunder.

'You.'

They started their agency in the third year of their stay in Nightshome. It started first as a lost-and-found and investigations agency, with Amara providing the services while Trixie did the administration and the logistics. They rented an apartment, near a relatively safer street. Steeltrains rumbled past hourly.

It paid the bills, in the form of skulls, tiny skull-shaped metal discs. It kept Amara fed. Her urges were hot in her. She was born to hunt. Red meat satisfied her and kept the urges from overwhelming her. She only let them loose when she was on a mission.

Clients ensured that they lived moderately comfortably, for Nightshome residents. Their major clients came from the renderers and the upper clans, people who wanted to keep their own dark secret urges secret. Their number-one client was Ah Long.

She hunted in flesh forests, in ruined renderer factories and along the dark streets.

'Feck, he's rich!' Trixie stared at their credit once, when Amara came back from a particularly tedious mission. She was good with counting.

Amara couldn't agree more, sucking on the chill marrow. He was arrogant, a typical rich man's son with appetites to fit his princely attitude. His voice was all she heard over the phone. She licked the blood off her lips, thinking wistfully about her skull bowl and vajira.

With the skulls they afforded her jacket and their tiny apartment, always rumbling when one of the steeltrains thundered past.

For a while, they lived as Nightshome residents. She hunted whenever she had a mission or when clients called them in the middle of the Nightshome night.

Now, their client stood in front of her. Cocky as a man who had just rutted.

She snarled, showing her dagger fangs.

Ah Long tsked at her. The darkness slithered about him.

A revelation slammed into her.

'You are a debased dragon,' she said matter-of-factly. 'Cast out from nirvana.'

'You are right, beast,' Ah Long nodded amiably. 'And you are cast out from the wheels of samsara.'

'I came here, because there were things to hunt. I am a protector.'

'I came here,' he mocked her, 'because I hunt things. Like you.'

'I will bring you back to the light. Release her.'

'See, you have succumbed to fleshy desires. You fell in love.'

He said 'love' as if it was a pit of poison.

'Nonsense.'

Where do debased dragons, their star-cores corrupted, go to? She wondered.

'Why me?' She held forth her vajira, its snarling face glittering with fangs.

'Why not? You are a dakini. I hunt dakini and feed on them.'

We are both beasts, she thought, *in human form and with human affectations.*

'Release her,' she said. She heard Trixie moan.

He replied by opening his skin and a dark draconic form slipped out, joining the darkness.

They ignored the scourers who scourged their bodies with barbed wire, so that they could reach enlightenment or whatever they envisioned enlightenment to be. They ignored the preachers who stood at corners, waiting for skulls to trickle into their bowls shaped from human ashes.

Trixie ignored them as she shopped at the meat stalls. She bought strings of hearts for Amara. She nibbled on meat sticks. There were a few vegetables on sale. They were wilted and wan. With no sun, they couldn't grow. Mushroom growers made fortunes.

For a while, they were happy.

'Release her,' she repeated. She smelled rich blood. The rope had cut into Trixie's wrists and her heartsblood was flowing out.

The corrupted dragon, once a glorious celestial serpent and a controller of the seas and winds, roared with laughter. The metal racks shook with the sound. Its shadow claws crushed bones beneath them. The fall had corrupted him as just it had released her.

'Never.'

She flew at the dragon, focusing her rage into an incandescent spear.

If it bleeds, I can still kill it.

The darkness met her, shielding its master from her full front assault. Her vajira went straight into its oily skin and cut deep.

It howled.

She howled in triumph and cut even deeper, even harder. It slashed back into her and light, her light, spilled from the wounds. The pain was more terrible than that of the preta's claws a few nights before. She howled and retaliated until the darkness writhed, its form dissipating.

'Release her,' she sang and her voice was the death of a thousand stars.

'Release her,' she sang and her voice was the flare of a thousand growing and dying galaxies.

'Release her.'

The dragon, corrupted soul, spat black darkness back at her. She blocked it with her skull bowl and the darkness transmuted into blood, red blood, fresh blood, splashing down harmlessly onto the tiled floor. The dragon cursed and flung himself at her, claws out, hatred spikes to maim and kill.

'You cling to flesh desires, beast.'

She laughed and the universe shook. 'At least I am honest.'

She plunged the vajira into his chest and the dragon screamed.

She ran, clawed feet, running and flying.

She was the hunter and she knew her prey was near.

She laughed and the whole universe laughed with her.

In one hand, she grabbed her vajira. In another hand, she held the skull bowl.

She supped deep of the skull bowl.

Her song filled the roiling skies.

'Amara?'

Trixie's voice was so soft as if she had long since passed into the death realm. She cradled her body and eased it down. Her wrists still bled.

Beneath her, the dragon was a twisted carcass. She had torn into him. He tasted rancid. She spat the flesh out. Let the renderers have a field day.

'Amara?' Trixie whispered. 'Oh, feck, I hurt.'

'I am going to get you healed,' Amara promised and carried her easily down, bounding across the tiled floor on muscled legs.

'Thank you,' Trixie's voice grew softer, but her heart beat strong.

They left the factory.

'Trixie,' the wolf smiled and there were stars in the sky.

'Uhm?'

'Call me Soinam.'

Nightshome's twilight lasted for hours, casting a weak orange glow on the flesh forests growing on its outskirts. A three-eyed wolf hunted, a dark shadow in the land of shadows. Her joyful laughter filled the forests , a song of the universe in motion.

Train Tracks

W. P. Johnson

The thing that I always ask guys is if they can get me glow. Scribbled in my father's notebook:

> *glow, aka, snot, rubber, soul, bright light. Knock offs include deadlights and slag (ecstasy cut with meth emulsified with gelatin and made into a hard jelly).*

I'm not saying I won't go home with someone if all they got is slag. But if they can get glow, I'll do anything.

Someone once told me that a pretty girl is never homeless. In the city of Philadelphia, the same goes for a pretty boy. Guys take me back to their place, tell me I can stay the night but I have to leave before morning. When I'm taking a shower they rummage through my bag and start asking questions about my father's notebooks and the worm drawings. They want to know why I still carry around a cassette player when an IPod can hold ten thousand songs.

Then they find the .38 and they just want to know when I'm leaving.

Normal sex isn't as good after you've had it on glow, even if it's a shitty batch and it's with someone you don't want to have sex with. A good batch makes me feel young, like I'm fifteen and having my first orgasm. It makes me so high I don't care who got hurt making the stuff.

Waking up, sober, I know it's not what I'm looking for. It's not nearly as strong as the glow I smoked when I was fifteen.

I keep looking. My father's notebook tells me where the warehouses are in South Philadelphia, the names of dealers and feeders, the descriptions of vehicles and cook rooms. I just need a key, someone lower on the food chain that can get me inside.

In Philadelphia, some guy with expensive tattoos and a

Rolling Stones shirt picks me up at a bar after last call and says he knows someone that can get anything, so I tell him that I want glow and that I want it to be the strongest glow he can get, the kind of stuff that I can feel from my head down to my toes.

We smoke it at his place and it's average at best. The guy gets off and asks if I want to get some pizza from Lorenzo's on South Street cause he's still wired and can't sleep. He brings back an eight ball of coke instead and we snort the whole thing in an hour. He asks me if I remember what my first time doing glow was like and I'm so cranked that I tell him everything, tell him who my father is, what the worm drawings are, what happened to Derrick, why I'm in Philadelphia. I talk until we're both sober and tired and my jaw is too sore and my mouth is too dry to kiss.

When the sun rises, I put my clothes on and don't worry about him following me.

Then it's just another day in the city.

Derrick was the first boy I ever got stoned with. He was a dealer, just dime bags, joints, sometimes acid when it was around. On the first day of school this fourteen year old girl got kidnapped right outside the bus stop so everyone had to pair up and we were put together at random. We started walking home together on the train tracks. There were no trespassing signs everywhere but the locals hunted when it was nice out. The air was still thick with the last wave of mosquitos and the thunderclap of a shotgun going off would toss a bucket of birds into the open sky. We'd always stop in our tracks, thinking somehow the path of buckshot was rushing past us like a kid on his dirt bike.

'Your dad ever let you shoot his gun?'

'We shoot clay pigeons sometimes,' I said. 'Scared me at first, but now I'm really good at it.'

'Cool,' he said. We stopped at a clearing between Logan Road and Kimble Drive and he left the tracks. Behind some trees was a patch of marijuana he had been growing.

'Ever smoke,' he asked.

'No. I mean… cigarettes, but not pot.'

'Wanna try it?' He was already picking some leaves off. 'It's better dry but I already sold all my stuff to Josh.'

'Okay.' A butterfly banged around in my stomach and I skipped off the tracks.

'I think Josh might be cutting my weed with catnip and selling it again, but whatever.' He ground up the leaves between his thumb and forefinger and packed it in a small glass pipe. Whispers of smoke crawled out from the edges as he ran a lighter over it. After taking a hit, he passed the pipe to me.

'Suck it… but not too hard,' he said, already giggling. 'You're good at sucking, right?'

'Shut up,' I said, grinning. I puckered my lips like I was going to whistle and slurped the stringy noodles of smoke.

'Hold your breath,' he wheezed.

I nodded, tonguing the back of my burned throat. He took the pipe and sucked in more smoke, making the embers glow. After a minute, I let the smoke go out in one giant exhale, raking my burnt throat with cindering nails. A fit of coughing choked me and I almost puked.

He nodded, patted me on the back as I spit up. The smoke slowly left his lips and he gave a couple of small coughs.

'Gotta cough if you want to get off,' he said, clearing his throat.

'Yeah,' I said, choking on air. We sat down and I felt nothing at first. Then time seemed to stop for a moment and random ideas fluttered by, brushing my thoughts for a moment only to leave just as quick.

'This is weird,' I said, still coughing.

'Just go with it.'

We sat there and laughed at nothing for an hour. More gunshots rang through the dense forest and we joked that they were God's farts. Another gunshot, another thunderous fart. My stomach hurt from laughing. We walked the rest of the way home, his arm slung over my shoulder at some point. When we reached Elkview Road, he let me go without a word and crossed the trestle to get to Walnut where his neighborhood was.

I had never crossed the trestle before. I kept thinking of *Stand by Me* and would get scared at the thought of having to jump off the side. The day after Derrick disappeared, I smoked his pot alone and walked the full distance of the tracks, not wanting to go home. I found his body at the foot of the hill where the river slid under the trestle. The back of his head looked collapsed, this flesh scoop of melted ice cream with wisps of hair. Several feet beside him was what looked like the molted skin of a gigantic snake, speckled with glowing slime.

No matter how many drugs I do, I can't forget his body.

At a swingers club in Philadelphia, this couple wants to take me home. A girl with black dyed hair, giant tits. A guy with a neatly trimmed beard and a cowboy hat. They remind me of this couple I knew back home and I start to think that when I get to their place, they'll ask me to put a dog collar on and play all sorts of head games, leave me tied up on their bed with a ball gag.

For once I'm just hungry and tired, not into scoring. Still, when we get there and I ask him if he has anything to eat he takes out a bag of coke and has his girl do a line off his cock, then asks me to do the same. I tell him no and he starts to get angry, asks me why I even came home with them in the first place if I didn't want to party. I get on all fours and blow the stuff off his hard on like a bunch of birthday candles. Minutes later I'm shoved outside and the door is locked behind me. My stomach rumbles.

'Whatever asshole,' I yell. I take out a bottle of wine that I managed to slip into my bag, drinking it as I wander around the neighborhood. There's a missing persons poster on every telephone poll on their block, some fourteen year old girl. She's been missing for five years but the poster looks fresh.

Around the corner there's an alley that isn't filthy and I sit down and drink the wine. A few cars pass me by without stopping, then one slows down, a red Toyota Camry, and a couple of guys stare at me for a long time, talking to each other. The alley light casts another decade on my face and after a few minutes they speed off, disinterested. I squint to read the license plate.

My father's notes: *2001 red Toyota Camry. Pennsylvania plates, DW62L.*

It's a match. I'm getting closer.

The rest of the wine goes quickly and I fall asleep on a bag of dirty clothes, dreaming of walking the train tracks home. Every time I reach the trestle in my dreams I stop, knowing that my friend is down there, knowing that I will never be able to forget the things that wait for me.

The next day at school, Derrick brought me a mix tape. It was all over the place with songs by Fugazi, Bad Brains, Deftones. It started with Smashing Pumpkins' 'Bedazzled' and ended with a Tool song. The tape was labeled with the words *Train Tracks*.

'Doing anything Friday?' he asked.

Looking over the tape, I couldn't help but grin.

'No. What's going on?'

The party was at Mike Bruno's house. Mike sold coke so people were always coming and going. He had a bunch of weird pets, like rats, snakes and tarantulas. He always joked that he fed all his victims to the rats and the snakes. It made me laugh until I saw the bullet holes in his living room. There were two guys from Philly that wouldn't stop watching me and Derrick. Every time they looked over at us I took another drink.

This Sophomore Tracy Sampson was fucking Mike and everyone at school started calling her Tracy Trampson. One night Mike and his wife were at a bar in town with Tracy on a dog leash and she couldn't say or do anything without their permission. She was at the party and she kept going up to the bedroom and coming back wide eyed, smelling like burnt rubber. At one point she walked up to me and said, 'You want to fuck me don't you?'

I said nothing and blushed, taking another drink of cheap wine. Tracy was wearing a wife beater and short shorts. She unzipped and showed Derrick and I that she wasn't wearing any panties.

'I won't fuck you,' she said to me. She turned to Derrick. 'But I'll fuck you if you want.'

She turned around and went back into Mike's bedroom, taking her shirt off on the way. Minutes later Mike and the two guys from Philly followed after. One of them had a giant burn that caked up on his head, the other a spotty beard with a mouth full of snaggle teeth and faded tattoos of names and dates that snaked obituaries up and down both of his arms. Mike's wife hopped off the couch and followed after them like a needy puppy. The bedroom door was left open.

The wine made me warm and fuzzy, uncaring. I told Derrick, 'You can go if you want dude. It's cool.'

'Huh?' he said, frowning. 'Oh, I'm not really into Tracy.'

'No? Saving your heart for someone else?'

'Maybe I am,' he said, giving me a sly smile. He walked towards one of the glass cases where a tarantula sat on a fake rock, waiting for another cricket to suck dry. 'Come here... I want to show you something.'

'What are you doing?'

He looked up the stairwell towards the bedroom to see if anyone was coming back. The bed creaked under the weight of several bodies, but nothing more than a few moans tip toed down the stairs. He slid the top off the tarantula's case.

'Derrick,' I hissed. 'Don't... I don't like spiders.'

'Shhh,' he whispered back, digging his hand in. The tarantula stood up, a disembodied high five with hair and fangs. He grabbed a small piece of scrap wood and brushed the spider aside. It scuttled away and Derrick lifted the rock, pulling out a small baggie. Chunks of rubbery snot were inside. He broke off a piece and put the bag back under the rock.

'Keeps people from getting into his stash,' he explained. The tarantula resumed its perch. 'Come on,' he said, walking towards the backyard. When we reached the end of the yard, he took out a pipe and smacked old ashes out of it, placing the rubber in its place.

'If that's crack or something, I'm not really into—

'It's not crack,' he said, running a lighter over it. Soon

enough the substance became luminous, a freshly cracked glow stick.

'Whoa,' I said. 'What is it?'

'It's new,' he said, watching the stuff turn bright green. 'Mike calls it bright light. Heard another guy call it slug, not sure why though. It's supposed to be like ecstasy, but kinda different. I haven't tried it yet.' He took a hit and handed me the pipe.

'I don't know Derrick… my dad—'

'Exactly,' he said. 'You know what that means right? You can pretty much do whatever you want and your dad will get you out of it.'

The wine made me feel too lazy to argue and without a second thought I took the pipe and sucked in the smoke as he ran the lighter over the glowing substance. It was thick and tasted sweet and salty. He took the pipe back and made it glow brighter. We passed it back and forth until it was a small ball of gray ash.

'Feel anything?' he asked.

'No. Not really. Maybe we should smoke more?'

'*Noooo*. Mike would kill me if he knew I was smoking this stuff. It's uber expensive.' He lit two cigarettes and told me to smoke one to cover up the smell. We walked back inside and sat on the couch of the living room, blowing smoke on our clothes to mask the scent. Another high pitched moan came from the bedroom, skin slapping against skin. We both rolled our eyes.

'Maybe it takes a while to kick in?' I said.

'Maybe. Try not to think about it.'

'Okay.' I took another sip of wine and laid my head back, the side of my leg brushing against his.

'You're a pretty cool kid, you know that?' Derrick said to me.

'Yeah?' I said, looking at the ceiling.

'Yeah. I think it's pretty cool that we got paired up like we did. We probably would've never been friends if it wasn't for that.'

'It is kinda cool when you think about it,' I said, smirking.

The drug took hold.

A flood of wet pleasure trickled over my lips, slithering down my throat and filling my stomach. Without touching myself I ejaculated with little tension and every inch of my body pulsed with pleasure, erasing all aches, pains, nervous feelings, all of it burned away by this orgasmic acid that coursed through my veins.

The brush of his leg against mine brought about a second orgasm, one that shuddered throughout my body. I quickly edged and came again. I was a drop of spit in someone else's wet dream, truly knowing the first moment of joy.

'God…' I shuddered.

'I feel it now,' Derrick said, slurring.

'Yeah.'

'What are you thinking?'

'I feel like,' I said, placing his hand on my leg. 'I want everything to touch me and for everything to be touched.'

'*Yes.*'

'Hold me.'

We held each other on the couch. At one point the man with the burned head and the man with snaggle teeth and faded tattoos came down the stairs holding Tracy between them. She was unclothed, grinning stupidly. A clear slime dripped between her legs. She kissed the air and glanced at us as she was taken away.

I wasn't afraid when I saw the two strangers carry Tracy away. All I could think was that I wanted her with us. I wanted Tracy's head between my legs and Derrick's tongue in my mouth. I wanted both of them inside of me.

They left, slamming the door shut behind them.

After that, I never saw Tracy again.

At a Japanese restaurant in Center City, I spot an older man at the sushi bar with dyed hair and leathery skin. He sneaks off his wedding ring and we slowly merge together after making idle conversation six spots removed. After dinner he offers to pay my tab and tells me that he's staying at a hotel down the street.

'Would you be able to get me something?' I ask.

'Anything you like,' he says, smiling bleached teeth.

'Can you get me glow?' I whisper.

He shrugs and takes out his cell phone, calls someone he knows in the city. The guy is only good for coke but he knows someone else who can meet us. Ten minutes later we're at a bar in Olde City and the old guy walks into the bathroom and comes out with his hand in his pocket. Back at the hotel, he starts to strip before I even get a chance to smoke the drugs.

'Where is it?'

'In my coat pocket,' he says, popping off his shoes. 'You want to smoke it right this second?'

'Yeah, if it's all the same.' I rummage through his stuff and pocket the wedding ring. After finding the drugs, I smack the old ash out of my pipe and pack the new stuff in. It smolders under the yellow tongue of my lighter and after a few seconds it begins to glow like a palm of smashed up fireflies.

'You know, I've never done that stuff before,' the man says, already down to his boxers. Even his body hair is dyed black and without clothes his skin looks one size too big for his skeleton.

'It can be pretty intense,' I say. The glow becomes brighter as the old man starts kissing my neck. I ignore him and take a toke.

'Isn't it made out of bugs or something?' he asks, nibbling my ear.

'Kind of,' I say, thinking of my father's notebook.

> *Unidentified species of gastropod. South American, only capable of surviving in warm climates. Ranges from 7-8 feet long, 200-300 pounds. Excretes a digestive enzyme to paralyze its prey, after which it then drinks the dissolved liquid. Defecates a highly concentrated form of MDMA.*

'If it's shit, I'd like to know what it is they're eating,' he says.

Cooks, also known as 'feeders', typically feed gastropods live animals (rats, birds). More concentrated forms seem to come from larger food sources (cats, dogs, pigs). Several cases of highly concentrated glow may be related to missing persons cases (Watson, Sampson).

'Yeah,' is all I manage to say.

He sits at the end of the bed and exhales green smoke. I take another hard toke and the smoke doesn't burn anymore. He starts kissing me hard, jamming his tongue into my mouth. Unbuckling my pants, he starts kicking both of my shoes off with the sharp claw of his toe nails.

The drugs hit.

'Jesus,' the old man says, twitching. He flops onto his back and lets go of me. 'I just came.'

'Yeah,' I say, drooling a little. 'It's pretty intense, huh?'

We both quiver several times as the echo of the first orgasm ripples through our bodies. Hours pass and the high starts to fade away. Even as I lay next to him, motionless, swimming in the flotsam of someone else's wet dream, I know that I have found my key to this locked door I've been trying to open.

The high fades and the old man is snoring next to me. I quietly sneak out of bed and grab the .38 from my bag.

Pressing it against his eyes, he blinks, shifting it away. The lights click on and I pull the gun back several inches so he can see what it is that's pointed at his face.

'Wake up,' I say, cocking the gun. 'You need to take me to your dealer.'

Derrick freaked out about Tracy missing. That same week, the two guys from Philly that were at Mike Bruno's party kept parking their car outside of Josh's garage where Derrick usually sold his drugs after school let out.

'They just parked and stared at me dude. What if they did something to Tracy and they want me gone too?'

'I don't know,' I said. We were sitting on a stump by the train tracks, kicking rocks in to the forest. 'Tracy's crazy,' I argued. 'She probably just ran away to Philly and is sleeping with anyone that'll get her stoned. I heard her say that a pretty girl is never homeless.'

'Maybe we smoked their stuff and they noticed that some of it was missing. Do you think they'd notice? I only took a little.' Sweat broke over his brow and he gave a nervous shake. 'Jesus, I'd pay them for what I took.'

'Hey,' I said, putting my arm around him. He shrugged me off but I held him tighter and he gave in, resting his head on my shoulder. At school we never held hands or looked at each other twice, but the walk home on the train tracks was our time, the place where we were safe to be ourselves, to not quite know what we were. He looked up, pressed his cheek against mine. Lips slid across towards my lips, kissing them. I didn't kiss back and he pulled away.

'Was that weird?' he asked.

'I… I don't know. I guess it's okay.'

'I'm really scared,' he said, resting his head on my shoulder.

'Me too.' I rested my lips on the top of his head and kissed his hair. 'It'll be okay. Maybe we can go to my dad… if it gets really bad, you know? Maybe it's my fault they're watching you in the first place.'

'Maybe.'

I frowned, lifting my chin off the top of his head. 'Well… you don't really think that, do you? No one at the party knows that my dad works for the DEA, right?'

Derrick spoke slowly, looking at nothing. 'I might have told Mike.'

I jumped up. 'Why did you tell him?' I whined.

'I don't know. I thought it was funny I guess. Getting the DEA's son stoned. Ironic, right? Mike flipped about it, so I told him I was just kidding.'

'Wow, that's fucking hilarious,' I said, walking away from him. A gunshot kicked some birds into the sky but I kept walking. Derrick called after.

'Come on dude, I didn't mean anything by it. It's just cloud talk, a bunch of bullshit.'

'Go fuck yourself Derrick.'

The next day, he didn't show up for class.

The old man calls in the order and there's a scheduled drop at a club in Old City. He gives me all the cash he has on him and I tell him that if I ever see or hear from him again I'll tell his wife everything. I keep the wedding ring as proof.

The dealer says he'll be in a tee shirt and jeans. He's going to go up to the bar, order a club with lemon and lime and pay with one dollar bills. If any of these details don't match, it's not him. Around one in the morning, a clean cut guy in a black tee shirt and blue jeans walks up to the bar, orders a club with a lemon and a lime and pays the bartender in one dollar bills.

He finishes and goes to the bathroom. I follow after. He's surprised when I open the stall door.

'Who are you?'

'I'm picking up.'

He shakes his head. 'No… you're not the guy I talked to on the phone.'

'If you don't want to sell, I can just—'

He rolls his eyes and starts digging into his pocket. 'Nah, it's whatever, but tell that guy that I don't deal with anyone unless I talk to them first.' He opens his palm, showing me the drugs.

'Same stuff as last time?'

'Yeah,' he says, confused by the question. 'Same stuff.'

'Know where I can get a lot of it?'

He smirks. 'Listen…'

I jam the .38 into his stomach and before he can even look down to see what it is, I cock it and my finger is sweating on the trigger. If he so much as burps, I'll put a hole in him that'll make him bleed so bad he'll be dead before they get a chance to plug it.

'Wait,' he says, shaking. He's clean cut, a suburban white kid slinging in the richer parts of Philly so no one really notices him. There's so much sweat on his face, I can tell he's never had a gun shoved into his stomach before.

'Take me to your supplier,' I say, pushing the gun deeper. 'Or I'll cripple you.'

'Okay,' he says, quivering. 'I'll do whatever you want. Just don't shoot me.'

We drive into Port Richmond and park outside the dealer's house. The kid calls and says there's a problem and that he doesn't feel safe talking about it over the phone. The dealer comes out and sits inside the car. He's rough looking, a few tattoos on his hands and face. When he sits down and notices me, he sneers at the kid. I've got the .38 leveled where his lungs are, the mouth of the gun flush against the back seat of the car.

He says, 'Who the fuck is this—'

I pull the trigger.

The kid starts to scream and the dealer is moaning, spitting blood. He's the type that's been shot before so I cock the gun.

'I've got five more bullets. The first one was to show you that the gun works and I don't mind using it. Now if you don't tell me who your supplier is, I'll keep pulling the trigger until its empty.'

'Fucking junkie,' the dealer says, moaning in pain.

'Next thing out of your mouth better be directions.'

'Okay,' he says, gritting his teeth. 'Okay, okay. I'll take you there.'

The white kid is so nervous that he runs a couple of red lights and I smack him across the head with the gun and tell him to slow down or he'll get us pulled over. A whisper of smoke drifts out of the front of the car where the first bullet exited.

'I'm bleeding really bad,' the dealer says, showing the first glimpse of fear.

'Then we better get this over with so I can let you go.'

We drive down Columbus Boulevard towards the shipping yards, passing the car impound and a dozen warehouses. The dealer tells the kid to turn left at the next road and park two blocks down the way. We pull up next to a large warehouse with boarded up windows but the front door is metal, locked, and it looks newer than the building itself.

'It's here,' the dealer says, tired. 'They make the stuff here.'

'Can you get me in?'

'No,' the dealer says, taking out his phone. 'I don't have a key, but I can call them.'

'Call them and say there's a problem and that you need to talk to them right now.'

'Okay,' he says, calling them. They pick up. 'Yo. Nah man, it's not that. Something's up. I can't talk about it over the phone. Can you come out? I'm out front.' He pauses a second. 'Cool.'

'They're coming out?'

The dealer sighs. 'Yeah… they're—'

I pull the trigger and his head explodes, his brains cherry pie smashed up over the dashboard. The white kid's face is speckled with blood and he screams until the gun goes off again and his blood paints the windows a fresh coat of red.

I get out of the car and wait by the door, hoping there's only two of them. I don't know where my fear is, where my pain and sadness are. All I have is the memory of Derrick's dead body face down in the dirt.

A car parked further down the street is the one I've spotted before, the one from my father's notebook.

'Small world,' I say, joyless and unafraid. I think I might be smiling, but the drugs have made it so I can't tell what my lips are doing.

On the night that I left, I broke into my father's office. The light was still on over his desk, pictures of the case spread out everywhere.

There were other victims. Kids, teenagers, all of them with the back of their heads missing, theirs skulls melted and collapsed. There were sketches and diagrams of the worm. A small baggie held a sample of its molted skin, the same skin I found near Derrick's body. Its mouth was lined with soft looking teeth, suckers, and an organ that excreted stomach acid while its mouth drank up the food it dissolved. A second sketch showed a metal table with straps, a series of vague lines pointing down to a bucket that sat below the foot of the table. The bucket was labeled with the words 'raw glow'.

All my father's notes were scribbled in a small notebook he kept on the case. Places, names, slang. *Glow is a sex drug*, he wrote, *a drug people would take in exchange for sex. It is similar to ecstasy, but more addictive than heroin.*

One of the cities he wrote down as a place of interest was Philadelphia.

Warehouses, abandoned buildings, somewhere near the shipping yards. Feeders can process the stuff anywhere if need be (given the situation and an isolated location, as several cases have indicated) but a clean operation would need a climate controlled atmosphere to operate within on a consistent basis so the worm does not die.

I put everything in my bag along with the loaded .38, some clothes, food, and the money I made off of selling Josh the rest of Derrick's weed that he had grown in the middle of the forest. I was about to leave when I noticed another evidence bag with Derrick's name on it.

A small cassette tape was inside with the word 'SORRY' written in black marker.

I placed it in my bag and tip toed outside of the house, walking the train tracks until I hit the first city.

The warehouse door bursts open and he stares at the car with bloody windows. I lift the .38. The old scabs have fallen off, leaving a pink blotch on his bald head.

'Hey,' I say to him.

He turns. Before he can see who I am, I pull the trigger, feeling nothing as I throw his face into the sky, a bucket of bloody birds. He falls to the ground, unknowingly clutching his ruined face, kneeling and still half alive as I walk pass him into the warehouse. The door locks behind me and it's only a short walk down the hall before I see a windowed door leading to the feeding room.

Inside, the man with snaggle teeth and faded tattoos is leaning back on a chair, smoking cigarettes while his feet are propped up on a table. Across from him is a teenage girl tied to a water pipe, blind folded and gagged.

A shotgun sits on the table in front of snaggle teeth.

Behind him on a tilted rack is the worm. It's strapped down to the table and a teenage boy is hung above its mouth, head first. The worm is pulsating, glowing, as it digests the boy's skull. A cylinder attached to the worm's tail is funneling all of its shit into a plastic container. I check the gun. There're only two bullets left.

I pause, trying to feel if I'm sweating, shaking. I feel nothing. All I think of is Derrick face down in a ditch under the trestle, the back of his head gone. I think about all the days we walked home together on the tracks, feeling the whisper of these memories.

The door flies open and snaggle teeth is quick. He jumps up from his chair and grabs for the shotgun. I aim for the head but miss, hitting his shoulder instead. He doesn't slow down. I run towards him as he pumps the shotgun, screaming as I aim my last bullet.

It pokes an ugly hole in his head and the shotgun sprays buckshot across a corner of the room as he falls back and dies, the shotgun still in his hands, twitching in death throes.

The tied up girl moans, shakes from the sound of gun fire. She digs her face into the crook of her arm.

'It's okay,' I shout, deaf from all the gun fire. I rush over to the boy that's tied up and try pulling him out of the worm's mouth. The thing's grip loosens and when the head slips out, it's nothing but melting bone fragments and jelly for brains dripping down the table towards the worm's hungry mouth.

I untie the girl. She won't stop crying. She sees the worm and the dead boy. Now she won't stop screaming.

'Come on,' I shout, taking her outside the room. She wants to keep going, to get out of here, but I tell her to just wait outside. 'I'll only be a second,' I promise her.

The shotgun is greasy from snaggle teeth's hands and a small pool of blood forms a dented circle around his body. My footprints are red as I step backwards from the worm and take aim with the shotgun. It kicks my shoulder hard and the worm's stomach explodes in a glorious burst of glowing guts that cover the walls with green pulsating light. Its toothy mouth keeps chewing the air as it quickly dies.

The shotgun is left in the pool of blood next to snaggle teeth's body. My father's gun stays with me.

After searching the warehouse for drugs, I leave.

It took me a day to reach the first town when I left home. It takes me about the same amount of time walking the tracks before I feel like I'm no longer in the city anymore leaving bloody foot prints.

The girl was afraid. She wanted to come with me. She kept telling me that it wasn't over, they'd find her again. I told her she was safe. But I knew she was right. It's never really over. As long as you remember all the things you'd wish you forget, it's never really over.

Somewhere along the way I burn my father's notebook with all of his leads and his theories. I bury the gun in a forest that slopes high above the train tracks. It's somewhere near West Chester where I finally decide to leave the tracks and hitch hike instead. A minute passes before this guy pulls over in a Camaro with Delaware plates. I tell him where home is and he says he'll take me as far as Kennetsquare.

'Do you need a place to crash tonight?' he asks, glancing at me now and again.

'No,' I tell him. 'I'm okay.' I look out the window, seeing a faint reflection of myself. I don't recognize the person I'm seeing in the window. 'I'm okay.'

'Well you don't look it,' he says, driving down Route One.

I shrug and pull out my tape player to listen to one of Derrick's mix tapes. I don't feel like talking anymore. After twenty minutes, I tell the man I need a pit stop. He groans and we pull into a WaWa where I go into one of the isolated bathrooms and rummage through my bag for all the rendered glow I managed to find at the warehouse. Under the bags of drugs is the SORRY mix tape Derrick never got to give me.

I place it in the tape player and hear the Pixies. My feet hurt, so I sit on the toilet while packing the glow, turning up the music as I smoke.

Eventually it hits me and it's absolute joy, my aches and pains fading away. For a moment my feet don't hurt anymore. For just a single moment, I forget everything and it's finally over.

Contributors

Hector Acosta has recently been testing out a theory, in which he's found that if he sits down and forces himself to write, eventually stories will fill up the blank page. He's currently thinking of setting up speaking engagements across the country to extol his new found theory. In the meantime, he continues to write. You can find on him on the web at hjacosta.wordpress.com – which he promises to start updating more.

Andrez Bergen is an expat Australian writer, journalist, DJ, and ad hoc saké connoisseur who's been entrenched in Tokyo, Japan, for the past 11 years. He published noir/sci-fi novel 'Tobacco-Stained Mountain Goat' in 2011 and the surreal fantasy 'One Hundred Years of Vicissitude' through Perfect Edge Books in 2012. He's currently working on #3, titled 'Who is Killing the Great Capes of Heropa?'

Bergen has published short stories through Crime Factory, Shotgun Honey, Snubnose Press, Solarcide and Another Sky Press, and worked on translating and adapting the scripts for feature films by Mamoru Oshii, Kazuchika Kise and Naoyoshi Shiotani. http://andrezbergen.wordpress.com/

Carol Borden is a writer who watches way too many movies and abuses her education writing about pop culture for the website, The Cultural Gutter (http://www.theculturalgutter.com). Some of her favorite articles have been collected into a book, The Cultural Gutter, available from Carnegie-Mellon University's ETC Press (http://www.etc.cmu.edu/etcpress/content/cultural-gutter). She also creates monster-themed art at Monstrous Industry (http://monstrousindustry.etsy.com). Some dialog from the movies M andfrom Metropolis were used in, 'The Blue Mark.'

Paul D. Brazill was born in England and lives in Poland. He is the author of The Gumshoe, Guns Of Brixton, 13 Shots of

Noir and Snapshots, and the editor of Drunk On The Moon and True Brit Grit. He writes regular columns for Pulp Metal Magazine and Out Of The Gutter Online. He is a member of International Thriller Writers Inc and the Hardboiled Collective, as well as editor-at-large for Noir Nation. His blog is http://pauldbrazill.wordpress.com

Born in Singapore but a global citizen, **Joyce Chng** writes mainly science fiction (SFF) and YA fiction. She likes steampunk and tales of transformation/transfiguration. Her fiction has appeared in Crossed Genres, Semaphore Magazine, Bards and Sages Quarterly and Everyday Fiction. Joyce also has a crowdfunded web novella entitled 'Oysters, Pearls and Magic'. Her urban fantasy novels are contracted under Lyrical Press. Her YA science fiction trilogy will be published by a Singapore publisher, Books Actually. Her website is found at http://awolfstale.wordpress.com.

Michael S. Chong was born a Scorpio in the Year of the Dog. He has lived in Toronto for most of his life but spent a few years in the Netherlands where he learned to love eating fries with mayonnaise. Now back in Canada, he enjoys the gravy and cheese curds of poutine but every once in awhile sentimentally slaps mayo on his frites. His story 'The Creep' is in the upcoming collection Masked Mosaic from Tyche Press.

Karina Fabian breathes fire, battles zombies with chainsaws and window cleaner, travels to the edge of the solar system to recover alien artifacts, and has been driven insane by psychic abilities. It's what makes being an author such fun. She won the 2010 INDIE Award for best fantasy for Magic, Mensa and Mayhem (her first DragonEye, PI novel) and the Global E-Book Award for best horror for Neeta Lyffe, Zombie Exterminator. She's an active member of Broad Universe and the Catholic Writers' Guild. When not writing, she enjoys her family and swings a sword around in haidong gumbdo. http://fabianspace.com

Richard Godwin is the widely published author of crime

novels *Mr. Glamour* and *Apostle Rising*. *Mr. Glamour* is Hannibal Lecter in Gucci, and was published in paperback in April 2012 by Black Jackal Books. The novel is about a glamorous world obsessed with designer labels with a predator in its midst, and has received great reviews. It is available at all good retailers. *Apostle Rising*, in which a serial killer crucifies politicians, and plays games with the police, is available in paperback and E Book, with some juicy extras. You can find out more about Richard Godwin at www.richardgodwin.net

Christopher L. Irvin scribbles about the dark and mysterious and dreams of one day writing full-time. His stories have appeared twice in the University of Maine at Machias Binnacle Ultra-Short Competition, The Undead That Saved Christmas Vol. 3 Monster Mash! and Dreadworks Journal. He lives with his wife and son in Boston, Massachusetts. www.HouseLeagueFiction.com

S.L. Johnson is a well-known, if seldom seen, recluse living in Connecticut. It has been rumored that she was a messenger for the French Resistance, going by the name of 'Le Noir Pigeon.' Or a rich Russian heiress, disowned by her family for falling in love with a poor Norwegian carpenter. Or a woman who took leave of her senses when she was jilted at the altar. Feel free to ask her any questions about her artwork. But not about her past. www.Sljohnsonimages.com

W. P. Johnson graduated from Temple University with a degree in English Literature. He is a writer of horror, weird fiction, and a member of the Horror Writers Association. You can follow him via the moniker americantypo through twitter, wordpress, and whatever other social media is popular this week. He currently lives in Philadelphia where he is researching his first novel, a horror story about stand up comedians.

Jan Kozlowski is a freelance writer, editor and researcher. Her first novel DIE, YOU BASTARD! DIE! was published in 2012 by John Skipp's Ravenous Shadows imprint. Her short horror stories have appeared in HUNGRY FOR

YOUR LOVE: An Anthology of Zombie Romance and FANGBANGERS: An Erotic Anthology of Fangs, Claws, Sex and Love, both edited by Lori Perkins and in NECON EBOOKS FLASH FICTION ANTHOLOGY BEST OF 2011. Her websites are: www.jankozlowski.com and www.butshekeepsanicelawn.com

K. A. Laity chose the stories for this collection after she was foolish enough to pitch the idea to 'the muse who punches you in the face' AKA Adele Wearing. She is grateful to Daz for doing the hard work of actually editing the stories. Her works include *Chastity Flame, The Claddagh Icon, Unquiet Dreams, Owl Stretching* and many many more. All-purpose writer, Fulbrighter, uberskiver, medievalist, flâneuse, techno-shamanka, Broad Universe social media wrangler, History Witch, and Pirate Pub Captain, she divides her time between Dundee & New York · http://www.kalaity.com

Jennifer Martin lives in El Paso, TX with her husband and two children. She writes horror, urban fantasy and paranormal stories and novels. You can find her at : j e n m a r t i n a u t h o r . w i x . c o m / w o r d i s a r t and www.facebook.com/author.jennifermartin

Jason Michel is the Dictator over at the joyfully irreverent Pulp Metal Magazine and the author of And The Streets Screamed Blue Murder! He lives in Paris. For his sins.

Leeyanne Moore is literary director for The Bridge Progressive Arts Initiative in Charlottesville, Virginia where she organizes readings and literary events. She has an MFA from Syracuse University and she has published short stories from her collection *The House With Chicken Feet* in *McSweeney's Internet Tendencies, The Alembic, Western Humanities Review,* and *redlightbulbs.* A lonely fabulist writer, she welcomes contact from other writers who like bizarre fiction too. Email her at leeyannemoore@gmail.com

Katherine Tomlinson is a former journalist who prefers making things up. Her stories have appeared online at sites like ThugLit, Shotgun Honey, Inner Sins, A Twist of Noir, and Eaten Alive as well as in the anthologies Pulp Ink, 2, Drunk on the Moon, and Alt-Zombie. She is the editor of the upcoming *Nightfalls* anthology. She lives in Los Angeles where she sees way too many movies. Find her work at her blog: http://kattomic-energy.blogspot.com/

Asher Wismer is an Editor for eNotes.com, living and working in Maine. He is a second-generation writer; his father Don Wismer published four science-fiction books in the 1980s. Asher's flash fiction is featured on the website 365tomorrows.com, and he has had three short stories published in anthologies from Wild Wolf Publishing ('December in Florida,' Holiday of the Dead), Matt Hilton ('Jobs Taken,' Action: Pulse Pounding Tales Vol. 1), and KnightWatch Press ('Safety in Numbers,' anthology title pending). 'Evil and Life' will be his fourth published short story.

Chloë Yates got her first taste of success pretty recently. In May 2012, her prose piece 'Don't Do it, Salvador' won the inaugural *Postcard Fiction Contest*, published at: http://kalaity.com/2012/05/23/writer-wednesday-post-card-fiction-prizes/ Then in October 2012 she won Fox Spirit Books' *International Talk Like a Pirate Day* Flash Fiction contest with her story 'Leave the Pistol Behind' http://www.foxspirit.co.uk/wp-content/uploads/2012/10/Leave-the-Pistol-Behind.pdf You can find her humorous, if somewhat macabre, poetry at http://www.short-humour.org.uk/6writersshowcase/6writersshowcase.htm and her occasionally vitriolic, sometimes sentimental blog at: http://chloe-yates.blogspot.ch/. Chloë currently lives in Switzerland with her bearded paramour, Mr Y, and their disapproving dog, Miss Maudie.

Adele Wearing is the driving force behind Fox Spirit and functions on the basic principal of jumping off cliffs with her eyes shut shouting 'geronimo'. She's been described as 'like a muse, who can kick you in the face' and that works so she's running with it. Adele lives with two cats and is constantly looking for a chance to take over the world.

Daz, the tireless copy-editor at Fox Spirit, lives, loves and bakes in darkest West Yorkshire. Currently peddling his wares for the excellent Crossroad Press and the inestimable Steven Savile, amongst others, Daz also has mid-range plans for World Domination (starting perhaps with the East Midlands) and becoming an Editor with a capital E. Can mostly be found @dazthreenine